Match Me if You Can

The School for Spinsters
Book Three

By Michelle Willingham

ARE YOU SIGNED UP FOR DRAGONBLADE'S BLOG?

You'll get the latest news and information on exclusive giveaways, exclusive excerpts, coming releases, sales, free books, cover reveals and more.

Check out our complete list of authors, too!

No spam, no junk. That's a promise!

Sign Up Here

www.dragonbladepublishing.com

Dearest Reader;

Thank you for your support of a small press. At Dragonblade Publishing, we strive to bring you the highest quality Historical Romance from some of the best authors in the business. Without your support, there is no 'us', so we sincerely hope you adore these stories and find some new favorite authors along the way.

Happy Reading!

CEO, Dragonblade Publishing

Additional Dragonblade books by Author Michelle Willingham

The School for Spinsters Series
A Match Made in London (Book 1)
Match Me, I'm Falling (Book 2)
Match Me if you Can (Book 3)

Dedication

To Sam, Katy, Stephanie, Elly, Christy, Thoeun, Richard, and Corrine: Thanks for making the workplace amazing and for the always funny existential dread conversations at 3:30 each day. Love you all!

Chapter One

"I 'VE NEVER HEARD of such a thing. A bride auction? What do you mean by this?" Her father sounded aghast as he spoke to his wife in the library.

Emma Bartholomew, who was eavesdropping, pressed her spine against the wall. This was clearly a conversation she was not supposed to hear. But she leaned in closer to the doorway, trying to learn what she could. Her thoughts sharpened with dismay, for it certainly sounded as if her stepmother was trying a desperate means of finding her a husband. But why? There was no reason for it.

Lucy lowered her voice for a moment, and Emma couldn't quite hear what she was saying. Then her stepmother continued, "Henry, we have to do something. And this will work, I promise you. You've been wanting Emma to be married for years now. This is an excellent way to find her a titled husband of wealth. She's certainly not going to find a husband on her own. It's been what—five years since her first Season?"

"She's not a painting, Lucy. We can't just . . . auction her off." Her father cleared his throat, and Emma took another step toward the doorway, leaning in closer. His voice held confusion, and he added, "I don't like this idea at all. It's probably illegal as well."

At least Papa was on her side. She took consolation in that, thankfully. He would never allow Lucy to sell her like an object. Emma took several slow breaths, listening intently.

"We're not hosting an auction for *Emma*, my dear husband," Lucy reassured him. "We will find something else to auction off. A painting or a statue. But whoever wins the auction will also win Emma's hand in marriage. And whatever price they pay for the painting, we will tell them that we will match it and add it to her dowry."

Her father mumbled something that Emma couldn't quite hear, but it didn't exactly sound like a dismissal. He wasn't considering it, was he?

Dear God, her stepmother truly did despise her. How could Lucy simply sell her off to the highest bidder? What person would do such a thing? And what suitor would ever agree to it, except a man who was unable to find a wife under normal circumstances? Which meant that her potential husband would be ancient, strange, or impossibly unattractive.

No. Absolutely not. She could never do such a thing.

"This is very unusual, Lucy," Henry said. "I cannot say that I approve. We will need to discuss it with Emma."

She nearly laughed at that. Lucy's idea of a discussion was simply to tell both of them what would happen and why. She never listened to their thoughts, and Emma was quite certain that this conversation would be no exception.

Behind her, she heard the heavy footsteps of a footman walking past her and into the library. She winced, realizing that someone, at least, was aware that she'd been eavesdropping. Rupert was a kindly footman, however, and probably would not tell her father.

"Ah, Rupert," her father said. "Be so good as to bring my daughter Emma inside."

Emma closed her eyes a moment. It was better to pretend she was passing by than for the footman to tell him the truth, that she'd been eavesdropping outside the door. Before Rupert could speak, she quickly walked four steps to the right and then circled left again to walk the remaining six steps inside the library. "Father, I was passing by, and I thought I overheard you asking for me?" She kept her tone calm and innocent, as if she had no idea what they'd been discussing.

To her right, she could smell the heavy lavender scent Lucy favored. Her stepmother bathed in it, packed her clothing with lavender sachets, and wore lavender perfume. Even now, the aroma made Emma faintly nauseous.

"Indeed, I did." Henry cleared his throat again. "Lucy and I were having a discussion just now. Have you ... given any thought to marriage?"

Bless her poor father's ignorance. Henry honestly believed that the reason why she hadn't married was because she wasn't interested. Emma tried to gather an appropriate response, but before she could speak, Lucy cut her off.

"Of course, she's thought of marriage, Henry. What do you think we've been spending money on all these years? New gowns, lessons—and none of it is working. It's time to change our strategy."

There was no denying the frustration in Lucy's voice. But Emma held fast to one hope—that Papa would never allow this so-called auction to happen. He loved her and wanted what was best for her—unlike Lucy, who clearly wanted to be rid of her. Even after five years, Emma had never truly understood why her stepmother seemed to dislike her so. From the moment they'd met, Lucy had tried to arrange a marriage for her—probably so she wouldn't have to be a stepmother at all.

"I would like to marry the right sort of gentleman," Emma said quietly. "But most of them are not interested in me."

It was the truth. She'd been a wallflower all her life, and that wouldn't change. She couldn't dance, conversation was nearly impossible, and she had to be careful that she didn't lose count of her steps. No man wanted her, and if that meant being a spinster, then such was her fate.

Yes, she *did* want a husband. And lots of children. But after being ignored by suitor after suitor, including the less-than-desirable men, she'd laid those hopes to rest.

"There are many men who do not care about your . . . eccentricities or your clumsiness," Lucy continued as if Emma hadn't spoken. "I have begun making a list of candidates, and I have decided to host an auction for your hand in marriage. We will say it is for art, but only unmarried gentlemen may come."

She was serious. Hearing it stated so baldly, Emma gaped at her in disbelief. "No. I will not be sold like livestock."

Lucy ignored her and turned back to Henry, "Emma can help select the guests. That way she does have some say in whom she will marry."

"That's . . . true," her father acceded. He seemed to ponder it a moment, which Emma had never expected. He was supposed to support her, not join in his wife's ridiculous scheming.

"I would allow it," he said, "but only if Emma is in agreement."

"Absolutely not," she said. "The very idea is awful." But she worried that Lucy would continue wearing down her father until he gave in, despite what he'd said. She sifted through ideas, trying to think of a way to change their minds. Why did she have to marry so soon? She'd already waited five Seasons. It was already July, so couldn't she simply finish the sixth Season and try again next year?

"I don't have to marry right away," she hedged. "I am still only three-and-twenty."

"You're becoming a spinster." Lucy sighed. "The longer you remain on the shelf, the worse it will be."

Spinster. The word struck her like a bolt of hope. Two of her acquaintances, Lady Ashleigh Pryor and Miss Violet Edwards, had sought help from Mrs. Harding's School for Young Ladies, also nicknamed the School for Spinsters. Both had spoken highly of the headmistress, and both women had married men whom they loved.

Emma had no such delusions that she would find anyone to love, but Mrs. Harding might be able to help her elude this horrid auction idea. Honestly, she was grasping at any means of an escape.

"Papa, what if I were to take lessons? I've heard good things about Mrs. Harding's School for Young Ladies. She's a matchmaker, from what I'm told. Would you allow me to try?"

Her father paused a moment. "What do you think, Lucy? I've not heard of this school before."

Her stepmother snorted. "The School for Spinsters? Really, Emma? Why would you believe that would work? We don't have years to transform you."

"It's worth a try," she offered weakly.

"We don't have the money," Lucy insisted. Then she corrected, "That is, we have to save the money for your dowry and the auction."

"But if I find a husband on my own, then there's no need for that," Emma said. She turned back to her father, hoping he would allow it. "Papa, what do you think? Would you let me try?"

"And . . . what sorts of lessons would you be learning?" her father asked. "You've already had a governess." He cleared his throat. "I thought you hated lessons."

"This is different," she insisted, though she truthfully didn't know what any of the lessons would be about. "Would you allow me to at least meet with her and ask questions?"

"I've heard it's very costly," Lucy interrupted. "And I see no reason for it. What could Mrs. Harding do for you that we couldn't?"

"It would be less humiliating than an *auction*," Emma pointed out. "Let me have a month or two of lessons. It might work." Though she didn't truly believe it, she was grasping at any means of delaying Lucy's ridiculous auction.

Her father didn't answer for a long moment. "Well, I suppose there would be no harm in getting information. Lucy could go with you."

"No," Emma answered quickly. Her stepmother clearly had her sights set upon this auction, and the last thing she wanted was Lucy's interference. But she softened her voice for her father's sake. "I mean, I wouldn't want her to be inconvenienced."

Lucy walked toward her husband and gave a soft sigh. "Dear Henry, you have such a kind heart. But I truly don't believe that lessons are needed in this instance."

"Papa, please." She wasn't above begging—not when it involved her future.

He seemed to consider it. "If it means that much to you, I suppose one month won't make too much difference." To Lucy, he added, "And that will give you enough time to plan this . . . marital auction, as it were. The two of you can find suitable candidates and determine whether any of them might be appropriate."

Though a month wasn't nearly enough time to deter Lucy from her plans, Emma saw no point in arguing further. Instead, she made her way toward her father and embraced him. "Thank you, Papa." She could smell the faint scent of sandalwood from his shaving soap, and the familiar aroma evoked the memories of when she'd sat in his lap as a young girl while he'd read her stories.

He sighed and hugged her back. "Go on, then. I'm certain you'll have to write a note to this Mrs. Harding and find out when you can pay a call."

Emma nodded and took a moment to calm her emotions. "Thank you." She nodded in Lucy's direction and then walked twelve steps to the doorway. Then she turned to walk the twenty-two steps to the staircase. On her way out, she overheard her stepmother remarking, "This isn't going to work, Henry."

"I know," he said softly. "But what else does she have except hope?"

CORMAC ORMOND, THE fourth Earl of Dunmeath, was running out of time. During the past six months, he'd asked twelve different young ladies for their hands in marriage, and all had refused. To be sure, he barely knew any of them. But all had been beautiful, with excellent dowries and good family names. As for himself, he wasn't very particular about what he wanted in a wife. As long as she didn't mind living in Ireland and accepting some of his . . . eccentricities . . . they would get along well enough. It didn't matter whether his wife loved him or not, so long as she was willing to bear him a child.

Because he was going to die quite soon.

His father had died seven years ago. Then, only three years later, his older brother had followed suit. Cormac had begun getting sick only last year, which made him worry about how much time he had left. The physicians believed it was an illness passed down through the male line—a theory that seemed to be accurate thus far since his sisters seemed to be well enough.

In her wild grief, his mother had ordered him to leave Ireland. She had inherited a townhouse in London from her mother, and she'd demanded that Cormac depart for England immediately so she wouldn't have to watch another son die.

He'd obeyed his mother's wishes, but the burden of familial responsibility weighed upon him. He didn't have the luxury of time, which was why he didn't particularly care whom he married. He needed an heir more than all else. His wife wouldn't have to endure his presence for very long. The physician had told him it was anyone's guess how long he would live. But Cormac didn't doubt that the fatal verdict was true.

He couldn't seem to concentrate, and he was always forgetting things. Headaches and terrible stomach pains plagued him, and there were days when he was so nauseous, he couldn't bear to eat. It was a sobering thought to realize that he would probably be dead before the year was out.

He tried to ignore it, tried not to let fear strangle the life out of his last few months. And so he'd made a vow that here—in

London—he would live each day to its fullest. He would do whatever he wanted, seizing every moment.

But what he wanted most was a wife and an heir. And, though it was possibly a lot to ask, he rather hoped he could hold a child in his arms before he was buried.

He'd tried to be entertaining during balls and soirees, trying to attract lovely young women whom he could marry. But inevitably, he would make one mistake or another that would put them off. Certainly, he couldn't remember names. And he often spoke whatever thoughts were on his mind, which tended to make women stare at him as if he were a madman. He wasn't trying to interrupt them. It was just that if he held back the words, he would forget them.

In the corner on a small end table stood an hourglass filled with sand. Cormac stared at it for long moments, as if it held the remaining hours of his life. For a moment, he lost concentration before he blinked and glanced around. He was sitting in his study surrounded by books. Three were open on his desk, while his grandfather's familiar green diary rested nearby as a reminder of home. He had four cups of tea in various places around the study, which startled him because he didn't remember having tea. Or were those from yesterday?

A knock sounded at the door. "Lord Dunmeath." His secretary, John Hawkins, greeted him, sounding out of breath. "You asked me to remind you of the Duke and Duchess of Westerford's ball this evening."

"This evening?" Cormac frowned. "But that isn't until Saturday."

Hawkins cleared his throat. "Today *is* Saturday, my lord."

Cormac frowned. "That can't be. It's Friday, and I'm supposed to be paying a call on Lord Scarsdale."

"That was yesterday, my lord. He sent a note when you didn't arrive. Remember, we spoke of it yesterday evening? I sent him an apology on your behalf."

Cormac paused a moment, wondering how he'd lost track of

the days. "Devil take it, Hawkins, why did you not remind me?"

"You weren't here, my lord. I thought you had kept your appointment, but you went out riding instead and didn't return until nightfall."

Cormac had no memory of that. It did seem that his episodes of forgetfulness were growing worse. With a sigh, he admitted, "Ah, you have the right of it, Hawkins. That was unfair, and it's sorry I am. Will you send for my valet?"

"He is waiting to help you dress, my lord." His secretary bowed and stepped backward. Then he paused and asked, "Is there anything else you need? Food or . . ." he paused and eyed the teacups, "something to drink, perhaps?"

"No, thank you."

Hawkins appeared uncomfortable, and Cormac waited for the man to speak. Clearly, there was something bothering him. "Is there something else?"

"No, my lord. It's just—have you eaten anything today?"

He tried to think, but the hours simply blurred together, and he couldn't remember. With a shrug, he said, "You can ask Cook to prepare something for me while I dress." He stood from his chair and stretched.

As he walked up the stairs to his bedroom, he tried to concentrate on the task of finding a bride. Somewhere, he had a list of eligible young ladies, though for the life of him, he couldn't recall where he'd left it. Miss Violet Edwards had been on that list. It had been so very disappointing that she'd married the Earl of Scarsdale. She'd been kind, quiet, and Cormac hadn't minded her stutter in the least. As for the other unmarried ladies—well, perhaps there were some who might suit him well enough.

He was indeed aware that he'd gained a reputation as the earl who wanted to be married. To his misfortune, he'd never been very good with ladies. They were rarely honest about anything, and he had often wished that they would simply speak whatever was on their minds.

Instead, he'd overheard many young ladies mocking him.

They thought he was desperate—which wasn't entirely true. Eager, yes. But the problem was, he didn't have the luxury of time to properly court a young woman. And the last thing he wanted was to admit to anyone that he was dying.

His valet helped him to dress, and Cormac held fast to a silent hope that tonight would be different. He would do his best to find an appropriate lady. Though he knew there were women who were . . . less attractive and had few prospects, he wanted to try again.

A knock sounded at the door, and he called for the servant to enter. Hawkins came inside with a silver tray, and another footman followed with food and tea.

"I've brought the post, my lord."

"Are there any invitations?" he asked.

Hawkins paused a moment. "There is one, I believe."

"Well, go on and open it. Read it to me, if you will," he said, holding out his arms so his valet could help him with his coat.

"It's from Mr. and Mrs. Bartholomew," the secretary said. He frowned, staring at the invitation. Cormac tried to remember what Miss Bartholomew looked like, but for the life of him, he couldn't recall her face. She wasn't from a noble family, but he thought she had a respectable dowry.

"I've no objection if you're wanting to write a letter accepting their invitation," he said, while his valet helped with his shoes.

"My lord, this invitation is . . . most unusual. I don't know what it is, precisely."

His secretary held it out, and Cormac stared at it. Was this an auction? He had no interest in acquiring paintings or furnishings. But something made him stop short.

Only unmarried gentlemen may place a bid upon this treasured family heirloom.

The auction winner will receive a priceless gift in return.

The item may be viewed at the Bartholomew residence.

Cormac read it again. "Unmarried gentlemen?" That, in itself, suggested that marriage was connected to this auction. Did it have something to do with Miss Bartholomew? He would ask her the next time they met. That is, if they had ever met the first time.

"Send a reply that I will attend." If nothing else, he would be curious to see what it was.

He picked up his gloves and hat and prepared himself for yet another ball. Perhaps this time, he might meet someone who would consider his suit.

"This is a foolish idea." Lucy sighed as the footman helped them from the carriage. "I don't know why you think this so-called school could help you at all."

Emma didn't expect her stepmother to approve, but she was at the end of her options. If attending Mrs. Harding's School for Young Ladies would grant her a month's respite from Lucy's plotting—and possibly an end to this ridiculous auction idea—she would do it.

She fervently wished her stepmother didn't have to accompany her, but her father had insisted.

"Father already gave his permission," Emma answered before she walked up seven steps to the townhouse and knocked.

"His permission isn't going to—" Lucy's words were cut off when a footman opened the door.

"I am Miss Emma Bartholomew, here to pay a call on Mrs. Harding," Emma said. She kept her voice steady, revealing none of her nerves.

"She is expecting you," the footman answered. "If you'll just follow me." His shoes clicked upon the smooth marble flooring, and Emma stepped inside to follow him. She counted twenty-four steps to the study, and as she stood at the doorway, she hesitated. Was she supposed to enter and wait? Or what was next?

Then the headmistress greeted them. "Good morning. I am

Rachel Harding."

"I am Lucille Bartholomew, and this is my stepdaughter Emma," Lucy answered.

"Please, come in and sit down," the matron invited them.

Emma took six steps forward and bumped into a chair before she managed to sit. She took a moment to steady herself, hiding her embarrassment at her clumsiness.

"I understand you are interested in becoming a pupil at my school," Mrs. Harding said to her. The woman's voice held an interesting blend of kindness and steel. Emma didn't know what she'd expected, but Rachel Harding did not seem to be an effusive headmistress bent upon false compliments. There was a no-nonsense demeanor that reminded Emma of her school days.

She repressed a shudder and told herself that this would be different. Her lessons here would be about finding a husband, not reading or writing.

"Well, my stepdaughter is unlikely to be a pupil here for very long," Lucy answered. "Emma has not had any offers of marriage in five Seasons. I don't anticipate there's any hope that she could learn anything at a school for young ladies—after all, she's not young anymore. But this was *her* idea, and she talked her father into giving her a fortnight's worth of lessons. After that—" Lucy laughed lightly. "Well, let us just say I have my doubts."

Mrs. Harding didn't seem to react to her stepmother's words. Instead, she kept her voice kind and asked, "And what are your thoughts, Miss Bartholomew?"

"I—"

Lucy cut her off. "She's terribly shy and clumsy. If you don't wish to accept Emma as a student, I'm certain we could make other arrangements."

Mrs. Harding stood for a moment and rang for a servant. "Would you care for some tea and refreshments, Mrs. Bartholomew?"

"Of course. I'd be delighted."

"Excellent. My partner, Cedric Gregor, will escort you to the drawing room. Emma and I will join you there momentarily."

"Oh, well I—" Before her stepmother could protest, the door opened wider, and a gentleman arrived. He wore all black, and Emma caught a different scent, almost like freshly cut wood.

"I would be delighted to escort you to enjoy tea, Mrs. Bartholomew," he continued. His voice had a charming air with a warm friendliness. "And on the way, I should love to hear all about your stepdaughter and how we can help her."

It was clear enough to Emma that they were removing Lucy from the room to talk to her in private. But it was done so smoothly, her stepmother could not argue without sounding belligerent.

"I will be there in a moment," Emma promised.

But after Mr. Gregor took Lucy from the room, he closed the door behind him. Mrs. Harding held her silence for a moment, as if staring at her. Then she asked, "Is this what you want, Miss Bartholomew? Or are you being forced into this schooling?"

"It was my request to come here," Emma answered. "I asked to take lessons, so that I may—" She stopped a moment, wondering if she should tell the matron about the auction. She decided to avoid it for now. "That is, so I might have a choice in whom I marry." Though truthfully, she wasn't certain whether that was possible. A month wasn't nearly enough time.

"Do you truly wish to be married?" Mrs. Harding asked. "Or would you prefer to remain on your own?"

"I would like to have a husband," Emma admitted. Though in all honesty, it was difficult to imagine. She wasn't like the other ladies of the *ton*, and men didn't seem interested in her at all.

"What sort of gentleman are you hoping to wed?" Mrs. Harding inquired. The matron opened her desk, and Emma heard the rustle of parchment and a pen being dipped into the ink.

"One who is . . ." Emma paused to think. Truthfully, she didn't think any man would want someone like her. She wasn't like most young women, pretty or vivacious. Instead, she relied on a rigid set of rules to get through each day.

"Kind," she answered weakly.

"What should he look like?" Mrs. Harding asked. "Do you have a preference?"

Emma shrugged. "His appearance doesn't matter. Though I would like someone who isn't the age of my father or grandfather."

"Do you want children?" Mrs. Harding inquired.

"Oh yes." That was very much a dream she wanted. "Or if he has children from a former marriage, that would be all right, as well."

She heard the scratching of Mrs. Harding's pen. "Are there any gentlemen who have your interest right now? Is there someone whom you would like to marry?"

"Oh, no one would marry me," Emma answered without hesitation. "It doesn't matter what I think."

"That wasn't my question," Mrs. Harding said. "I asked whom you would *like* to marry."

She shook her head. "I can't really say. I don't know any of the gentlemen of the *ton*, to be honest. They don't speak to me. They hardly even know I'm there."

Mrs. Harding sighed, and her pen bumped against the wood as she set it down. "Miss Bartholomew, you should know that we do not accept every potential student at our school. We have an outstanding success rate with our matchmaking. But only young women who are willing to learn, who are willing to try, can become pupils here. Are you that sort of woman, Miss Bartholomew?"

Emma nodded. "I *am* willing to learn, yes."

"Good. Then I have an assignment for you. A task you must complete before I will consider accepting you for lessons at my school."

A sudden uneasiness filled her. She'd mistakenly believed that Mrs. Harding accepted all students. Both Violet Edwards and Lady Ashleigh had found husbands, after all. For the first time, a sliver of doubt poked her like an invisible splinter. What if they did not accept her as a student? Would she be forced into this auction? Panic took hold, twisting her stomach into knots.

"If this is truly something *you* wish to do," Mrs. Harding continued, "then we can help you. But your task is this. You must attend a ball within the next week. You must speak to five gentlemen and make conversation. During this time, you will determine a list of what you do or do not like in a husband, and you will return to me on Monday next with this list. Do not bring your stepmother with you. After that, I will determine whether you may join my school."

Five gentlemen? Emma managed to refrain from immediately refusing. She was trying to become a pupil at this school as a means of delaying the auction—not because she actually believed there was any chance of marriage.

Mrs. Harding was essentially asking her to be publicly humiliated. No man would speak to her, even if she initiated conversation. Not to mention the harrowing task of navigating the intricacies of a ballroom. She was far more comfortable as a wallflower.

The matron was still waiting for an answer, so Emma hedged, "I—I understand."

"Very good. Now we will go and join your stepmother. Do try to join in our conversation without letting her speak over you," she said firmly.

Emma nodded, though she didn't know how such a thing was possible. With every moment, she saw her escape plan starting to crumble. What if Mrs. Harding refused to take her? What could she possibly do to prevent herself from being sold off like a horse at auction?

She simply didn't know.

Chapter Two

CORMAC HAD ATTENDED two balls during the past week, but thus far, he'd had no luck in finding a potential bride. His memory seemed to be getting worse, and it was only because of Hawkins's reminders that he'd managed to keep the household together. Tonight, he could feel another terrible stomachache coming on, and he fought to push it back. He had promised himself that he would keep searching for a wife—and he intended to keep that vow.

Tonight, he was attending a ball hosted by Lord and Lady Scarsdale. The earl and his new countess had been married only a few months, but during that time, they had managed to rebuild the family's fortune. Cormac had considered courting Scarsdale's sister, Lady Melanie, but thus far the lady had ignored his offers of marriage. Perhaps tonight he would have better luck.

The ballroom was beautifully decorated with flowers everywhere. The musicians played lively dance sets, and Cormac studied the young ladies, trying to determine who might be a good candidate.

"Oh, look who's here. The Earl of Marriage." Lady Persephone, the Duke of Westerford's daughter approached and cast him a disparaging look. She wore a gown of pure white, embroidered in silver, and her blond hair was adorned with diamonds. "Lord

Dunmeath, why do you persist in trying to find an English bride? You would have better luck in Ireland."

He knew the sort of vain, coquettish woman Lady Persephone was. She delighted in tormenting the wallflowers and believed that her father's wealth would solve all problems. "I might indeed," he answered. "But then I'd not have the pleasure of meeting so many young ladies."

Her face narrowed in a frown and then turned to a sly smile as she beckoned to two other ladies. "Miss Cooper, Lady Chelsea, were you both aware that Lord Dunmeath is looking for a bride?"

Cormac didn't recognize them, but one of the other young women tittered. "*Everyone* knows he's looking for a bride. If you put your dog in a gown, Lady Persephone, he would probably propose to her as well."

Lady Persephone laughed prettily and waved her hand in dismissal. "I wish you luck, Lord Dunmeath."

He ignored her taunting and turned his back on Lady Persephone. She, at least, was one young woman he would never ask to wed.

His gaze passed over the other young ladies—Miss Abrams . . . Lady Diana . . . and then he saw her. Miss Barnes. Or was it Bartley? Dash it all, he couldn't quite recall her name, but the young woman stood near the edge of the ballroom, quietly observing the others.

Cormac knew there was something he was supposed to remember. Something he was meant to ask that was connected to this young woman, but for the life of him, he couldn't recall it. So, he passed through the crowds of people, making his way to her side.

"It's a lovely evening, isn't it?" she said to a gentleman passing by. The fellow glanced at her with surprise but gave no answer.

"That's three," he overheard her muttering to herself. "Two more."

Two more what? In spite of himself, his curiosity got the better of him. He took a few steps closer, and then saw her speak to another gentleman, "Hello."

The man didn't even spare her a glance but continued toward the opposite side of the room.

"And four," she continued.

Was she . . . counting the number of times she spoke to a gentleman? Or the number of times one spurned her? What precisely had she meant by "two more"? On impulse, Cormac went to stand beside Miss Whatever-Her-Name-Was. "Four what?" he asked.

She jolted at the sound of his voice and turned to face him. "I'm—sorry, but did you say something, sir?"

"I was asking you what you were counting," he remarked.

Beneath her breath, he thought he heard her say, "And that makes five." But after that, she said, "Oh, nothing really. It was a wager from one of my friends. She dared me to speak with five gentlemen and claimed that I couldn't do it. I believe you have just helped me win."

He smiled at that. "An interesting wager, to be sure. What is your prize?"

Her cheeks colored, and she said, "I'm not certain yet. I'll find out, Monday next."

Cormac studied the young lady closely. She had long black hair pulled into an elaborate arrangement with curls resting on her cheeks. Her green eyes were striking against her pale complexion, and he found her rather lovely, even though she preferred to remain apart from the others. Her gown was nondescript—a short-sleeved, high-waisted white frock with a blue sash. Yet, it seemed that her eyes drifted toward the ballroom, almost as if she were thinking of something else. Or perhaps *someone* else.

Then he thought a moment and asked, "Have we met before?"

"We have, but you probably don't remember me. I am Emma Bartholomew. And, if my memory serves, you are Lord Dunmeath. From Ireland, I believe?"

"You do have an excellent memory," he complimented her. Which would be a great benefit if this lady would consider him. "My home is near Kerry. Have you ever been to Ireland?"

"No, I haven't."

It was the first time any of the young women in London had spoken to him for more than a few sentences, and he warned himself not to make any mistakes. "It's lovely there," he admitted. "Very green it is, with fields as far as the eye can see."

"What brings you to London?" Her gaze drifted back to the ballroom.

Cormac hesitated, unsure of what to say. If he told her he was seeking a wife, she might believe he'd scorned the women of his homeland. And although he'd already considered many of the young ladies in Ireland, word had gotten out about his family curse. Many were superstitious and refused to have anything to do with him—not if he was going to join his father and brother in an early grave.

His mother's demand that he leave Ireland had forced him to visit the infamous marriage mart of London. The city was indeed filled with heiresses, and there were many ladies to choose from, to be sure. He could only hope that he would find the right woman to bring home again.

"My mother forced me to come," he admitted. "She has a townhouse here, and she asked me to see about the property. I have to make a decision on what to do with it."

"Is it in good condition?" she asked.

"Not too bad," he admitted. "But I've yet to decide whether to sell it. Unless my wife wants me to keep it, that is."

She faltered at that. "Oh, you're married? I didn't realize."

"No, not yet. But if you're willing . . ." He let his voice trail off, keeping the teasing tone. Instead of laughing as most women did, she appeared shocked.

"I—don't know you, sir." She backed away from him and stumbled as she bumped into the wall.

"Oh, you needn't pay me any heed," he said quickly. "I wasn't being serious."

She stopped trying to back away, her face turning bright red. "Oh. Of course, you weren't." The expression on her face was of a woman accustomed to being ignored and overlooked. It bothered him to see it, and he tried to apologize again.

"I didn't mean to embarrass you." In a moment of rare inspiration, he asked, "Would you care to dance?"

"I could never." The words burst forth from her, and she appeared horrified at the idea. His own sense of embarrassment rose up, and he realized that the young lady didn't like him at all. He'd made a mess of things, as usual.

"Oh. Well, do forgive me if I've offended you, Miss Barnes."

He gave a hasty bow and turned away, only to hear her murmur, "It's Bartholomew."

ON MONDAY, EMMA arrived at Mrs. Harding's School for Young Ladies with the full intention of enrolling as a pupil. She had brought a bank note her father had given her for tuition and also a small trunk of her belongings. She'd done exactly as the headmistress had asked and was prepared for whatever lay ahead. Or, at least, almost everything. She hadn't made a list of gentlemen because her handwriting was wretched. Most of the time, she paid the housekeeper to write notes for her because otherwise, the recipient could barely read it.

To her surprise, instead of meeting with the headmistress in the library, Mr. Gregor led her outside to the garden. She counted sixty-two steps to the end of the hall and four stairs down into the tiny garden where Mrs. Harding was waiting.

Emma hesitated before approaching, but at last, she took a seat upon a stone bench. The headmistress cleared her throat. "How was the ball on Saturday?"

For a moment, Emma thought of Lord Dunmeath. He'd had brown hair, and she hadn't been able to tell what color his eyes were. At first, she'd been stunned that he'd even spoken to her. No one ever talked to her.

"I spoke with five gentlemen, as you asked."

"And?" the headmistress prompted.

"Four of them didn't answer me but continued walking to the other side of the room."

"And the fifth?"

An unexpected blush warmed her face. "Lord Dunmeath spoke with me for a time. He asked me to dance with him." She'd been so shocked by the invitation, she'd turned it down, unwilling to consider the possibility of dancing with a gentleman.

"And did you?" Mrs. Harding asked.

She shook her head. "I . . . don't dance well. It's not a skill I have."

"Conversations also seem to be a challenge for you," the matron noted.

Emma couldn't deny it. Lord Dunmeath couldn't even recall her name by the end of their conversation, so clearly she'd made a poor impression.

"What would you say are your strengths?" the headmistress asked.

Leaning up against a wall, she wanted to say. But instead, she answered, "I can play the pianoforte."

Mrs. Harding wrote that down. "What else?"

Emma shook her head. She didn't know what to say when the simple truth was, she wasn't very good at anything.

"And what about your list of possible husbands?" Mrs. Harding asked. "That was one of your tasks, was it not?"

Emma flushed. Yes, it was, but she couldn't have come up with a list if her life depended on it. "I'm sorry. It's hard to imagine husbands when you don't know the men." With a heavy sigh, she continued, "I honestly can't say where I should begin."

The matron set down her quill. "Miss Bartholomew, I can only help you if you want to be helped. You must face your worst fears, whether it be conversation or dancing. And if you become a student, I can promise you that you won't enjoy your time here. This isn't a school where we teach you about the latest hairstyles or fashions. It's about confronting your greatest weaknesses."

Emma didn't know what to say, so she simply held her silence.

Mrs. Harding waited for a reply, and when there was none, she said, "I don't think you should take lessons here, Miss Bartholomew. Not if you've already decided they won't work."

Emma was about to protest when she realized the woman was right. She'd given up on the idea of a marriage based on love years ago.

But if she didn't do something to stand up for herself, her own family would ridicule her. She could indeed protest and refuse to be part of Lucy's auction. But then she might end up being sent away. Or, more likely, word would spread about how she couldn't even find a husband when her family had tried to sell her. She would be utterly humiliated and there would never be a chance of finding a true match in London.

"I do want to marry," she admitted. "And I would love to wed a man who loves me. It's just that . . . after five years, it seems impossible. Even if I wore diamonds and the latest gowns—or even if my dowry were exceptionally large, I just don't think there is anyone who would like me."

"And if we found someone for you, would you consider the match?"

"I might," she conceded. Though she couldn't suppress her apprehension, she asked, "Would you allow me to try a few days of lessons? And if it doesn't work, then I won't have wasted your time."

Mrs. Harding seemed doubtful. "No one can get results so quickly," she cautioned. "Even if you gave it your best effort, it's far too soon."

"I would try very hard," Emma insisted. "I know that I'm not exactly the sort of woman a gentleman would want to marry. But if you could help me, I *am* willing to change myself."

"It's not a matter of changing yourself," Mrs. Harding explained. "It's about building your confidence. And that simply doesn't happen in a matter of days."

Emma opened her reticule and withdrew the banknote. "Two weeks, then."

Mrs. Harding exchanged a glance with Mr. Gregor. "If I agree to this, you must obey my rules. No questions asked."

"I will," Emma promised. "I can even start this afternoon, if you like."

Mrs. Harding let out a sigh. Then she accepted the bank note and said, "One week. If you have shown progress, you may continue a little longer. If not, I will return the remaining tuition."

"Thank you." Emma didn't care what they asked her to do. If she had to dance, she would stumble through it. If she had to make conversation, she would try her best.

"Mr. Gregor, please escort Miss Bartholomew to her room." To Emma, she said, "I will send for you when it is time for your first lesson. In the meantime, get some rest. You're going to need it."

Emma had no idea what she meant by that, but a sudden thrill of excitement hummed within her veins. For the first time, it felt as if she were seizing control of her life instead of doing as she was told.

And one way or another, she would end her stepmother's hopes for this auction.

"WHAT DO YOU think?" Rachel Harding asked her business partner Cedric Gregor. "I want to hear your impressions of Miss Bartholomew."

"Her looks aren't bad," he hedged, "but there is something unusual about her. I've heard her counting beneath her breath whenever she is walking anywhere. She seems to be a young woman who needs to be in control at every moment."

"And she cannot control a husband," Rachel countered. "Perhaps we should begin by creating chaos. If she can learn to be more adaptable, then it might help her to become less rigid."

"She's afraid," Cedric predicted. "Disrupting her life may cause her even more suffering."

"But we both know she needs to be broken before we can help her," Mrs. Harding said. "She needs to abandon her bad habits."

He gave a nod, and then asked, "Did you have anyone in mind for her?"

"Begin with Lord Dunmeath," she suggested. "I've heard rumors that he cannot remember anything. A man like the earl would drive Miss Bartholomew to madness. I am interested to see how she would respond."

"I'll see if I can arrange it," he answered. "Who else?"

"See if you can find gentlemen who are carefree and kind," she suggested. "Let me know who else might suit."

Cedric inclined his head. "Shall I send for the dancing master?"

"Indeed. As soon as possible." But even beyond the lessons, Rachel knew she would have to dig more deeply. Emma Bartholomew had not become a rigid woman of control for no reason. Her task now was to discover that reason and help the young woman gain the confidence to stand up for herself.

"I will see it done." He paused for a moment and studied her. "There's something else. Sir Brian Lucas sent a note. I presume he wants to pay a call on you."

She tensed when he set the note down on the table. A few months ago, Sir Brian had come to her asking for help with matchmaking only to reveal that he was interested in her. His unexpected courtship had rattled Rachel, for she wasn't ready to face another relationship. One terrible marriage was enough for a lifetime—and she couldn't imagine trying again. She had tried to put him off, but the baronet would not be dissuaded.

"You know I am not interested in being courted." She left the note alone, ignoring it.

"As you say. But he *did* ask for your help in matchmaking. You have other ladies who are looking for a husband. Is it wise to ignore a potential suitor, even if he's not for you?"

She grimaced, for Cedric had a point. "Why are you always the voice of reason?"

He sent her a wicked smile. "Because I am an excellent business partner, and I would never turn down an opportunity for money. Now, write a reply to his note, and in the meantime, we'll decide whether our Miss Bartholomew can be coaxed into softening her rigid control."

Rachel thought a moment, wondering about the best way to proceed. It did seem that social situations were one of the young lady's greatest weaknesses. Which meant that she needed to be forced into it so she could practice. "We should host a dinner party for a group of gentlemen," she suggested. "It doesn't matter who they are. Pick anyone you like—hire them, if need be. She needs to speak with each of them."

"She's going to fail," Cedric predicted. "Is that what you're hoping for?"

"Yes. And that is how we will begin—by finding her failures and addressing them." She held no delusions that Miss Bartholomew would find a match. But the dinner party would be a good way of identifying the young woman's difficulties.

"I'll make the arrangements. I presume you want this dinner tomorrow evening?"

"If at all possible." She glanced at the note she didn't want to open. "We'll host it earlier so if any of the gentlemen are already attending a ball, it won't interfere with that."

"I'll notify Cook."

Rachel waited until after he'd left before she reached for the folded note. She didn't want to answer the note at all, though courtesy demanded it. Sir Brian seemed to believe that they had known each other once, that he was part of her past. Yet, she didn't remember him at all. Her only memories of the past involved a husband she would rather forget.

She broke the seal and opened the note. There was no letter, no words except his signature. But Sir Brian had sent her a pressed forget-me-not. The dried blossom did seem to tug at a long-forgotten memory, though she couldn't quite grasp it.

It wasn't fair to lead him on, to let him believe there was any hope. She lived her life in a different way now. It filled her with a quiet joy to watch shy young ladies blossom into confident women who were adored by their husbands. They would find the happiness and love that she'd never known.

And it was enough.

THE FIRST DAY had been rather disastrous. Not only had Mrs. Harding left her a list of instructions, but Emma had no idea where anything was. Instead, she'd ignored the list and had taken the time to explore the house instead. She'd counted steps, learned where all the rooms were, and made every effort to avoid being caught.

Oh, she knew that avoiding the list would anger the headmistress, but she didn't want to admit her reasons just yet.

But after she'd returned from exploring, Mr. Gregor had knocked on her bedroom door and advised her that Mrs. Harding was waiting downstairs to escort her to the dining room for supper.

"Will I need to change my gown?" Emma asked.

"That won't be necessary." But even though his tone was neutral, she questioned whether she was in trouble.

"Is she . . . angry with me?" Emma asked tentatively.

"Should she be?" Mr. Gregor said nothing more, but she followed him down the stairs and they walked thirteen steps toward the dining room.

Before they reached the doorway, he stopped, and Mrs. Harding, who was waiting for them there, spoke quietly. "Miss

Bartholomew, there will be several dinner guests this evening. Your task is to speak to each of them. It must be a true conversation, not simply saying hello. Get acquainted with the gentlemen and be memorable."

Emma had no idea what the headmistress meant by memorable, but she realized something was amiss when Mrs. Harding added, "Our guests are wearing blindfolds. I do not want them to form judgments before they know you. So, you must use conversation to draw their attention."

Why would Mrs. Harding do such a thing? Then her heart sank when she realized the truth. If they could not see her, then they would have no idea who she was—which made it less likely that they would ignore her. It also made sense why there was no need to change her gown, for the men would never know what she was wearing.

"Gentlemen, may I present Miss Mary Smith," Mrs. Harding began as she led Emma into the room. "That is not her real name of course, but your task is to guess who she is."

And Emma realized that she, in turn, would have to learn something about each of them.

"It's a brilliant idea," she heard one man offer. "I shall enjoy this game very much." His voice held a hint of a lilt, and she recognized him. Cormac Ormond, the Earl of Dunmeath. Emma half-wondered whether he would remember her at all.

"A fascinating notion," said another man. "But I know every eligible young lady in London. It won't be hard to guess who she really is."

Emma didn't recognize this man's voice, but then Mrs. Harding nudged her. Oh. Right. She was expected to speak to them.

"Good evening." Her voice came out softer than she'd intended. The headmistress did not look pleased, and Emma spoke louder to the guests. "I look forward to conversing with you."

Which was an utter lie, of course. She didn't know the first thing about having a conversation with an unmarried gentleman. What on earth should she say? Perhaps she could talk about the food.

Emma took her seat at the head of the table, and the footman stepped forward with the first soup course. A moment later, someone placed a blindfold over her eyes. At first, Emma had to resist the urge to take it off. The fabric felt like wool and itched. And in the darkness, she could no longer see her food or drink.

It almost made her laugh at the absurdity of this dinner.

She heard the sound of a liquid being poured into her cup. But when she reached for her glass, it was no longer in the same spot. Or had the drink been given to one of the other gentlemen? She wasn't certain.

Emma took a moment to take her bearings. First, she placed her napkin in her lap. Then she arranged her silver until she knew where her fork and spoon were. Her glass was located at the top of her soup bowl instead of to the right, so she moved it.

"Miss Smith," one of the gentlemen dared, "tell me something about yourself. Something no one else in London knows about you."

In a way, she was grateful for the suggestion of conversation. "I'll have to think," she answered. But the truth was, she couldn't think of anything interesting. Her life was a tightly knit pattern of meals with her family, insufferable balls, and walking outside with her father's dog. She didn't read, didn't do needlepoint, nor did she paint.

"I do play the pianoforte," she offered.

"Nearly every young lady does," another responded. "Do you sing?"

Though she supposed the gentleman was trying to learn more about her, she felt as if he'd given a slight criticism. "Very badly," she admitted. "Our dog would howl if I tried to sing."

"What sort of dog is he?" she heard Lord Dunmeath ask.

"He's a spaniel." Though truthfully, he was her father's dog. Bertie was a sweet animal, but he mostly lay beside the fireplace and snored. He tolerated the walks, but because of his age, she suspected he didn't enjoy them.

Emma reached for her spoon and found the edge of her bowl before dipping it into her soup. The warm vegetable soup was comforting and provided a distraction while she searched for another conversation topic. For a moment, she fell silent, slipping back into the familiarity of not speaking. Although she knew she was supposed to be engaging and vivacious, she had no idea where to begin. She didn't talk to gentlemen. She knew nothing of how to converse.

But then, Lord Dunmeath offered her a respite. "Miss Smith, I suggest that each of us should be telling you something about ourselves. One at a time, around the table."

She was grateful for the suggestion and answered, "That sounds like a good idea." The other gentlemen murmured their agreement, and Emma turned to her left. "Might I suggest that the gentleman on my left begin?"

"Ah yes." She heard him set down his spoon and he said, "I enjoy reading books. Do you have a favorite novel or author?"

"No," Emma answered. "I can't say that I enjoy reading." There were too many memories when she'd had her knuckles rapped as a young girl. Her governess had given up eventually, but she'd made it clear that she thought Emma was the most ignorant girl she'd ever attempted to teach.

"Oh," he said. "I must admit I'm surprised. I rather thought that since you had come to this school, you were most likely a bluestocking."

"Far from it," Emma admitted. She'd never been very good at school. It had taken years to hide her ignorance from others.

Then the next gentleman spoke, "I enjoy hunting. Do you shoot at all?"

"No," she answered. "My aim is terrible."

The third gentleman was Lord Dunmeath. He began by saying, "I like new experiences. Taking walks early in the morning or buying food from a street vendor. Sometimes I'll go about my day with no plans at all, except the ones I make at the last minute."

The very idea horrified her, for Emma found familiarity and comfort in routines. Each day, she ate the same breakfast, nearly the same luncheon, and at night, she fell asleep at the same time. "That sounds . . . interesting," she responded, though it was a blatant lie.

Then he continued and asked, "Tell me, Miss Smith . . . do you wear spectacles?"

The blood rushed to her face, and her skin went icy. For a moment, she had a sense that he had guessed her darkest secret. It startled her, but she managed to blurt out, "No, I do not."

At least, not anymore. Not since her stepmother had thrown them out, claiming that attractive women didn't wear spectacles.

His silence felt like an unspoken judgment. But really, her stepmother had been right. The spectacles hadn't helped anyway. She could barely see anything at all—only colors and vague shapes. And reading was impossible. She'd given up at the age of nine. Her governess had despaired of her lack of education and had eventually quit.

Although Emma rather hoped Mrs. Harding wouldn't discover the truth of her poor vision and illiteracy for a few more days, she knew the headmistress would be horrified when she found out.

Mrs. Harding had already been angry with her for refusing to write a list. But Emma's penmanship was terrible, for she couldn't see the letters she'd printed. And likely the headmistress would be furious to learn that Emma had ignored her list of instructions. But how could she admit that she couldn't read them?

"I believe it's my turn," the last gentleman said. "I enjoy playing cards. Do you enjoy whist, Miss Smith?"

"I've never played," she admitted. "So, I really couldn't say."

The footmen brought in the next course. From the delicious roasted scent, she guessed it was chicken. She found her fork and knife, located the edges of the plate, and began to eat. While she understood that Mrs. Harding was trying to draw her out, to force her to converse, the dinner was becoming increasingly uncomfortable. Eventually, the men began to talk amongst themselves, leaving her out of the conversation. Until she heard a voice near her ear.

"I didn't mean to offend you."

She jolted at the sound of Lord Dunmeath's voice. It was rare that anyone could sneak up on her—she'd trained herself to listen closely to all sounds. But she'd been distracted trying to eavesdrop on the others.

"You didn't offend me," she said quietly.

"It's just that . . . well, never mind."

"Go on," she said dully.

"Well, I took some time to be thinking about your answers. Someone who needs spectacles would not enjoy reading. I used to hate it as a child until my tutor gave me a more interesting book of fairytales." He moved to the other side of her chair. "And then, too, I suppose you'd not enjoy shooting or anything that involves straining your eyes. It was simply a guess."

It had been a very good guess indeed. And she realized that he'd also noticed how she'd grown silent, and he'd made an effort to speak with her.

The pine scent of his shaving soap fascinated her. A sudden rush of nerves made her blush. For if she had to decide on suitors, Lord Dunmeath was indeed a possibility.

She didn't know what prompted her to say it, but she confessed, "I did wear spectacles as a child, though I don't anymore. They didn't help my vision at all." She dropped her voice to a whisper. "I cannot see anything close up, and it's mostly colors and shapes."

She waited for him to express his horror, but instead, he remarked, "I must admit, I admire you for being able to navigate a ballroom or even a meal. I suspect half my food is on the floor after wearing this blindfold, to be sure. 'Tis a miracle I was able to find your chair." She didn't know how to respond to that, so he ended by saying, "It's my hope that we might become better acquainted, Miss Smith. If you're willing." Then she heard him moving back to his seat.

None of the other men continued the conversation, so she finished her dessert course and waited for them to leave.

Mrs. Harding returned and asked the gentlemen. "Has anyone guessed the identity of Miss Smith after your conversation with her earlier?"

At first, there was a slight discussion amongst the men. One guessed that she was Lady Beatrice. Another guessed that she was Miss Edwards, only to be corrected that Miss Edwards was now the Countess of Scarsdale. She waited on Lord Dunmeath to reveal her identity, but he remained silent.

Mrs. Harding's tone held a trace of annoyance. "None of you has guessed? After all this conversation?"

Then she heard Lord Dunmeath speak at last. "I know who it is, but I fear I'm dreadful with names."

"And what do you believe her name might be?" the matron prompted.

He held his silence a little longer, and then sighed. "I know it's wrong, but possibly Miss Cooper?"

The sting of embarrassment hung over Emma. But then, what had she expected? Clearly, she'd made no impression at all on these men—not in person, and not when they were blindfolded. Her shoulders slumped forward, and then she heard Mrs. Harding say, "Incorrect. I fear none of you has guessed the identity of our mystery lady. Thank you for joining us for supper this evening. I will show her out, and Mr. Gregor will let you know when you may remove your blindfolds."

Emma felt a hand on her shoulder, and she stood from the chair. Mrs. Harding took her hand and guided her from the room. She counted sixteen steps until they reached another room. The matron brought her to a chair and bade her to sit down.

Several seconds ticked by until finally, Mrs. Harding said, "This isn't going to work, Miss Bartholomew. Not if you aren't willing to try."

"I did try," she started to argue.

"Not one of the gentlemen had any idea who you were. And after one failed attempt at conversation, you simply gave up."

"I didn't. It was just that—none of them were interested in talking to me."

"Do you presume that Lady Persephone or any of the ladies of the *ton* would sit back and allow men to ignore her?"

"No, but—"

"If you cannot break out of your habits, then I fear we are done before we've even started."

At that, Emma pushed back. "And how would you know what happened at the dinner? I did speak to Lord Dunmeath."

"I know what happened because I never left the room," Mrs. Harding answered. "I was there the entire time. I saw precisely what you did—and didn't—do."

At that, Emma's face flushed. "None of the men wanted to talk to me," she murmured. "I didn't know what to say."

"So, you gave up."

The judgment in the woman's voice bothered her deeply. Yes, she'd given up. She was so accustomed to feeling awkward and unwanted that she'd fallen back on familiar habits. Even after Lord Dunmeath had come to speak with her, despite the hopes she'd gathered . . . she didn't truly believe that it would work. After all, the earl had asked half of London to wed him already. Why would he have any real interest in her? Especially when he couldn't be bothered to remember her name.

And yet, she couldn't deny that Mrs. Harding was right. If she didn't do something, she would find herself being sold off into marriage soon enough.

"I suppose I did give up," Emma admitted. "I didn't like being the center of attention."

"What sort of husband do you want?" Mrs. Harding asked.

She took a long moment to think about it. "Someone who lets me be who I am. Someone ordinary, who doesn't expect me to plan grand parties or be in charge of a large household. I shouldn't marry a man with a title."

"And why not?"

She shrugged. "I'm not able to handle all the responsibilities. It's too much." Her cheeks flushed with embarrassment at her ignorance.

"Does it have anything to do with your eyesight?" Mrs. Harding asked. "When was the last time a physician examined you?"

A flush came over her at the realization that the matron had overheard her quiet conversation with Lord Dunmeath. She lowered her gaze and admitted, "Years ago, when I was seven. He told my father I would be fully blind by the time I turned eighteen."

"And are you?"

She shook her head. "Not yet. But one day, I fear it may happen."

The matron fell silent for a long period of time, and Emma couldn't quite tell whether it was pity or whether the woman was trying to decide what to do.

"Has your sight become worse over the years?"

Emma shrugged. "I don't really know. But I can only see things that are farther away. And even then, it's mostly colors." Truthfully, she couldn't recall ever being able to see properly. Whatever that meant. She knew how to count steps in familiar places so she would find the doorways. She knew colors, but even when she was close to someone, she couldn't quite make out all their features.

"Why didn't you tell us this when you first arrived?"

Emma's skin grew cold, and she suppressed a shiver. "Because whenever anyone learns that I cannot see well, they presume that I am incapable of doing anything at all. If I say nothing, they assume I have a ladies' education."

"And do you have an education?" the matron prompted.

She felt sick to her stomach at the prodding. "I can't read, if that's what you're asking. I didn't write your list because I cannot see the letters I am printing. I couldn't read your instructions this morning."

"I noticed that you ignored them," she said. "You were walking around the house instead."

"It was the only thing I could do," Emma admitted. The sting of humiliation washed over her. "I can't paint with watercolors or do needlepoint. If you ask me to locate Italy upon a map, I would have no means of finding it, not even if the name was printed on it." She shook her head, holding back hot tears. It humiliated her, admitting all that she couldn't do. But she saw no reason to hold back anymore. Most likely, the matron would now refuse to take her as a student.

"Conversations are difficult for me because I have nothing to talk about," Emma continued. "I've never traveled anywhere or done anything." Despite her attempts to keep her emotions under control, the tears finally escaped. "I'm sorry. It's just that . . . it's so hard. What man wants a wife who is practically blind?"

Against her hand, she felt the headmistress press a handkerchief into her palm. "I think I misjudged you, Miss Bartholomew. And hearing what you've said has made me reconsider your lessons."

Mrs. Harding paused for a moment and said, "I believe part of your lessons should be receiving an education on all the things you wanted to learn but couldn't."

The woman's sudden kindness only made her tears come harder. Emma struggled to gather her thoughts amid her sobs and admitted, "I would be grateful."

"Then we will begin in the morning."

"There's something else," Emma interrupted. She wiped her tears away and admitted, "My stepmother has planned an auction. She intends to invite unmarried gentlemen to bid on a piece of art, but whoever wins will also win my hand in marriage." Her voice held a tremor, despite her efforts to control it. "I can't let them do this. Please help me."

Mrs. Harding let out a heavy sigh. "Unfortunately, I did hear of this from rumors around London. My source tells me that your stepmother has already sent out the invitations."

"Oh no," Emma breathed. Humiliation washed over her at the thought. It meant that Lucy had made the decision without consulting her husband. "I thought I could talk her out of it. It's . . . part of the reason why I came here."

"If it is still your wish to be married, I can send several suitors to become your tutors," the matron suggested. "Then you can get to know them and decide if you like them." She paused a moment. "Unless there is someone else who has already caught your interest?"

Emma thought again of Lord Dunmeath, but then she was afraid to get her hopes up. Most likely the earl wasn't truly interested in her—only curious.

And so, she answered, "No one in particular."

"Then we will choose a few candidates," Mrs. Harding finished. "In the meantime, go and get some rest. Tomorrow will be very busy indeed."

Emma supposed it was good that her secret had now been revealed. But even so, what man wanted a wife who couldn't read, handle the household accounts, or write letters? Her time was running out—and she worried that there wasn't enough time to escape this auction.

Chapter Three

C ORMAC'S STOMACH WRENCHED with a vicious pain. His vision had grown dizzy, and he'd been unable to sleep or eat. He couldn't remember the last time it had been this bad. His senses were so overwhelmed he simply lay in the darkness, trying to do nothing but breathe.

The attack had come on suddenly, without any warning. He'd tried to distract himself from the pain by rereading his grandfather's diary. The stories of his family's past were familiar, and his father Brandan had added his own tales over the years. In many ways, it was a way of remembering his father. There were sometimes notes written in the margins, reminders that Brandan had written about family birthdays or gifts he'd meant to buy for them.

The words caused a fresh ache of pain, even though it had been seven years. As a boy, Cormac had wanted nothing more than to be like his father. But the illness had struck hard and taken his loved ones far too soon.

His mood grew despondent, for he didn't want to die. He was only six-and-twenty. He'd barely lived a life at all, and he had a household in Ireland who depended on him. His little sisters needed him. His mother needed him.

Yet he could do nothing except lie in the dark in his study.

Hawkins had offered to help him upstairs to his bedchamber, but he'd refused. The thought of walking made him nauseous, and the thought of being carried—was humiliating. He had nothing left but his pride. At least if he lay back on the settee with a blanket, he could rest.

"Sir, I've brought you a headache powder in water," Hawkins offered, keeping his voice low. "And some fresh bread. It might help."

He had no desire to eat, but he knew he had little choice. Bitterness cloaked his mood, even as he choked down the food and the bitter powder in water.

"You also received an invitation to pay a call at Mrs. Harding's residence in the morning," Hawkins said. "She said something about matchmaking?"

Cormac steadied himself. He wasn't certain he would be well enough by then, but he did need help finding a wife. Although, at this rate, he might be dead by Christmas.

"Shall I send your regrets, my lord?" Hawkins suggested. "I doubt if you'll be well by morning."

He already knew he would not. And yet, if he was able to stand or walk around, he would force himself to go. Even if his head was pounding, he would try. If he stayed within these four walls, he might go mad.

His thoughts drifted back to Miss B. Or whatever her family name was. He'd lied about knowing who she was, for he hadn't wanted to embarrass her. But the truth was, he'd noticed the moment she'd withdrawn from the dinner conversation. The other gentlemen had already dismissed her, and he'd sensed the awkwardness she was feeling.

Cormac had experienced the same isolation himself as a boy, and it drew him closer to her. He remembered the night he'd spoken to her at the ball. She'd had a softness in her features, and he'd had a sense that she was seeing beyond what everyone else saw. And now he knew the reason behind that distance in her green eyes, though last night she'd revealed more than she'd intended.

Despite knowing about her vision problems, it didn't make him pity her. Instead, it provoked his curiosity. He wanted to know more about blindness, to understand how she navigated such a complex world as London. Honestly, he didn't know if he could manage it. And he was convinced that no one else knew of this, which fascinated him.

"Write a note, if you would, and tell Mrs. Harding I will try to come," he said. "If I can."

"There are four other invitations for this week," Hawkins continued. "Two are balls, one is a musicale, and the last one is the auction. Do you still wish to attend?"

He'd nearly forgotten about the auction. "Write a reply of yes to all." If he didn't feel better by then, he would send a note of regrets.

But as he lay back on the settee in the darkness, he knew he would have to take desperate measures if he meant to see his heir before he died.

CORMAC WAITED IN the drawing room, feeling as if he'd gone three rounds in a boxing match. He'd barely slept, and he felt weak and exhausted. Even so, he didn't want to waste any opportunity to find a bride. Miss B was the best option he had, and he would not turn his back on her.

Mrs. Harding arrived at last and greeted him. "Lord Dunmeath, I'm so glad you've come. Are you still interested in finding a bride?"

"I am, yes." He tried to keep his voice friendly, though he felt as if he'd just crawled out of his own grave.

"At the supper party the other night, what did you think of our Miss Smith?" she prompted.

"I knew her," he admitted, "though I could not recall her name. I liked her, though."

"Her real name is Miss Emma Bartholomew."

"That's right." She was indeed the young woman who'd been counting off gentlemen to speak to the other night. "I remember her now."

"Miss Bartholomew will be having a dancing lesson today, and I would like you to be her partner. The dancing master, Mr. Brown, will be here soon."

The idea of spinning in circles made his stomach twist, but Cormac warned himself that this was a chance to know the young lady better. "All right."

He followed the headmistress up a flight of stairs to a small room that he supposed was meant to be a ballroom.

The young lady stood on the far end of the room. She wore a lovely day dress that was the pale pink of a spring rose. It contrasted against her dark hair, and he complimented her when he greeted her. "You look lovely this morning, Miss—"

"Bartholomew," she finished. "I know you can't seem to remember my name."

"I've never been good with names," he admitted. "I apologize." Though, to be fair, he was far more focused on settling his stomach and calming the illness when he felt so terrible.

She sighed. "Lord Dunmeath, I know you don't really want to be here. I can manage alone with the dancing master if need be. Though, to be honest, I don't know why Mrs. Harding is having me take lessons. The idea of dancing in a ballroom horrifies me."

"Let us sit and talk for a moment," he suggested. It was a good excuse because he needed time to gather his strength again. "Did you ever want to learn how to dance?"

"My tutors tried to teach me when I was growing up. But it was too easy to bump into things—and other couples. I gave up. I found it easier to pretend that I didn't like dancing. Which, I suppose, is true."

"How do you get around houses?" he asked. "It does seem easy enough for you."

"I count steps," she admitted. "And I walk slowly when I can."

The idea intrigued him, and he couldn't help but ask, "How many steps is it from here to the doorway?"

"Fourteen," she answered.

He considered that and asked, "What about from the door to the stairs?"

"Seven steps forward and then twelve to the left." Then she said, "Lord Dunmeath, if you don't mind, I'd rather not converse about all the steps. It makes me feel as if I'm being tested. I get around as best I can, and I'd rather not be pitied."

"Forgive me then, *a chara*. It's only my ignorance that's showing." He tried to keep his voice lighthearted, hiding the pain that kept rising up. His head was aching again, so he stopped trying to smile. In a way, it was a relief not having to feign an expression he didn't feel.

Instead, he studied her features, noting that her dark hair was braided and pinned up. Her expression held an invisible shield, as if she didn't want to answer any questions about her vision. Wallflower or not, no one could deny that she was beautiful.

His curiosity continued, and he asked, "Are you angry that Mrs. Harding wishes you to learn to dance?"

"It's not the first time I've been forced into it," she admitted. "When I was young, a tutor tried to teach me country dances, but I couldn't keep up. It was too complicated."

He could see how that would be a problem with swift dancers and switching partners. "There are other, easier dances you could try." Not to mention, his stomach was still aching with a vicious, throbbing pain. He didn't think he could manage the dizzying steps of a quadrille or anything faster. "Perhaps a waltz, I'm thinking." A slow one, where he didn't have to move quickly.

"I simply don't see the point," she answered. "What purpose is there in dancing?"

He supposed she wouldn't understand if she'd never indulged. "Perhaps I can show you, if you're willing." He didn't ask permission but took her gloved hand in his. "Stand up and move beside me."

She did, but her demeanor was stiff and uncertain. When he drew near, he noticed that her scent reminded him of honeysuckle blossoms. He wondered whether it was a fragrance she wore, or whether it was soap from her bath.

He let go of her hand and said, "Place your right hand behind your back." When she obeyed, he touched his own hand to hers, resting them against her spine. She seemed nervous, as if she'd never held a man's hand before. "Now you'll be taking my left hand, and I'll hold it over here. Like so." He took her left hand in his and drew it to the side. "After that, we'll be walking forward together. Right foot first, then left. Imagine we're taking a stroll."

Her green eyes seemed troubled, but at least she seemed willing to try. He walked with her slowly, giving her time to get adjusted. But he grew aware of the warmth of her gloved hand against his and the curve of her waist. "Smaller steps," he urged. "Again, right . . . then left. Right . . . then left. We're just going to be strolling across the room while you get used to it."

When she seemed comfortable with those steps, he said, "Now, turn toward me, and I will raise our left hands high." She did, and he lifted her hand, holding it up while he moved his right hand to the small of her back.

"Put your right hand on my shoulder," he said. "If you would, please."

"This feels like I shouldn't be this close to you," she admitted.

"It's like an embrace, isn't it?" For a moment, he held steady, letting her get used to his hand against her body. "I think that's why men and women enjoy waltzing. It gives you the chance to see if you like being so close to someone."

"I—I don't know if I like it or not." Her face was flushed, and for a moment, he thought about kissing her. Her mouth interested him, and he suspected she'd never been kissed before. Now that would be an enjoyable lesson—to spend hours teaching her how to kiss. He imagined stealing the slightest touch, letting the warmth of his mouth press against hers. The very thought heated his blood, making him yearn for more. For a moment, he indulged himself in the idea of courting this woman. He found her lovely, and she did seem to be a potential wife candidate, even if she was shy.

She took a breath, as if trying to calm herself. "What happens next in the dance?"

"From here, you'll take smaller steps while I move you in a circle."

"What kind of steps?" she asked.

He thought a moment, and then an unexpected laugh broke forth. "To be honest, I've no idea. Women's skirts are so long, I could never quite tell what they were doing. I don't think it matters so very much."

"It does matter a great deal," she protested. "If I move the wrong way, I'll step on your toes and fall."

At that, he realized she'd come up with an excellent solution. "That's a very good idea, actually. Go on and step on my toes. Both of them, if you please. I'll move my feet in the correct patterns, and you can learn them by feeling the direction instead of me trying to teach it badly."

"I'll crush your feet," she argued. "It's not a good idea. Nor is it very proper."

"I'll only suffer for a wee bit. Go on, then."

She stepped on his feet, and he tested out a step or two. Her weight was hardly anything at all, but he grunted, "Never mind then. You were right about my feet."

In spite of herself, she started laughing. "You're not serious."

"I might be." He groaned again with mock pain. It was good to hear her laugh for the first time. Cormac began moving her through the pattern of the waltz, despite her feet being atop his.

"Did you never dance with your father like this?" he asked.

"No, never. He wasn't much of a dancer." But she seemed fully concentrated on the steps. He kept it very slow, both for her sake and his own lingering pain.

"Are you ready to try it on your own?" he asked. "We'll march forward first."

"I will probably be terrible." But she stepped off his feet and moved beside him once again. They took four steps, and she turned to him, keeping their left hands clasped above their heads while his hand was on her spine.

Her face was so close to his, he could easily have stolen a kiss. From the way her breathing grew unsteady, he suspected she felt something as well. Heat seemed to emanate between them in a silent invitation for more. He suddenly imagined unbuttoning her gown slowly, tracing the silken line of her back.

"Lord Dunmeath, I—" She started to pull back, but he held her hands a moment longer.

"You're doing very well," he said. "Now perhaps next time when I'm inviting you to dance at a ball, you might say yes."

But her expression faltered. "Why are you helping me, Lord Dunmeath? I am grateful to you, but . . . are they paying you to be here?"

"No. I agreed to come and help."

"But why?"

I need a wife and I'm running out of time, he almost said. Instead, he answered, "Because I am a curious man. I'd like to know how you've managed to survive all this time. No one seems to grasp the challenges you face every day, simply by walking into a room. It intrigues me."

"I don't have a choice," she pointed out. "But then, I suppose I am lucky to have any sight at all. Sometimes when I feel sorry for myself, I imagine those who cannot see anything."

"Does your family know?" he asked.

"They don't know how bad it is. They think I can see most things and that I am only clumsy."

"What is it you see when you look into this room?" he asked.

She paused and thought a moment. "I see the sunlight from the window over there. I see dark shades of your clothing."

"Can you see my face?" He wondered whether she had any

idea what he looked like.

She shook her head. "Not really."

He couldn't imagine such an existence where he couldn't see someone's face. It bothered him to know that she would never know what anyone looked like. But there weren't any words he could think of except, "I'm sorry to hear it."

"I can still see you," she said quietly. "Just in a different way."

He didn't understand what she meant. Then she continued. "You have dark hair, and you're taller than me. Your shaving soap reminds me of fir trees at Christmas." After another pause, she said, "You walk around and stop frequently, as if you're thinking of something. And right now, you're in a great deal of pain, but you don't want to admit it. And it has nothing to do with my feet on yours."

Her quiet conclusion startled him. "How could you be knowing such a thing?"

"Your voice. You sound as if you haven't slept in at least a day, if not longer."

"Not since the supper party," he admitted. "I often get . . . very bad headaches." It wasn't quite the truth, but it sounded better than confessing the stomach pains.

"I'm sorry. I know many women who suffer from those. I've heard that a quiet, dark room can help."

He nodded and then realized she probably couldn't see the nod. "It does, aye. But I haven't slept or eaten well in some time." For a moment, he wished he could confess the truth to her, that he was dying. But it would only frighten her off, and right now, this woman was the best marital prospect he had. He liked her a great deal. Yet, he sensed that she would not be one to rush into marriage.

The dancing master, Mr. Brown, arrived at that moment, along with two other couples. Miss Bartholomew seemed disconcerted, but Cormac murmured, "It's only Miss Cooper and Lady Chelsea. And I believe that's Lord Malfield and Mr. Alan Goodson."

"You remember their names, but you don't remember mine?"

He didn't miss the chiding in her voice. "I could be wrong. And I can't say why your name won't stick in my memory. But I suppose it's because . . . when I'm around someone like you, my thoughts scatter. The others mean nothing to me. Whereas you've captured my full attention. It may be that's the reason why."

EMMA COULDN'T STOP the wayward thrill that passed over her, even knowing that Lord Dunmeath probably didn't mean anything by it. It was a throwaway remark, one that held no import.

But no man had ever said anything like that to her before. *Don't let yourself believe him.* Lord Dunmeath had been kind, but he'd admitted that he was only here to satisfy his curiosity. To him, she was like an unusual creature, one who fascinated him with her blindness.

A knot settled into her stomach when Mr. Brown asked them to form two lines. *Oh no.* It was country dances again.

Emma swallowed hard, already knowing what was about to happen. With so many people in such a small space, undoubtedly she was going to make a mess of herself. But Mrs. Harding had been adamant about these lessons. Did she want her to face her worst fears? Was that it?

"Don't be afraid," came the voice of Lord Dunmeath. "I'm going to stand across from you. And I'm going to talk you through every moment."

He took her hand and led her to the end of the line, which ensured that they would be last. The dancing master instructed the men to bow and the ladies to curtsy. That part was easy enough. But when the patterns began, Emma's nerves tightened. She felt lightheaded, and with so many scents and the sound of so many feet, she started to grow disoriented.

I don't want to be here.

She took a step backward, wondering if she could safely escape when Lord Dunmeath's voice interrupted. "After you step toward me, keep your hand in mine and turn in a circle," he said quietly. "You'll end up on the opposite side of the line."

She hesitated, but finally took a few awkward steps forward, and he used his hand to turn her in the right direction. "Perfect. Now step back and we'll do the same with your other hand."

His deep baritone voice had an Irish lilt that offered friendly encouragement. She swallowed hard but obeyed his instructions. When his hand touched hers, another flare of heat slid through her.

"We'll be switching partners now," he said gently. "Take a slight step to your right and hold out your hand. The gentleman will take it and turn you twice in a circle."

Emma had no time to think, but she took one step and held out her hand. Thankfully, a gentleman took it, and as Lord Dunmeath had predicted, he turned her in a circle.

"Left hand," she heard him say, and when she turned with her left hand, the gentleman took it and led her in a circle once again.

"Right hand," she heard again, and when she stretched hers out, the others rested their hands atop each other. Lord Dunmeath reached back for her other hand and discreetly guided her into a larger circle. She was utterly lost in the patterns, but she was aware of him. The scent of his skin allured her, and she realized that she was letting herself become too vulnerable.

It brought back memories of balls years ago, when she'd mistakenly believed that she would meet a gentleman, dance with him, and fall in love. Instead, she'd been unable to follow the steps and dancing became a means of humiliation. Today would probably be no different.

She reminded herself that Mrs. Harding had asked Lord Dunmeath to be here. He wasn't here to court her. And the fact that he'd asked so many other young ladies to wed him—but not her—was evidence enough. She couldn't allow herself to dream of something that wouldn't happen.

Mr. Brown went to the pianoforte and began playing another song. Emma struggled to remember what was next. Some of the couples had switched places, and to her dismay, she realized that Lord Dunmeath was no longer her partner.

For a moment, she stumbled but then held out her right hand for her partner. In, then out. Spin, then switch places and hands. She silently recited the instructions to herself over and over, trying to memorize them.

But with this gentleman, she felt only tension and unease. His scent was heavier, of bergamot. Her partner grasped her hand firmly, but she sensed an unspoken arrogance about him—as if he believed he were better than her.

Was this supposed to be fun? Emma knew she was starting to get the steps right, but all she could think of was trying not to embarrass herself. The familiar panic knotted inside her stomach, and she started to lose her place. The moving shapes and colors made her dizzy, and she took a few steps backward. "I'm sorry. I need a moment to catch my breath."

"An excellent idea," Lord Dunmeath said from nearby. She hadn't known he was so close, and the thought unsettled her.

She couldn't tell if there were any chairs in the room, but she walked toward the closest wall.

"Miss Bartholomew, I would ask you to please rejoin the ladies," Mr. Brown called out. "Mrs. Harding gave instructions that you are to remain for the entire lesson."

"If you'll give me a moment, I will try again," she answered. Though she kept her voice calm, the familiar sense of being flustered was overwhelming. All she wanted to do was leave the room. And yet, she'd promised Mrs. Harding that she would try the lessons.

She heard footsteps approaching, and the gentleman stopped a short distance away. In a low voice, Lord Dunmeath asked,

"Are you all right?"

She nodded, even though it was a lie. She had no desire to do this again. Dancing was terrible. Well, except perhaps when she'd waltzed with him earlier. That hadn't been so bad. The earl stood beside her, and his pine scent made her want to bury her face into his coat. She imagined what it would be like to have his arms around her once again.

Don't do it, her brain warned. She couldn't dare give herself hope. Five Seasons had taught her that much. Better to push back the wayward daydreams and face what was real.

"Are you wanting to stop?" he asked.

She did, but to admit it was to admit her cowardice. "I'll manage. I was just . . . starting to forget the patterns."

With a sigh, Emma started back toward the blurred colors. She walked to the very end of the line where she could see no one, and thankfully the dark shape of Lord Dunmeath stood across from her once more.

She steadied herself, keeping track of right and left, but when it came time to switch positions, she started to get disoriented again. Which way was her partner? She tried to move to the right, but suddenly there was no one there. A slight titter of laughter came from one of the ladies, so she attempted to go left. Once again, there was no partner. She didn't quite know what to do, so she waited. A moment later, someone took her hand and spun her around. He let go too soon, and she bumped into one of the ladies.

"Sorry," she murmured.

But when she turned the other way, she collided with one of the gentlemen. "I beg your pardon."

The slight laughter happened again, and she tried to pretend as if it didn't bother her. "Forgive my clumsiness," she said lightly. "I suppose that's the reason why I need dancing lessons."

She tried again with the dancing patterns, but it soon became clear that Lord Dunmeath was no longer across from her. Where had he gone? She couldn't understand why he would suddenly leave.

"Now, let's try it faster." Mr. Brown changed the tempo of the music. The next thing Emma knew, a gentleman grabbed her hand and swung her in one direction and then another. As she'd feared, she started bumping into people more frequently. It almost felt deliberate, until finally she gave up.

"I'm sorry. I'm just not able to—"

"Now, Miss Bartholomew, you really must try," the dancing master insisted. "It's simple. Just follow your partner. One, two, three."

"I did try," she said. "But I think this is more difficult than—"

"It's not hard at all," Lady Chelsea said. "Anyone can do it." Her voice dripped with disdain, and Emma stepped back.

Anyone but me, she thought. There was no way to respond to her insult, so she held her silence.

"Honestly, it's no wonder she's a wallflower," Miss Cooper remarked, as if Emma weren't standing right there. "She doesn't even make an effort to dance with anyone."

Why would the woman say such a thing, except to be cruel? Her cheeks burned with embarrassment.

"I . . ." she started to say, but then her words died down.

"It's because she can't bloody well *see,*" Lord Dunmeath snapped. "She can't see any of you or any of the patterns. For someone who is practically blind, I think she's doing better than any of you ever could."

Oh God. Her stomach twisted with humiliation. Why had he said that in front of everyone? Her face burned crimson, and Emma pushed her way past them, counting steps until she thought she was near the doorway. But the blur of a white doorway against a white wall made it so the threshold wasn't where she'd imagined. In her haste, she crashed right into the wall.

Damn him for spilling her secret. She found the doorway and went into the hallway. After counting steps, she reached around until she found the stair banister and hurried down the steps.

Emma had no idea where she was going, but anywhere far from here was good enough for her. If the guests talked, then soon everyone in London would know. It was bad enough being unable to see, but she'd managed to keep it hidden for years. Everyone believed that she didn't *want* to dance—not that she couldn't see.

Lord Dunmeath's betrayal sliced through her. Why had she been so stupid as to confess the truth to him? She should have known better than to trust him.

"Seeking an escape, are you?"

She heard the voice of Mr. Gregor, and she stopped on one of the stair treads.

"Please. I just need a few moments to myself." And when she was alone, then she could have a good cry and decide what to do next.

"Garden or library?" he asked.

"The garden." Though it was growing late in the summer, there might still be some blooms left. Privacy meant the most to her now.

Mr. Gregor took her hand and rested it on his arm, leading her down the end of the hall. Twenty-four steps later, he opened the door, and she felt the sunlight on her face.

He guided her down four stone steps, and then remarked, "If you walk about . . . let's say twenty paces, there's a stone bench on the left side."

"Thank you," she whispered, taking her hand from his arm. She walked across the grass, counting the steps, until the scent of roses deepened. She turned toward the left and saw a grayish form that contrasted against green shrubbery.

She made her way toward the bench and sat down. The weight of discovery infuriated her, but what could she do about it now? She could only hope that the others wouldn't share the secret.

But part of her knew they would. It was delicious gossip, was it not? Poor, blind Emma.

No, she wasn't fully blind. But she didn't want to be pitied or treated differently.

The sound of footsteps approaching caught her attention. When the footsteps stopped, she guessed that it might be Lord Dunmeath. He paused a moment and seemed to think about what he wanted to say. Only, she didn't want useless apologies. Instead, she wanted him to understand the magnitude of what he'd done.

"Miss Bartholomew, I truly am—"

"You had no right," she cut him off. She turned to face his shadowy figure and crossed her arms. "I've kept this from the *ton* for years. It was *my* secret to keep, not yours to tell."

"I am realizing that now," he said woodenly. "And you cannot know how very sorry I am."

"Your apology means absolutely nothing. The four of them will go and tell everyone they know." In an exaggerated tone, she whispered loudly. "Remember that pathetic wallflower Miss Bartholomew? Well, it turns out she doesn't dance or talk to anyone because she's blind. Imagine!

"Oh, the poor dear," Emma mocked herself. "She'll never get a husband now.

"Have you heard the best part?" she continued. "Her stepmother is hosting an auction. Are you in need of a bride? Well now, you can buy one. If you win the auction, you'll win her hand in marriage."

He seemed stunned at her words but didn't respond. She didn't need his pity anyhow. Furious tears streamed against her cheeks. "You ruined my chances of finding someone real, Lord Dunmeath. You took that from me."

That was what hurt most of all—the loss of hope. She'd always doubted her ability to find a husband. But now it was truly over. Once everyone knew, they would shun her even more.

The earl's silence gave her no indication of what he was thinking. Finally, he said grimly, "You could marry me."

The words were an invisible blow. It was the first marital

proposal she'd ever received, and it was from a man who didn't really want to wed her—it was intended as a weak apology, nothing more. He didn't mean it.

"I don't want to marry you," she shot back. "Why would I want to marry a man who humiliated me?"

"I am truly sorry." His words had a soft finality to them, shadowed with regret. "I meant only to defend you."

"Just go," she said wearily. "Find yourself a bride and go back to Ireland."

"What can I do to make it right?" he asked. "Is there anything?"

She shook her head. "You cannot take back the words. Just . . . leave me alone. I don't want to see you again."

THE NEXT DAY, Cormac returned to Mrs. Harding's. Oh, he knew Miss Bartholomew was furious with him for what he'd said—and she was right to be angry with him. The words had been born of impulse and a desire to defend her, not an intention to reveal her secret. But he never should have disclosed her blindness. It was his fault, and he needed to atone for what he'd done.

Her confession about the auction was startling, but not entirely surprising. He'd already guessed that it had something to do with marriage. But it didn't sit well with him that her family was prepared to auction her off—if that was, in fact, what they meant to do. The invitation he'd received had made a veiled reference to it, and he now understood why she was seeking her own escape. It was likely the reason she'd come to the School for Spinsters.

Cormac's head was pounding, and the rattling of his carriage through the streets only made it worse. He'd brought an arrangement of flowers with him. They might not do any good, but he hoped she would enjoy the blossoms and might reconsider accepting his apology. The truth was, Miss Bartholomew was his best hope for finding a bride. And he couldn't let her slip away because he'd spoken careless words.

He liked her, and she was the only woman in London who had truly talked with him for longer than a few moments. He liked the way she spoke her mind when she was with him, but he also sympathized with her difficulties. He knew exactly what it felt like to be an outsider—and how it was to be treated as less than a person. Absently, he rubbed the scar on his wrist.

Perhaps that was why she'd caught his interest. She was determined to be independent and didn't want to accept help from anyone. It revealed an inner pride and strength.

But she'd missed out on so much of life—reading stories, playing cards, hunting. And he questioned whether there was a better way to offer an apology than with flowers. His mind spun off with ideas, darting from one to another. He wondered if there was a way for her to experience everything she'd missed out on.

The carriage lurched through the streets, and his stomach twisted with nausea. It made him question how much longer he truly had to live. Perhaps it was already too late to marry and sire an heir. A bleak sense of failure passed over him before he pushed the self-pity aside. It would do him no good to think about his own demise. Better to move forward and try to repair the damage he'd done.

When he arrived at Mrs. Harding's school, the footman at the door informed him that Miss Bartholomew was not receiving.

"Is she ill?" Cormac inquired.

"She is otherwise occupied with lessons," the man explained. He had already started to close the door when Cormac stopped him.

"Will you give these to her?" He held out the bouquet of lilies. "And if you don't mind, I would like to wait until she is finished with her lessons. I need to speak with her."

The footman took the flowers and paused. "Are you certain you wish to wait, my lord? It could be hours."

"If you have a library, I can find something to read," Cormac suggested.

The servant opened the door and said, "I will let Mrs. Harding and Mr. Gregor know you are here. The decision on whether you may stay rests with them." He led Cormac down the hallway toward the library. "Would you care for tea or any refreshments?"

"I would like that very much, yes."

The footman paused a moment and then nodded. "Someone will be with you shortly. Please, make yourself comfortable, my lord."

After he closed the door, Cormac began searching through the book titles. He found a book of fairy stories that she might enjoy, and he got so caught up in perusing the titles that at some point, he realized a servant had brought tea. After he poured a cup, he realized it must have been there for a while since it had gone cold.

There came a knock at the door, and Cormac called for the person to enter. Instead of Miss Bartholomew, he saw Mr. Cedric Gregor, Mrs. Harding's business partner.

"Good morning, Lord Dunmeath," the man said. "I must admit, I'm surprised to see you here."

"After I made a terrible mess of everything and offended Miss Bartholomew yesterday?" he asked. "Aye, I know."

Mr. Gregor regarded him with a raised eyebrow and merely crossed his arms.

"You're right," Cormac said. "But I'm wanting to tell her how very sorry I am. I need to atone for what I said."

"The lilies are a good start," Mr. Gregor said, "but do you truly wish to court Miss Bartholomew? Or is it only pity?"

It wasn't pity—not at all. But even though he had offered a proposal, she hadn't believed him. Which, he supposed, was to be expected.

"I am wanting to court her," he admitted. "But I'm also aware that she does not like me very much. I hurt her without intending to."

"Mrs. Harding and I have discussed her lesson plans, and they have changed significantly. It is our belief that she may need far more time before she is ready to wed anyone." Mr. Gregor's gaze passed over him, and for a moment, it seemed as if the gentleman sensed Cormac's illness.

"That may be," he acceded. "But I do owe her an apology. And if it's all the same to you, I'll wait here."

"So, you plan to apologize and then leave?"

Cormac shook his head. "I need to talk to her."

"You cannot undo the things you said," he continued. "The question is what action you will take now. Will you defend her in the *ton*? Or merely spread more rumors?"

Cormac stood from the chair, his own frustration rising. "I already tried to defend her, and it failed. Then I offered an apology and asked her to wed me. She refused."

"And are you surprised by this?"

"No." He paused a moment, "But I'm wanting to make things right if I can. And perhaps find out what I can do to help her."

Mr. Gregor crossed his arms and leaned back against the wall. "Why not choose another debutante? You have a title and wealth enough, it seems. Why her?"

Because there was no time. And also because the other ladies had already refused. But he didn't want to reveal that to Mr. Gregor, so he answered honestly, "I like Miss Bartholomew. She suits me well enough."

A slight smile tipped the man's mouth. "I've heard it said that you've asked women to wed you within an hour of meeting them."

True enough. But he needed a better answer than to admit he was dying. Instead, he answered, "Most women do not want to live in Ireland. It seems to me that if she isn't wanting to live somewhere else, it's best to find that out sooner."

"They might consider marrying you if you gave them a better chance to know you." Mr. Gregor sent him a chiding look. "Why are you so eager to wed quickly?"

Cormac didn't quite know how to answer that, but he avoided the whole truth. "I do need to return to Dunmeath. I've responsibilities back at home." He hoped the reason would shut down the man's questioning.

Cedric Gregor studied him for a long moment, as if searching for answers. "I would advise—if you are truly interested in wedding Miss Bartholomew—that you take the time to get acquainted. After you apologize, that is." He paused a moment. "I shall send her to the library—without telling her you are here—and then it is up to you to win her forgiveness."

"That's fair enough." Cormac inclined his head. "I will do my best."

After Mr. Gregor had left, Cormac explored the library titles, running his hands over each book spine. It reminded him of the first story he'd read—about a boy and his dog.

But it wasn't the story that remained fixed in his memory—it was the moment when he'd actually been able to read it on his own. His new tutor, Mr. MacPherson, had taken pity on him. Instead of beating him when he couldn't finish his lessons as the others had done, he'd taught Cormac how to use a piece of paper and slide it down the book to keep the sentences separated. He'd chosen adventure stories and fairy tales, and when he'd offered Cormac the chance to try new stories in French and German, it had startled him to realize that he was good with languages.

He wondered if anyone had ever read stories to Miss Bartholomew. Did she know what it was to get lost in a world of heroes and adventures? Somehow, he suspected not. He was beginning to consider new ways of courtship, showing her all that she had missed while growing up. That is, if she would give him the opportunity to try again.

It was nearly half an hour before the door opened, and Miss Bartholomew entered the library. She took a few steps inside and glanced around.

Cormac stared at her, and before he could speak, she asked, "What is it you want, Lord Dunmeath?"

"You look . . . beautiful, Miss Bartholomew."

He'd always found her pretty in an unassumed way—but today, her deep blue gown brought out the blue in her eyes. Despite his headache, he found himself captivated by her. A sudden rush of attraction pushed away the pain, provoking a new desire. He wanted to touch the edge of her jaw, to lean in and feel her breath against his mouth. Then he wanted to discover the shape of her mouth by kissing her, tracing every part of her lips.

"Here. I brought you these." He offered her the flowers, and she seemed uncertain about them, though she took the bouquet and lifted them to her nose.

"Thank you."

There was no denying the wariness in her voice. Flowers weren't enough to fix the mistakes he'd made. But he'd been truthful with Mr. Gregor, for he liked Miss Bartholomew a great deal. And as far as he was concerned, if he could convince her to accept him, he need look no further for a wife. He could give her a title, a grand estate, and even wealth and servants to look after her every need. And for whatever time they had remaining before he died, they could try to conceive an heir. But first, he had to convince her to forgive him and grant him another chance.

He struggled to find the right words, and the apology tangled up inside him. "You really are quite lovely."

Her face flushed, and she remained standing near the door. "Mrs. Harding brought the modiste and a hairdresser to style my hair. I don't know what they did with it. Something with curling tongs."

He studied her and described it for her. "It's still long and dark brown. They've twisted and pinned it up, and there are small pearl combs tucked within it. Some longer strands are curled beside your face."

Her expression turned wistful, and she said, "They gave me this ballgown to try on. I know it's blue, but that's all."

"There's some embroidery on the bodice," he said. "It looks like an intertwined pattern." The gown she wore skimmed the edges of her figure, baring her arms and revealing every curve.

He wanted to unfasten those buttons to see more of her lovely skin.

He took a step close to her and took her hand, drawing it to her own bodice. "Here. Trace it with your fingers."

For a moment, he rested his hands upon hers, just at her waist. At this close distance, he could smell the honeysuckle scent of her skin. She froze, almost fearful of his nearness. He kept his hands where they were for a moment longer, but he could see the light rise of goosebumps on her arm. He probably shouldn't have touched her, but he'd wanted her to "see" the gown in her own way.

"It is pretty," she admitted. Her cheeks were blushing, but he didn't release her wrist.

He wanted to continue touching her while fumbling for the right words. "I came to beg your forgiveness," he said. "I wasn't feeling well, and I did a poor job of defending you while you were dancing. I am sorry for it."

She sighed and set down the flowers on a nearby table. For a moment, she looked at him, but her expression held disappointment. "I know I'm supposed to accept your apology and tell you that no harm was done. But you did tell them my secret, which you had no right to do."

"I didn't mean to say it," he admitted, "and I *am* angry with myself."

She didn't soften. "I don't know how I will attend a ball in the future when everyone is staring at me. I kept that secret for years. But now, everyone will know that I cannot see."

Her voice trailed off, deepening his guilt.

And Cormac realized the lady would not be so easily won. "I made a mistake, aye," he acceded. "But you're wrong if you're thinking that I'll stand aside if anyone says a word against you. Especially after it was my fault."

He took a step closer and reached for her hand again. She wore gloves, and yet he kept her hand in his.

"Don't," she ordered, stepping back from him. "I can't think when you're this close to me."

"What is it you want from me, *a chara?*" he asked.

"What I *don't* want is your pity or guilt." She closed her eyes. "And I don't need your Irish endearments."

"I called you my friend," he clarified. "But I meant what I said yesterday. I do need to marry and return to Ireland."

"Then I bid you good fortune in finding a wife." She took another step backward.

The conversation wasn't at all going the way he'd imagined it would. "I was hoping you might change your mind." He stepped between her and the door, wanting her to listen. "You want to avoid your stepmother's auction, don't you?"

Her face fell. "I . . . well, of course. But I don't know you. And you don't know me."

"If you tell your stepmother that you're already engaged, then the auction will not happen," he offered.

"But we're not—"

"*She* doesn't know that, now does she?"

She froze in place, frowning. "Are you suggesting that we lie to her? That we tell the others we are engaged to marry?"

"We could," he agreed. "Or it could be real, if you're wanting it to be."

Chapter Four

EMMA DIDN'T BELIEVE him. How could Lord Dunmeath ever want a wife like her? She couldn't manage anyone's household, much less become a countess—not truly.

"I can't," she told him. "I'm sorry." But the truth was, she was afraid to put any of her hopes on him. Or anyone, for that matter. In five Seasons, no man had ever shown interest before. Why should it be any different now? She was starting to realize that, no matter how much she might want a family of her own, she wasn't ready for marriage. Not yet.

"I should go," she said suddenly. "Mrs. Harding will have more lessons for me." She stood up suddenly and nearly knocked over an empty teacup. From the clatter of porcelain, she suspected Lord Dunmeath had steadied it before it could fall.

"Will I see you at any of the balls this week?" he asked.

Emma thought wildly of the impending auction her stepmother had planned. "I don't know yet." She turned around and stumbled over the chair before she got her bearings and counted the eight steps to the doorway.

Before she left, he reminded her, "My marriage offer stands, *a stór.*"

But she couldn't think of that now. He had lured her in with his compliments and that honey-and-butter voice. She'd wanted to remain in his embrace when he'd described her gown, covering her hands with his own. Even now, she couldn't stop thinking of how it had felt when he'd rested his hands on her waist. The heat of his touch had sent her senses scattering like smoke in the wind.

Lord Dunmeath's footsteps drew close to her, and she caught the scent of pine and male skin. For the slightest moment, he stayed where he was, beside her in the doorway. But then, he walked away and left her alone.

Emma felt a sudden sense of emptiness, but she chided herself for daring to believe there could be more. He'd come to apologize, and that was all. His offer of marriage wasn't real. She simply couldn't believe him.

Despondency cloaked her as she walked from the doorway toward the stairs, counting the steps as she went. Before she reached them, Mrs. Harding called out to her. "Miss Bartholomew, may we speak?"

She turned and waited for the matron to approach. "Of course."

"Come into my study." She started to guide her with a hand on her shoulder, but Emma interceded.

"It's all right. I can follow your steps."

The headmistress dropped her hand away. They walked alongside one another until they reached the study. Inside, Emma could smell the lingering aroma of tea, and she heard a cat purring to her right. "Please, sit down."

She found a chair and heard Mrs. Harding pulling out a sheet of paper. "I've arranged for you to attend a ball tomorrow evening. Am I correct that, aside from Lord Dunmeath, you had no interest in the gentlemen who were here for supper the other evening?"

Her face flamed as she thought of the Irish earl. But she guarded her heart fiercely, knowing it was folly to imagine more. For now, she answered Mrs. Harding's question. "The others weren't quite right for me." But more than that, she'd sensed that they had no interest in her.

"I've asked Mr. Gregor to find other candidates and ensure that they will be present during the next ball you attend," she continued.

She didn't know what else to say except, "Thank you."

"In the meantime, we must ensure that you wed a very wealthy gentleman. You will need a secretary to handle the household accounts on your behalf."

Emma was starting to feel uncertain about all this. A wealthy nobleman could have any heiress he wanted. Why would he want someone like her?

"After we introduce you to the new gentlemen, you must try your best to make conversation with them. We may only be able to stop your stepmother's auction if you find another possible husband."

Her thoughts wandered back to Lord Dunmeath's offer, but Emma said nothing of it to Mrs. Harding. "I will try. But what if Miss Cooper or Lady Chelsea tells everyone that I am blind?" The very thought was humiliating, not to mention untrue.

"Lord Dunmeath has agreed to ask you for a waltz. If the others see you dancing, then we believe it will help to dispel the rumor. Others may dismiss it as only a falsehood. I have also asked Lady Ashleigh and Lady Scarsdale to help you. They are former pupils of mine."

Emma knew that already, for it was because of the women's recommendation a few months ago that she'd even heard about Mrs. Harding's School for Young Ladies.

But although she knew Mrs. Harding was trying to help her, familiar self-doubts intruded. What good would it do to attend this ball? She was convinced that the rumors would only humiliate her more.

And yet, if she didn't make a strong effort to find someone, she might be forced into a match she didn't want.

"You seem nervous," Mrs. Harding said.

"I've many reasons to be nervous. Especially after that dancing lesson." She shuddered and hoped in vain that she would not be expected to dance again.

Mrs. Harding asked, "I would . . . strongly advise you to consider Lord Dunmeath as a possible husband. That is, if you wish to marry."

"I don't know," Emma murmured. "Ireland is so very far away." It was only an excuse. The truth was, it had nothing to do with the physical distance and everything to do with how she felt so uncertain around the earl. She didn't understand what sort of man he was. One moment, he was easy to talk to, as if they'd been friends for years. And the next, he betrayed her to strangers. Although he'd apologized today, she didn't know if she could ever trust him.

"He has asked for our help in finding a bride," Mrs. Harding said. "If you are not interested in him, then we may consider him for another student in the future. Would that bother you?"

"No, of course not."

But despite her answer, a sudden rush of dismay came over her. Now where had that come from? She barely knew the earl. He could marry whomever he wished. Heaven knew, if she agreed to wed a man like him, she would be nothing to him but a disappointment and a burden.

And yet . . . an unexpected, possessive mood coming over her at the thought of him with someone else. Which wasn't fair to him at all.

"Or would you consider him as a possibility?" the matron prompted again.

Emma pushed away the confusing thoughts and said, "I don't know."

Mrs. Harding remained silent for a long moment as if she were thinking about it. At last, she inquired, "Miss Bartholomew, are you certain you even *want* to be married?"

"Yes," she said softly. "But the problem is . . . I'm not certain that anyone would want to be married to me."

A MOUNTAIN OF letters and invitations lay atop his desk. Cormac glanced at a few but didn't open them. Instead, he stood and walked over to the bookshelf by the window. He'd brought a few books from Ireland with him, but his grandfather's diary meant the most to him because of the familiar family stories and anecdotes it contained. It was falling apart after so many years, with a cracked spine and loose pages. Someone had tried to repair it almost eight years ago with a new cover, but even the new paint was crumbling now.

His father had written most of his stories in Irish, but whenever Cormac read them, it evoked childhood memories of sitting on Brandan's lap, eating warm slices of bread and drinking milk.

He missed his family. And although this house held traces of his grandmother's childhood, she had died years ago. He'd only been to her house in London a few times over the years, and he'd never met his great-grandparents. It was strange to think that they'd turned their back on their only daughter so easily. And after she'd married his grandfather, Celeste had never returned to London again. He wondered if she'd ever been homesick.

Would his bride feel the same way if he brought her to Ireland?

His thoughts drifted back to Emma. He couldn't deny that she'd captured his full interest. And despite his hurried proposal, he didn't want her to say no like all the others had. He felt protective of her and wanted her to consider him.

He knew what it was like to be mocked by others and treated as if he knew nothing. During his entire childhood, he'd been beaten by his tutors and teased by the other boys. He understood how Emma felt about being isolated from the rest of society, for in Ireland, he'd known the same loneliness.

But instead of fighting back, she'd hidden herself away. And although he didn't know if they could ever be more than friends, he didn't want her to fade into the background. He wanted to see if she could emerge from that protective cocoon to spread her wings and become something more.

Since he had so little time left to choose another marital prospect, he found himself wanting to help Emma. He'd done what he could to apologize, but would it be enough?

His secretary entered the study and said, "My lord, will you be attending the Duke of Westerford's ball this evening?"

"Aye," he answered. "Miss Bartholomew is supposed to attend, so I've heard."

His secretary offered a slight smile. "Will she be our new Countess of Dunmeath?"

"With a bit of luck, perhaps." He stood from his chair and stretched. "What do they say about her? Have you heard any servants' gossip?"

"Only that she has been out for five Seasons, and no one has asked her to wed."

That wasn't entirely true, Cormac mused, though Miss Bartholomew hadn't taken his proposal seriously. He walked toward the doorway and told a passing footman to send his valet to him.

"What else do you know about Miss Bartholomew's family?" He thought of the mysterious auction. "Are they in financial trouble?"

His secretary shrugged. "Not so far as anyone knows. She has a decent enough dowry, if that's what you're asking."

But Cormac was really wondering why Emma's parents had conceived of such a strange notion as an auction. It was unheard of.

"There was another invitation from the Bartholomew family," his secretary said. "About the auction."

"I thought we answered that one already," Cormac answered. "But I will speak with Mr. Bartholomew about it, if I see him tonight." And if he could manage it, he would try to coax her father into abandoning the idea of an auction and instead, give permission for him to marry Emma.

The way he saw it, he could wed her by special license so her family could be there, and then they could return to Ireland. He could also try to arrange a few days near the seaside by way of a holiday.

But even as he dressed for the ball, he sensed that Emma would not be so easy to convince. And as the familiar headache took hold, he realized that desperate measures might be called for.

If the auction *did* take place, he had to do everything in his power to win.

"YOU'RE NOT STANDING among the wallflowers tonight," Lady Ashleigh MacNeill announced. She took Emma by the hand and said, "You're coming with Lady Scarsdale and me."

Emma felt rather bewildered, wondering why the two women had agreed to Mrs. Harding's request to help her. She knew they were both former students, and both had made exceptional marriages. Though she'd met the two ladies before, this was the first time they'd truly spoken to her at length. There was a warm friendliness from them that could not be denied.

She didn't know quite what to say, but she let Lady Ashleigh lead her onward while Lady Scarsdale followed.

"Y-yes," Lady Scarsdale said. "W-we will see to it that you have a w-wonderful time tonight."

Emma suddenly realized that the women were a shield, protecting her from those who might make fun of her. It eased some of her tension.

"I do like that gown," Lady Ashleigh said. "That shade of rose is stunning against your hair."

"Thank you," she murmured. The silk was indeed lovely though she felt slightly self-conscious about the neckline and her bared shoulders. She wore long gloves, and yet, it felt as if she were pretending to be someone else.

"M-Mrs. Harding told us about the auction," Lady Scarsdale said.

"Yes, and we intend to help you avoid it entirely," Ashleigh finished. "We'll do our best to find someone for you."

A pang caught her heart at their willingness to help her. She was hardly more than a stranger to them, but the two women seemed sincere in their efforts. "Please don't think me ungrateful, but . . . why would you go to so much trouble for my sake? We hardly know each other."

"I know w-what it is to be a w-wallflower," Lady Scarsdale said. "And what it is to be mocked."

"Mrs. Harding's school changed my life," Ashleigh answered. "I am glad to help someone else. Especially after I was such a coward before."

An ache caught in her throat, but Emma said, "Thank you both so much."

"Don't thank us yet," Ashleigh cautioned. "We're only getting started. Violet, who is the first gentleman on our list of husband candidates?"

"Viscount Richford," she answered. "H-he is standing over b-by the refreshments."

Ashleigh turned in that direction and asked, "What do you think of him, Miss Bartholomew?"

Emma couldn't hide her smile. "I can't see him. You'll have to describe him for me."

"I am an idiot," Ashleigh sighed. "Sorry. He's taller than you with light brown hair. A little older, perhaps in his forties. He has a beard and mustache, and his smile is nice enough."

"He's a w-widower, isn't he?" Violet asked.

"I believe he came out of mourning last year," Ashleigh said. "What do you think? Would you like to meet him?"

"I suppose so." But in all honesty, she was hoping that Lord Dunmeath would arrive. He'd promised to come tonight to assist her. And although she didn't trust him, she wanted to see whether he would keep his word about defending her from idle gossip. She'd wanted to believe that he would help her—and yet, he wasn't here.

Emma followed the women toward the refreshment table, but as she walked, she could feel a tingling sensation—as if she were being watched. The crowds parted for them, but she sensed people staring. Her face flushed, and she tried to ignore it.

"Lady Scarsdale," Emma asked. "It seems like everyone is looking at us. Or am I wrong?" She wondered if Miss Cooper or Lady Chelsea had spread rumors or lies about her.

"It's p-probably nothing," Lady Scarsdale said. "Your g-gown is quite lovely. That may be why."

"Do you want me to find out?" Lady Ashleigh inquired. "I could make discreet inquiries. My husband could learn whatever it is you wish to know."

"Please," Emma answered. "I would be grateful." Although she had come here tonight to meet other suitors, something felt unusual, almost uncomfortable.

"Oh dear," a snide female voice said. "I didn't realize my family had invited *everyone* to our ball."

Emma recognized the voice of Lady Persephone, the Duke of Westerford's daughter. Normally, she escaped Persephone's notice but not tonight, unfortunately.

She took a breath and ventured politely, "Thank you for the invitation, Lady Persephone."

"Oh, *I* didn't invite you," the woman sneered. "It must have been my mother. She does like to be charitable."

Her words were a razor, slashing any enjoyment Emma might have felt. Right now, all she wanted to do was leave. Instead, she took a deep breath and turned away.

"Enjoy your evening," Lady Persephone called out. "I'm certain that Lady Ashleigh and Lady Scarsdale won't mind leading you around the room like a pet out for a walk. At least it will keep you from being a wallflower."

"Violet, did you hear anything just now?" Without waiting for a reply, Ashleigh answered her own question. "No? Neither did I."

Before the woman could say anything else, Violet and Ashleigh took Emma's hands and skirted her away.

Ashleigh let out a sigh. "I'm so sorry for what she said. Persephone has always been horrid. I doubt if any man will ever want to marry her." She looped her arm in Emma's. "Are you all right?"

"I'm fine," Emma managed. "It was just words." But more than ever, she wished she were anywhere but here.

"Now, I thought Lord Dunmeath was supposed to be here this evening," Ashleigh began. "Wasn't he?"

"He was, but I haven't seen him," Emma answered. She didn't know what to think of his disappearance other than to wonder if he'd had more headaches. But his absence bothered her more than it should have. It was entirely possible that the flowers and the apology had meant nothing. She pushed back her own feelings of regret, telling herself not to rely on him.

"Wasn't he s-supposed to dance with you?" Lady Scarsdale asked. "If he doesn't come, m-my husband will help."

"Help with what?" a male voice asked. Emma detected a soft laugh and guessed that the earl had come to join his wife.

"Mrs. Harding has asked us to help Miss B-Bartholomew," the countess said. "She will n-need to meet the right gentlemen."

"Of course," Lord Scarsdale agreed. "Whatever she needs."

"I am willing to help as well," came another man's voice.

"Cameron, I'm so glad you're here." Ashleigh sounded delighted. She lowered her voice and Emma guessed she was giving instructions to her husband, asking him to find out why everyone was staring.

"In the meantime," Ashleigh continued, "Miss Bartholomew, we will ensure that you have many dancing partners."

"Oh, please, not dancing," she begged. "It's too complicated for me."

"Then we will introduce you to several suitors, and you may converse with them," Lady Ashleigh suggested. She paused a moment and murmured, "Oh dear."

"What is it?" Emma didn't have a good feeling about this. "Is it Lord Dunmeath?" The moment she asked, she could have kicked herself. It made her sound as if she'd been waiting only for him.

"Your stepmother is here," Ashleigh said. "Did you . . . want to speak with her?"

Oh no. Emma grimaced at the mention of Lucy. "I'd rather avoid her."

"Food it is, then." Ashleigh took her hand. "And Cameron, will you and Lord Scarsdale see to it that Lucy Bartholomew cannot possibly see Emma?"

"Consider it done," her husband answered. Then he murmured to Ashleigh, "Will you save a dance for me later?"

She sighed and answered, "I wish I could save all of them for you. You're far more interesting to talk to."

Her husband gave a soft laugh, and Emma could almost hear the love between them. Would she ever know something like it? She could only hope so.

Lady Ashleigh led her through the crowd and into the next room. Emma could smell the tables of food, and her stomach rumbled. She couldn't quite see the food choices, but before she could choose something, a male voice said, "Good evening."

She couldn't tell whether he was speaking to her or Ashleigh, so she glanced in the direction of her friend.

"Good evening, Mr. Durham," Ashleigh answered. After a brief pause, she asked, "Have you met Miss Emma Bartholomew?"

"I have not had the pleasure."

His voice was deep and pleasant, but Emma sensed that Ashleigh didn't like the man. She couldn't quite put her finger on why. But after Ashleigh made the introduction, Emma answered, "Good evening, sir."

"I am glad to finally make your acquaintance," he said. "I've been very curious about an invitation I received from your family."

Her face burned scarlet, for she knew exactly what he was referring to—the auction.

For a moment, she panicked, wondering what she could say to make her escape. "I . . . don't know what you mean, sir."

He laughed softly. "Everyone's talking about it. And I, for one, am looking forward to placing a bid very soon."

Thankfully, he left, and Emma closed her eyes, wishing she were anywhere but here.

"I'm so sorry for that," Ashleigh said quietly.

"I don't understand why he would say he was looking forward to placing a bid soon." Emma could feel his mockery, and she turned to Ashleigh. "Do you think something has changed?"

"It must have." Ashleigh guided her away from the food and back toward the main ballroom. "But I don't know how."

"Ashleigh," Violet warned.

The young woman let out a heavy sigh. "I see Mrs. Harding walking toward us, very fast. Whatever she's learned, it can't be good."

Emma wondered what the headmistress could possibly want, but she sensed she was about to get the answer to her questions. She saw a maroon blur coming closer. And when the headmistress reached them, she was nearly out of breath.

"Miss Bartholomew," Mrs. Harding said, "It seems that your stepmother has made a change in the auction date. It begins tonight."

Chapter Five

C ORMAC LAY IN bed, his body wracked with pain and weakness. He didn't know what had caused the onslaught of illness, but he lay in the darkness of his bedchamber. His mood grew despondent, and he gripped the edges of the sheets, wondering what in God's name he'd done to deserve this suffering. Or his father and Finn, for that matter. The illness was utterly merciless.

His mother had voiced her own suspicions of poison, but how was that possible when he'd left everyone behind? All his servants were new—he'd hired them in London. None had connections to Ireland.

Then, too, if he were being poisoned, whoever was trying to kill him in Ireland would have done so in a single dose. No, this was different. There were days when he started to improve, when he was enjoying life, only to be followed by several more days of agonizing illness. He had no doubt that this was simply the disease that had claimed his father's and brother's lives.

He was supposed to be at another ball tonight, helping Miss Bartholomew. And yet, he could barely bring himself to move.

I really am going to die, he thought. He wasn't going to have the opportunity to be a husband or a father. And the frustration and grief caught him in a morass of pity and anger at the unfairness of it all.

A soft knock came to the door. "My lord?"

"Leave me be," Cormac muttered. "I can't go tonight."

Hawkins opened the door slightly, a candle in his hand. "My lord, shall I send for a physician?"

He didn't answer, for what good would it do? The physician would only bleed him or make him drink foul potions that he would simply bring back up again.

"No," he said quietly. "Just let me lie here and sleep."

"Is there aught I can do to help?" his secretary asked. "Should I send word to anyone?"

Cormac was about to refuse and then thought better of it. "Aye. Send my apologies to Miss Bartholomew. Tell her it's sorry I am that I can't be there."

He hated the thought of his weakness, but if he was going to die soon, perhaps it was better that she didn't rely on him.

"Is she . . . going to be your wife, my lord?" Hawkins asked.

"Unfortunately, she's already refused my proposal of marriage once." He covered his eyes with his hand and added, "Don't be worried about it. We have time to figure that out later."

"But you *do* wish to marry her?" Hawkins prompted.

"I like her," he admitted. "And she'd make a fine wife, to be sure. But she's a stubborn *cailín,* and I don't know if I've time enough to win her consent. Not as sick as I've been." He said nothing of dying, though he supposed his secretary suspected it by now.

"What about the auction, my lord?" Hawkins dared to ask. "Would you bid upon her?"

"It won't come to that," he answered, "but aye, if it did, I would place the highest bid before allowing some other gentleman to hurt her." After that, he ordered Hawkins, "Leave me. Rest is what I'm needing now."

Hawkins paused as if he wanted to say something more but then held his silence. "Aye, sir. I hope you feel better."

Cormac curled on his side, fighting against the familiar pain after the door closed. He hated that he'd become such a helpless wretch.

You could go to the ball anyway, his conscience suggested. And for a moment, he thought about it. If this truly was the end of his life, the last thing he wanted was to spend it curled up, waiting to die.

Hawkins had left some dry toast on the table beside his bed. Cormac reached for it and forced himself to take a bite. He ate slowly, hoping he could keep the food down.

It did seem to ease the gnawing in his stomach. He decided to see if he was capable of walking downstairs. If he could manage it, perhaps he would try again.

The second piece of toast went down easier, and he drank a cup of cold tea with it. Cormac took several deep breaths before he swung his feet to the bedside and stood. The room swayed, but he seized the bedpost to regain his balance.

Better. He breathed slowly, steadying himself before he took a few steps toward the bedroom door.

By God, if he was going to die, he'd rather go out swinging his fists at Death than to cower in his bed alone.

"WHAT ARE YOU talking about?" Emma demanded. "The auction wasn't supposed to be until next week."

"Apparently, your stepmother sent out a change," the headmistress answered. "Tonight is the viewing. Of you."

"No." The thought horrified Emma. "She can't do this. I am not something to be bought. This is illegal."

"I agree," Mrs. Harding said. "But if she is questioned, she will only claim that they are selling a painting or another work of art. There is no crime against auctioning that."

She knew the matron was right. Lucy would never admit the truth about her plans. "I have to leave," Emma insisted. "I can't stay here."

"I have a coach waiting outside," Mrs. Harding offered. "It can bring you back to my house, and we can reconsider our plans. I will stay a little longer. We need to know what your stepmother intends to do next."

"I'll go now," Emma agreed. But as she walked with the matron to the doorway, she couldn't help but feel a twinge of remorse that Lord Dunmeath had not come.

But then, she should have known better. His proposal was born out of an apology, not because he liked her. And yet, she couldn't suppress her foolish disappointment that he'd gone back on his promise.

"My footman Ned will escort you back to the school," Mrs. Harding promised. "Wait here for him, and I will see you there."

Emma waited among the other ladies, and soon enough, a footman approached. "Miss Bartholomew?" he asked.

"Are you Ned?" she inquired.

"I'm here to escort you," he answered. "If you'll just follow me."

It was dark outside when she got into the hackney, and there was a slight delay with the driver. But soon enough, the wheels rumbled through the city streets.

Emma glanced outside at the darkness, expecting to arrive at Mrs. Harding's within a few moments. But to her surprise, the hackney continued driving. Had the coachman taken a wrong turn? Where was the driver taking her?

She knocked on the window, trying to get the driver's attention. Though it was difficult to see, she realized there were two drivers. Or was one of them the footman? Strange.

Her instincts tightened, and she wondered if she was in danger of some kind. Where were they going?

"Pardon me!" she called out. "You've gone past the school already." But either they ignored her, or they couldn't hear her. Instead, they continued going in another direction.

She was starting to grow afraid. And when she tried to open the door while the carriage was moving, it seemed to be wedged shut.

Her blood turned icy, and she struggled to catch her breath. But panic would do her no good. She needed to concentrate and figure out where she was.

Emma knew she couldn't rely on her limited vision—not in this darkness. But she knew exactly how long they'd been traveling and which directions the carriage had turned. As a child, she'd gone out driving with her father many times, and she'd made a game of trying to guess the streets. She had a fairly good mental map of London.

For a moment, she closed her eyes, and then realized they were just past Mayfair. She tried to listen to the sounds to determine where she was, but there were too many noises of horses and carriages.

She had no doubt her stepmother was behind this. But it made little sense.

Her questions died off a moment later when the carriage came to a stop. The door lurched open, and one of the men ordered, "Get out."

Emma didn't move. "Who are you, and where are we?" she demanded.

"It don't matter who we are," one said. "We were paid to bring you here."

"By whom? What are you talking about?"

They didn't bother answering her questions, but one of the men reached in and grabbed her. He hauled her forward, and Emma started to lose her balance before the driver caught her.

"Don't be trying to run," he ordered.

She was torn between hysteria and laughter. Where could she even go? She couldn't see well enough to flee. And if she screamed, her rescuer might be even worse than her kidnappers. They started to bring her toward a modest townhouse she'd never seen before.

Another carriage pulled up, and Emma heard the horses stop. She slowed her pace, and the men stopped walking as well.

"Bring her inside," came the voice of her stepmother Lucy.

In a way, it was a slight relief to hear Lucy's voice. At least she wasn't being kidnapped by a highwayman or brigand. Her shoulders lowered and some of her fear drained away.

"Why am I here?" Emma demanded. "What's happening?" She couldn't understand why her stepmother would go to all this trouble.

Lucy unlocked the door to the house and opened it. "Take her inside."

The interior of the dwelling had a musty odor as if no one had lived here in years. Emma couldn't make out anything beyond a large table on one side of what must have once been a kitchen or a dining room.

"This is the house where I was born," Lucy said. "My brother lives here now." To the men she said, "Bind her hands behind her back. Then you may go."

Emma tried to fight against them, but their strength easily overpowered hers. It felt as if her hands were bound by cloth instead of ropes. Then she heard the sound of clinking coins, and the men departed.

"I don't understand what this is. What have you done?" she demanded.

"If you do as you're told, all will be well," Lucy promised. "The auction will begin soon." Her tone sounded pleased, and she added, "You have several bids already from tonight's ball."

"You cannot do this," Emma protested.

"Oh, but I can, and I have." Lucy seemed pleased with herself. "I did not go to all this trouble of arranging this auction only for you to spoil it."

"You want me to be married so I'm gone from your household," she said quietly. "I understand that. But there is no need for this humiliating farce of an auction. I already have one offer."

"Oh, this isn't about marriage," Lucy said. "That would be easy enough to arrange."

Emma fell silent, not understanding what her stepmother

meant. "If it's not about marriage, then what is the reason for this?"

"Your father has almost nothing left. We're nearly destitute, and this auction was our way out."

"What do you mean?" This was news to Emma. She'd had no idea their finances were so dire.

"I mean that we were going to have the men bid on a painting, and in return, they would receive your hand in marriage."

"And you were going to give them their money back after I married one of them," she finished. "I overheard you talking to Papa."

"No, I was never going to give the money back," Lucy said. "I was going to use the funds to pay off your father's debts. And if anyone questioned it, I would simply say that I sold them a painting. It was never about you, Emma."

It was thinly disguised theft, she realized.

"Why am I even part of this?" she asked. "Why not simply sell the paintings?"

"Because no one wants to buy a painting. But gentlemen find the idea of bidding on a young woman positively exhilarating. They will pay a great deal of money, and I've arranged for a meeting with the archbishop in the morning for the special license. Or your bridegroom can take you to Scotland. It doesn't matter to me."

Emma straightened her spine. "I won't do it. You cannot force me to wed."

Her stepmother sighed. "Do you *want* your father to go to debtor's prison? I'm trying to save him, Emma. I don't think you want him sent away to work off his debts. Henry would never survive prison or hard labor." Her stepmother paused and added, "He doesn't have a title or a seat in Parliament. The only reason we ever received invitations at all in London was because of my mother's friends. They took pity on us."

A cold grip settled upon her when she realized Lucy was right. Her father would die if they sent him to debtor's prison.

"This is the best way to save him," Lucy continued. "And to save our family."

"Does he know?" Emma asked. She couldn't imagine her father agreeing to this.

But Lucy sighed again. "He does. It was his debts that caused most of our problems. We owe thousands. And to be honest, you have no dowry at all. This is a last, desperate effort."

"No one wanted to wed me in the past," Emma felt compelled to point out. "Why would anyone offer now?"

"I have three bids so far," Lucy said. "I sent out invitations to every bachelor in London over a week ago. The men have been talking of little else."

So there had never been a choice about avoiding the auction. Lucy had already done it. Tears pricked at her eyes, and it was all Emma could do to keep from breaking down. "Do you hate me that much, Lucy?"

"No," her stepmother answered softly. "I love your father that much. And I will do anything—anything at all—to save him from prison or worse." She reached out and touched Emma's shoulder. "Wouldn't you do the same?"

IT HAD TAKEN everything in him to attend the ball. Cormac felt as if he'd battled a dragon, and he didn't want his weakness to hold him back. But he'd never guessed that Emma would already be gone. He strode through the crowds, searching for her face, but there was no trace of her. Instead, he saw Lady Scarsdale.

"Forgive me, Lady Scarsdale. Have you seen Miss Bartholomew? I was supposed to meet her here this evening."

"She l-left an hour ago," the woman replied. Her voice was cool, and her expression held sadness. "Mrs. Harding was to meet her back at the school."

"Was she all right?" Cormac asked. He suspected she would be angry with him for being late.

"I couldn't say." Lady Scarsdale turned to walk away, and Cormac cursed himself for not arriving sooner. He was questioning what to do when suddenly, he saw Mr. Gregor.

The man appeared uneasy, and as soon as he approached, Mr. Gregor asked Cormac, "Have you seen Miss Bartholomew, Lord Dunmeath? Did she return to the ball?"

"I haven't seen her, no. Lady Scarsdale told me she went back to the school."

"Miss Bartholomew never arrived at our school." His voice held concern, and he added, "I came back to search for her."

Cormac tensed, fearing the worst. "What about her mother?" he asked. "Do you think this was related to the auction?"

"Possibly." Mr. Gregor paused and said, "I heard rumors that she had already begun accepting bids. Do you think . . .?"

"I'll go to her house right now," Cormac answered. He didn't bother to consider other options, but Mr. Gregor hurried to his side. "Wait, my lord. We need more information about where she is."

"No," he snapped. "I have to stop this from happening." He shrugged off the man and hurried back outside. Within a few minutes, he was inside his carriage on the way to the Bartholomew residence. He paid the driver to go faster, hoping to God he could get there in time.

His stomach lurched, but he pushed back the pain. It was an hour before midnight, and his mind flooded with self-loathing. He should have arrived earlier, regardless of his illness. If he had, he could have escorted Emma back. Instead, she was at her stepmother's mercy—and he couldn't let that happen.

It was strange to realize that Miss Bartholomew meant something to him though they'd only become acquainted recently. And he didn't want her to fall prey to this auction. He had to get there in time to stop it from happening. His careless words had already caused enough problems for her, and the last thing he wanted was for her to be trapped in a marriage she didn't want. Although she'd already refused to wed him—and likely still wouldn't agree to a match—he had to do something to help her.

When the coach arrived at her residence, he was startled to find the house dark with no other coaches nearby. If the auction was indeed happening, as rumor had it, then surely there would be many vehicles. Nonetheless, he hurried to the door and knocked hard. No one answered, not even a servant. True, it was quite late—but surely a footman or a maid would answer.

After no one did, he was forced to return to his carriage. It was then that he remembered Hawkins telling him this evening about the invitation from the Bartholomew family. Cormac had mistakenly thought it was the one he'd already answered—but now he realized that a new one had been sent out. Damn it all, he was losing time.

Woodenly, he returned to his carriage. He should have opened the invitation earlier. His carelessness had cost him—and perhaps Emma as well. He was about to drive home when another carriage pulled up beside his. Mr. Gregor bolted outside and held out the new invitation. "It's here."

"Thank you." He gripped the man's hand and gave the address to his driver. He could only hope that he wasn't too late.

EMMA SAT IN a chair on a small, raised platform. Beside her was an easel with a landscape painting. She doubted if it was valuable at all, but of course, she knew that the male guests weren't truly here to buy art.

She couldn't move, could hardly breathe. Her skin felt frozen, and the men were all a blur of dark coats and white cravats. She didn't know who was here or whether they were simply entertained by this spectacle.

Her stepmother remained quietly in the background while another gentleman presided over the "auction."

More than anything, Emma wanted to run away from this humiliating spectacle. She still wore the rose ballgown that exposed her shoulders. Her stepmother had taken down her hair, and it hung down her back in soft waves, as if she'd just awakened from sleep.

God help her, she hated everything about this. And yet, what could she do? She couldn't let her father be sent to debtor's prison. It would kill him, without a doubt.

Her stepmother had admitted the true reason why she was doing this—and Emma couldn't deny that an auction was indeed a quick way of raising money. But it was so very wrong.

She wanted to cry, and yet she was afraid to let a single tear fall for fear that she wouldn't stop sobbing. Her stepmother claimed that whoever won the auction would receive the marriage license, and they could marry discreetly in a few days.

But what sort of man was so desperate that he had to buy his bride? Someone awful, she decided. Or hideously ugly. Someone who enjoyed watching others suffer.

Emma gripped her hands tighter together, wishing there were a way out of this. For the past hour, she'd wracked her brain, trying to think of another way to earn money. Anything. Would Lady Scarsdale or Lady Ashleigh loan her funds, just enough to help them out?

"Gentlemen," a baritone voice began. "I understand that preliminary bids were offered earlier this evening. I can tell you that the bidding on this lovely work of art—"

Emma sensed every eye in the room was staring at her, and it only intensified her anxiety. It was far worse because she truly couldn't see any of the men. She didn't know who was here, and her fear began to accelerate.

"—will continue at one hundred pounds."

There was a slight buzz, and her hearing seemed to fade in and out as the bidding increased. At first, it was only one hundred and ten pounds, but soon enough it was up to two hundred.

I'm going to faint, she thought. *I can't bear this.*

Because Lord Dunmeath wasn't here. He hadn't come to the ball, and now he'd abandoned her at this auction. She should have known better than to put any hope in him. He didn't keep his promises. Whether it was absentmindedness or illness didn't matter; he would only let her down.

Men continued to bid, and it took all her willpower to remain sitting with a neutral expression. This wasn't at all the way she'd wanted to find a marriage. It was horrifying and humiliating. A rebellious thought intruded—why did *she* have to pay the penalty for her father's mistakes? Yes, she wanted to help him, but this was a lifetime sentence that went well beyond paying debts.

But she didn't see another way out. Her father didn't have a title or a means of escaping debtor's prison. And no one else wanted to wed her. What else could she do but endure the nightmare?

"Four hundred," the auctioneer said. "Do I hear four twenty-five?"

Her palms were sweaty, when suddenly, she heard the door fly open. Another male voice spoke up and said, "Six hundred."

But the new bidder wasn't Lord Dunmeath. She didn't recognize the man's voice, nor did anyone say his name aloud. Who was he, and why had he bid so much? The worry and anxiety twisted her stomach in knots.

After that, the bidding began to escalate. Three gentlemen were bidding against one another, and Emma held her breath as the amount climbed to one thousand pounds.

They went back and forth, more and more, until at last the final bid came in from the latecomer for twelve hundred pounds. She felt chills rise all over her body. Something was happening with Lucy and the auctioneer—perhaps something involving a bank note payment. But then she heard the man speak again. His voice was nothing like Lord Dunmeath's.

"She comes with me right now," he said quietly. "Along with the marriage license and the painting."

"A moment, please," Lucy answered. "I need to speak with my stepdaughter."

Emma's breathing was shaken, and all she could wonder was

to whom she'd been sold. What sort of gentleman was he, and what would happen to her now? He had brown hair, a beard, and was taller than she was, but that was all she could see.

What if he were cruel? Would he force himself upon her or hurt her? The room seemed to tip as dizziness washed over her. She'd been so stupid to imagine that Lord Dunmeath would come in at the last minute and save her. He might not even have known about the change in the auction date or the location.

But it didn't matter now, did it? Someone else had stepped in and outbid the others. And if she refused to marry the gentleman, he might allow her father to be sent to debtor's prison.

Her heart ached, for she'd wanted to believe in Lord Dunmeath. She'd wanted to imagine that he would follow through with his promises. But he hadn't.

Her mind was numb with sadness and dismay. She could hardly conceive of what had just occurred.

"Emma," she heard Lucy say. "Walk with me, won't you?"

Lucy placed a warm woolen shawl around her and led her forward. "You're very brave, my dear. It's going to be all right, I promise you."

"No, it won't." Her voice sounded like a shard of glass. "You've sold me to a stranger."

"You know we had no choice," Lucy said. "But I believe you will be happy as a married woman. He *chose* you and was willing to pay twelve hundred pounds. Don't you think that sounds promising?"

"I want to go home," she pleaded. "At least give me time to pack my belongings." More than that, it would give her time to plan an escape.

"I'm afraid . . . I can't do that," Lucy apologized. "It was a condition of the auction. You'll be going home with your new . . . fiancé."

Emma froze as her stepmother's words struck hard. Clearly her suitor believed that she would share his bed this night.

"I will not." It took an effort not to raise her voice and instead feign a calmness she didn't feel. "I participated in this farce for my father's sake. But if you think I am going to go off with a stranger tonight and let him do as he pleases, you're very much mistaken. I am not a lightskirt."

"Miss Bartholomew," came the voice of the gentleman. "May we talk for a moment?"

Though his voice sounded kind, something inside her snapped. She couldn't bear to imagine going through with marriage to a stranger. It was well past midnight now, and all she wanted to do was find a corner, draw up her knees, and cry.

The gentleman waited for a moment, but she couldn't quite determine whether he meant for her to follow him or not. It didn't matter. She intended to stay right here.

"I do hope that you will consider this proposal. You see, I—"

"There is nothing to consider." Her words came out cold. "You bought a painting, sir. Take it with you and go."

He let out a slow breath. "That's . . . not exactly what happened." Before he could continue, two men came on either side of her and seized her arms.

"Where do you want her, sir?" one growled.

Emma struggled against the men, but they overpowered her easily. "Let me go!"

"My coach is just outside," the gentleman said. "I am sorry for all this. I had hoped we could speak in private and discuss the matter."

"There's nothing to talk about, is there?" she shot back. The men were rough, and she fought to free herself. Panic washed over her at the thought of what would happen now. And worse, Lucy was doing nothing to stop it.

"We'll take her to the coach for you," the man said. Emma gasped when they dragged her toward the door. Before she could scream, the other man tied a handkerchief tightly around her mouth to prevent her from making a sound.

Dear God, this wasn't a marriage proposal—it was an outright abduction. She struggled against the men as hard as she could, but her new suitor only opened the coach door while the men forced her inside. Her screams were muffled, and he joined her inside before the door slammed shut.

"I apologize, Miss Bartholomew. Believe me, this is not at all what I intended." His voice held kindness, utterly at odds with his actions. "Be that as it may, I can promise that you won't be harmed."

Emma stopped struggling, for what good would it do anyway? It didn't seem that her husband-to-be intended to rape her. But something was very odd.

"I've made all the preparations and sent word. At any moment now—"

The man never did seem to finish a sentence, for just then, the carriage door opened again.

"What in the name of the saints have you done?" a man's voice demanded. "Jesus, Mary, and Joseph, Hawkins."

Was that Lord Dunmeath's voice? Shock suffused her at the realization that he was here. Muddled thoughts blended as she wondered what was happening now.

"Well, sir, I didn't think you wanted someone else to bid on her so I . . . bought her for you."

Bought her? Emma blinked in the darkness. She could hardly believe what she was hearing. So—this man had bid on her on behalf of Lord Dunmeath? A rush of air filled up her lungs when she realized the earl hadn't abandoned her after all. And yet . . . why hadn't he come for her himself? She sagged back against the carriage seat, overwhelmed.

Lord Dunmeath gripped the man's hand and said, "Thank God. Whatever I'm paying you, Hawkins, I'll double it. Especially after what you've done. Now untie Miss Bartholomew. She looks like she's been trussed up for Christmas dinner. That wasn't necessary."

"Very good, sir. It wasn't my idea to keep her bound, but I fear she wasn't being very cooperative."

"I can't imagine why," Lord Dunmeath mused with a trace of

irony. He slipped into the carriage and sat across from her. "Are you all right, Miss Bartholomew?" He reached back and unfastened the gag.

"You came." Her words came out hoarse, and the tears welled up again. She didn't know whether to be furious with him or grateful. Every emotion within her was strung so tightly, she felt as if the slightest word would crumble her into pieces.

"Hawkins is my secretary," the earl explained. "It's my fault that we didn't know where the auction was. It's grateful I am that he found the new invitation and bid on my behalf." He reached back to untie her ropes.

Her skin was chafed and raw, but he was gentle as he loosened the ties. "Will you let me take you away from here? Or if you'd rather go back to Mrs. Harding's school—"

She could only nod at first, wanting to be anywhere but here. And yet, she didn't know what his intentions were, nor did she fully trust him. "I'd be grateful to go to the school."

The other gentleman, Mr. Hawkins, added, "My lord, I took the liberty of putting your name on the marriage license beside hers. Are there any other preparations I should make?"

"Not yet," the earl answered. "I believe Miss Bartholomew should have some say in this."

THEY DROVE THROUGH the streets for a time, but Cormac didn't push her to make a decision. Clearly, she'd been through hell this evening. Just as he had. Even now, he was barely hanging on to his own strength. He'd eaten so little, the slightest movement made him dizzy.

"I'm sorry I was late," he said. Inwardly, he thanked God that his secretary had read his mail and learned what was happening with the auction. He couldn't imagine what might have happened otherwise.

Cormac reached out to take her hand, meaning to reassure

Miss Bartholomew. But then he realized she wasn't wearing gloves. Her hands were cold, and he felt the slight abrasions on her wrists where her hands had been bound. He raised her wrist to his mouth, as if he could soothe the hurt away. She gave a soft cry but didn't pull her hand away.

"Emma," he breathed. He needed to speak her name, to reassure her that everything was all right now.

"Don't," she whispered. It was then that he realized she was holding onto her emotions by a thread.

"Are you hurt?"

"No." She closed her eyes and leaned against the side of the carriage. "Just take me back."

He heard the disappointment in her voice and knew better than to ask her about marriage. He blamed himself for not being there. He'd let her down tonight, both at the ball and at the auction.

"Why did your family do this to you?" he asked. "It wasn't necessary."

"Our family is in debt," she answered. "Lucy told me my father could be sent to debtor's prison—and he would die if that happened. This was her way of trying to pay off what we owe."

He'd never imagined her stepmother would do such a thing—or that Emma would agree to it. "I already offered to wed you before," he said quietly.

"Even with the money you bid, I don't know if it will be enough to save him." Her voice was weary, filled with hopelessness. "And I have no dowry."

"The money be damned," he said. "You're worth a hundred times that." He meant it, for she had a courage he'd never imagined. Cormac took her hands in his and insisted, "I will help you. And your family."

She withdrew her hands from his. "Lord Dunmeath, find another heiress to wed. Someone beautiful with a dowry who can be the sort of wife you need."

But there was no time for that. His days were numbered, and

he needed to marry immediately.

"And what if the woman I want to marry is you?" he asked. "Would you not consider it? I could save your father and take care of you."

"I can't," she whispered. "Don't ask that of me."

"Why can't you?" he demanded. "Aye, I've made mistakes. But I deserve to know why you won't be giving me a second chance."

"Because I can't rely on you," she blurted out. "I don't trust you."

Her words were an invisible blow he hadn't expected, and he fell silent.

"You said you would be at the ball tonight. And you weren't." In her voice, he heard the quiet censure. "Then you weren't there at the auction. Your secretary had to place a bid on me so I wouldn't be auctioned off to someone else."

"I had my reasons," he said. Namely that he'd been so sick he could barely get out of bed. But he didn't want to admit his weakness to her. Was it better for her to believe him to be absentminded or dying? He didn't know.

"You're not a man I can depend on," she said softly. "I can't marry you."

Her words bothered him more than he'd imagined they could. He liked Emma, and he'd thought he could give her a happy life with whatever time he had left. He'd never considered that she would truly not want him.

Aye, he understood why she felt the way she did. He *had* let her down. More than once. But that was beyond his control. He was dying, and every day was a gift to him. Was it so terrible that he wanted to spend his last weeks with someone he considered a friend? But it sounded as if she didn't even consider him that.

"What if . . . we come to an understanding?" he offered. "You want to save your family from debt. I want the chance to change your mind. Allow me to court you and show you that I can be a different man."

The carriage pulled to a stop in front of the school, and she started to move toward the door.

"Flowers and empty promises won't make me change my mind," she said. "I'm sorry, Lord Dunmeath. But I cannot marry you."

Chapter Six

EMMA DIDN'T SLEEP all night. She simply stared into the familiar darkness, wondering what to do next. Because Cormac had been the one to win the auction, it had granted her a slight reprieve. But by refusing to marry him, she was doing nothing to help her family's debts. The guilt settled its invisible weight across her shoulders, making her wonder what to do.

She'd spoken the truth when she'd said that she didn't trust him. One moment he was at her side, causing all sorts of unexpected feelings—and the next, he disappeared with no word of explanation, only apologies.

It made her wonder why he wanted to marry her at all.

Was there a reason for his absences? She'd noticed pain edging his voice before, and last night it had sounded similar. Yet, he seemed unwilling to tell her the truth. He had simply accepted the blame with no explanation.

A knock sounded at the door, and when she called for the person to enter, a maid said, "Good morning, Miss Bartholomew. Would you like to have breakfast with Mrs. Harding in the dining room? Or would you rather have a tray in your room?"

The thought of spending the day in this room sobered her so she answered, "I'll go downstairs, if you could help me dress."

She chose a day dress that was a gentle shade of green, and

once she was ready, the maid helped her brush and style her hair. Emma had no idea what was done to it, but she did feel better prepared to face the day and what lay ahead. She was afraid to imagine facing Lord Dunmeath again, but she'd been honest with him. How could she marry a man who was here one day and gone the next?

She walked down the stairs but soon realized that Mrs. Harding had already eaten and departed. Emma picked at her toast and eggs, feeling the restlessness rising within her. Papa was going to be held accountable for his debts, and she had to do something.

Guilt weighed upon her, for her stepmother had tried to help him. The auction, though humiliating, had been Lucy's effort to solve their problems. But now Emma was unraveling all her efforts by refusing Lord Dunmeath.

She pushed her food aside, needing something to quiet her mind. She counted the steps toward the staircase and then made her way to the music room that connected to the ballroom. There was a pianoforte there, if she remembered correctly. Though it had been weeks since she'd played anything, it was just the sort of distraction she needed.

When she entered the room, she saw a large, blurred shape on the opposite end that turned out to be the pianoforte. She smiled, tracing the edges of the instrument. Then she took a seat, first removing her gloves before she found the familiar keys with her fingers.

Here, at least, no one noticed her blindness. She could play the keys and know that the sounds would rise and fall together in pure music. And so, she closed her eyes and gave in to the moment, playing a simple minuet that she'd learned as a child. It always took a long time for her to learn a song, for she could not read the music. But she could hear it, and over the years she had improved her ability to match what she heard.

As she played, she questioned whether she was being selfish in refusing Lord Dunmeath. He was the only man who had ever offered for her. She doubted she would find anyone else willing to marry her. Why then, did she keep pushing him away?

It was fear, she realized. Fear that if she said yes, she would be forced into an unfamiliar life for which she wasn't ready. And she didn't want to one day resent him for that or for his being an unreliable partner. Better to let him go.

Light footsteps entered the music room, and she heard Mrs. Harding say, "I understand that Lord Dunmeath won the auction last night."

Emma stopped playing and let out a breath. She could hear the mild frustration in the headmistress's voice. "His secretary did," she corrected. "Lord Dunmeath didn't arrive until after the auction was over." She paused a moment and added, "I'm not going to marry the earl. I refused him."

"May I ask why?" Mrs. Harding inquired gently. "Has he been cruel to you?"

"Not . . . exactly. Thoughtless, perhaps."

The headmistress waited for her to continue, but Emma didn't know what to say. Somehow telling Mrs. Harding that she couldn't depend on the earl seemed wrong. And she could already read the matron's judgment.

Lord Dunmeath wasn't a cruel man. Forgetful, perhaps—and she sensed that this wouldn't be the last time he'd let her down. But even more than that, she didn't want to give herself false hopes that this could be a happy marriage. Even if he tried to become more trustworthy, there were her own faults to consider. She could never imagine becoming a countess.

Which meant that one day, he would come to resent *her*. And the thought hurt, for she could do nothing to restore her sight. If she dared to wed Lord Dunmeath, one day he would break her heart.

"Many men are thoughtless," Mrs. Harding said at last. "And yet, he *did* offer to help your father." The headmistress thought a moment longer and added, "But that isn't the only reason you refused him, is it?"

Emma closed her eyes and shook her head. "I can't do the things other wives can," she confessed. "I would be expected to run his household, and I don't know if I can manage that. I could marry a merchant or a knight—but not an earl."

"You're afraid," Mrs. Harding deduced.

Emma nodded. "I would become a burden to him, and that's not what I want. I'd rather marry someone who leads a quiet life, someone who has no expectations of me."

She could bring nothing to this marriage. And it was far better to refuse him and remain in the wallflower life she'd always known than to reach for something she didn't deserve. She would think of another way to help her father.

"Lord Dunmeath is waiting for you in the ballroom," Mrs. Harding said. "With a marriage license, so I understand. And he told me he has already paid off your father's debts."

Emma went icy cold at the revelation. "He did what?"

"It seems he didn't want to accept your refusal."

She blinked a moment, trying to understand. Why had he done such a thing? He knew she didn't want to marry him. But now she was beholden to him. Whatever his intention had been, it seemed as if he was trying to take away her choice. And that wasn't acceptable to her—not at all.

"He shouldn't have done that," Emma protested. "I told him I didn't want to marry him."

"Do you want me to send him away?" Mrs. Harding asked.

"No. I will speak with him." And hopefully she could convince him of all the reasons why they should not marry.

"Wait here, and I will tell him you are ready."

She did, but instead of waiting in silence, Emma began to play another more complicated piece—the third movement of one of Beethoven's sonatas, which gave her the opportunity to express her frustration. She only knew the opening phrases, but it gave her the means of attacking the keys.

The moment Lord Dunmeath entered the room and drew close, she smelled the familiar scent of pine—likely from his shaving soap. He stood beside the pianoforte, waiting for her to finish. When she forgot the next line, her hands stilled.

"You're quite good, Miss Bartholomew. I enjoyed hearing you play." His deep baritone slid beneath her defenses, and she tried to ignore the way her heart warmed to his compliment.

"Thank you. But it doesn't change the fact that I cannot marry you."

"Miss Bartholomew . . ."

"No, let me speak," she said, cutting him off. "While I appreciate what you did to help my father, I am not going to change my mind," she said. "I will repay the money as soon as possible."

"I don't think you understand my reasons." His voice remained even, as if he were trying not to make her angrier.

"You want a wife. And for some reason, you won't accept my refusal to wed you." It sounded clear enough to her.

"Could we speak frankly, Emma?" he asked softly. The intimate use of her name caught her unawares, and it disconcerted her.

"I thought we were." She'd given him her reasons—the only problem was that he wouldn't accept them.

"No. I've been avoiding the truth, and I suppose it's time that I told you everything." There was an edge to his voice that deepened her discomposure, making her wonder what exactly he meant to say.

But he continued, "And in turn, I want you to tell me the truth about why I'm not the husband you want. I want to know the real reasons for your refusal—and stop telling me to wed someone else. There isn't time for that."

"What do you mean, there isn't time?" Something in his words struck her as unusual.

"I will explain everything in a moment," he said. "But first, I want to know if you dislike me. Is your reason for refusing marriage about not wanting to live with me or share my bed?"

Her face flushed scarlet at that. "Y-you truly are being frank, aren't you?" But when she imagined being intimate with a husband, Cormac didn't displease her. Quite the opposite, in fact. Though she couldn't see him very well, the slightest touch set her on edge. His voice drew her in, and the smell of his skin made her want to lean closer.

"I don't dislike you," she admitted. "But I don't trust you."

He reached out to take her hand. Though she wanted to protest, her words fell silent when his thumb stroked the edge of her palm. The slight caress made her imagine him touching other parts of her body. Her breasts ached against her chemise, and between her legs, she felt a warmth beginning to blossom.

"Then what can I do to earn that trust?" he asked.

His fingers laced with hers, and she decided that if they were going to be honest, she might as well say everything.

"I do want to be married. And perhaps have children one day," she confessed. "But I always imagined marrying someone with a very small household. Perhaps a merchant or a knight, at most. You're an earl. If I became a countess, I could never do what is expected of me."

"All I would expect of you is to join me at meals, offer companionship, and try to give me an heir as quickly as possible."

She blinked at that. Though it wasn't an unexpected desire for any husband to want an heir, she sensed a slight desperation in his words. It meant he would want to share her bed often, and the thought frightened her.

But still, she forced herself to answer him with the truth. "I cannot read, Cormac." Speaking his first name brought an intimacy that she hadn't expected. "I can barely write. I cannot manage the accounts, and I doubt if I could find my way around your home in Ireland. You're asking me to leave everything behind and become mistress of a household where the servants would see me as incompetent."

She pulled her hand back. "I've worked so hard to keep my blindness a secret. But everyone in your household would know. They would feel pity . . . and they would wonder why you lowered yourself to choose a wife like me."

An ache caught in her throat, and she added, "You would come to despise me. And I don't want that."

His silence unnerved her, but she felt a sense of relief that she'd told him the truth at last.

"So, if I were a man of no consequence, you'd marry me?"

"I . . . I suppose I would." But as soon as she spoke the words, the guilt returned. "What I don't understand is why you keep insisting that *I* be the one to marry you. There are other women."

He let out a slow sigh and finally spoke. "As I said before, there's no time. There's only one thing I'm wanting in the world, Emma—and that is to be a husband and a father."

It was a mirror of her own dream, but she sensed something darker within his words. Something forced her to wait, to let him finish speaking.

"I can promise you that if you marry me, I will never come to despise you. I would be grateful for each and every day as your husband. And if we are blessed with a child, nothing would make me happier."

He reached for her hand again, but this time it was as if he were seeking strength from her. "I know you think I am irresponsible and forgetful. I've let you down when you needed me. And it's possible—even probable—that I'll do so again. But it's not because I didn't want to be there."

"Then why?" she asked softly.

"It's because I'm dying, Emma. It's unlikely that I'll last through the end of the year."

For a moment, she couldn't speak. Words of protest rose to her lips, but she could say nothing. For she sensed that this wasn't an exaggeration. She recognized the pain edging his voice, and even now, she could hear the exhaustion in his tone.

"So, when you said there's no time . . ."

"I mean exactly that," he answered. "I don't know whether I'll last until winter or whether I'll die next week."

The solemnity in his voice brought an unexpected wave of sadness. "How can you be certain? Did you see a physician?"

"Many," he answered. "And they all agree that it's a disease passed through the male line. My father died, as did my older brother Finn. When I grew ill, my mother sent me here." He paused and added, "She questioned whether we were being poisoned. But I arrived in London with no one. I hired servants a few weeks later. And no matter how hard I've tried, the illness keeps coming back."

He waited for her to speak, and when she could say nothing, he added, "So long as we are being frank, I can tell you that this will most likely be a temporary marriage. After it is over, if you do not conceive a child, my cousin will inherit. That is, if he doesn't become sick as well."

"You want me to give you an heir," she said slowly, releasing his hand. The thought unnerved her, for she'd barely imagined being married, much less becoming a mother.

"I do," he said. "And in return for your hand in marriage, I've paid all your father's debts." He waited a moment and asked, "Would you consider it?"

"I don't know," she hedged.

And truly, she didn't. In one way, he'd taken away her choice. If she refused, it made her an ungrateful person, for he'd given her the gift of her father's freedom. But on the other hand, it felt as if she barely knew Cormac—and he'd given her no time to truly know the sort of man he was. While she understood his desperate desire for an heir, it felt rather like she was selling her body in exchange for her father's debts.

He took her hand again, as if gathering strength from her touch. "I don't want to die, Emma. Nor do I wish to burden you with my illness. But the past few days have made it clear that my time is ending."

"What if I cannot give you a child?" she asked quietly.

"Then I can die knowing that I did everything I could." He drew her hand to his cheek, and beneath her fingertips, she felt the rough stubble. It seemed like an invitation to touch him, and she used the moment to explore his features. She could see the dark brown color of his hair, but she closed her eyes and traced the edges of his face. He had a strong jaw, a straight nose, and full lips. Her fingers slid down his cheeks to his chin, and he turned his face, pressing a kiss upon her palm. She reached out to touch his hair and noticed that it was roughly cut against his collar, slightly longer than was fashionable.

"What color are your eyes?" she asked.

"Gray," he answered. Then he drew her hands to rest upon his shoulders. He said nothing about her touch, but it did seem that he understood it was her way of seeing him.

His hands came up to frame her face, and before she knew what was happening, he leaned in and stole a kiss. His warm mouth claimed hers, and a sudden rush of sadness flooded through her before it transformed into something different. It was as if he'd reached inside her and pushed away the thousands of doubts until all there was left in the world was him.

His mouth coaxed hers, his tongue tracing the edge of her lips, asking the silent question of whether she would open for him.

And when she did, everything changed.

The kiss grew hotter, and he pulled her so close, she could feel every line of his body. It had become more than his lips upon hers—it was an invitation.

His hands moved down to her hips, and she could feel the hard strength of his body pressing against her. He tempted her to break past the boundaries of her reticence to surrender to the forbidden.

Emma didn't want to believe he might die, though she'd heard the rough exhaustion in his voice before. She was afraid to take such a risk, for she wanted more time to know this man. But there wasn't time, was there?

She let out a slow breath, wondering if she dared to take such a leap of faith.

CORMAC HAD NEVER imagined kissing Emma would be like this. He'd expected her shyness, but the touch of her hands on his face, as if she were learning every edge, every line, drove him mad. He imagined her exploring his body with those sensitive hands, and it nearly sent him over the edge.

He drew back and noticed that her lips were swollen, her blue eyes bright. Her dark hair was tangled about her face, and there was a becoming flush to her cheeks.

"Do you have an answer for me?" He moved his hands to her waist, keeping them there lightly if she wanted to pull away.

"I have more questions than answers," she admitted. "My brain is spinning."

"What does your heart tell you?" He sensed that the kiss might have tipped the balance in his favor.

"The wise answer would be no. There are so many things that could go wrong," she said.

"Don't be wise," he said, leaning in to steal another kiss. "Be very, very foolish."

A sudden laugh broke out before she turned somber. "Lord Dunmeath, I am grateful for what you did for my father. But—"

"Don't say no—not yet." He cut her off before she could finish the sentence. "I suggest we draw up a marriage contract between us. You tell me all the things that you don't want and tell me what you do want. We will make an arrangement out of it. I have only one condition of my own, besides needing an heir."

She studied him and asked, "And what is that?"

"We cannot fall in love." Though he understood that Emma had a soft heart, he already knew he was dying. He didn't want her to grieve for him, nor did he want to fall in love with her, knowing that they would never have a future together. "Friendship would be best, considering how little time we have."

Her expression turned pensive, and she seemed to consider it.

At last, she answered, "I suppose we'll need paper if we're to draw up a contract, won't we?"

Her answer brought a rushing sense of relief. "And a pen and ink."

"I will want Mrs. Harding or Mr. Gregor to witness our contract," she said. "Since I cannot read it for myself."

"A reasonable request," he said. "But if we could draw up the terms first and then have them witness our signatures later, perhaps that will give us time to discuss anything we might be disagreeing on?"

"All right." She waited while he found paper, a pen, and opened the inkwell. He dipped the pen in the ink and wrote, *We will not fall in love.*

"What is your first condition?" he asked.

"First, do not reveal my vision difficulties to your staff," she said. "Let me try to find my way around. They will eventually learn the truth, but at first, I don't want them to judge me by my failings."

He wrote it down but said nothing. She didn't know how very large his home was, and it would take quite a lot of time for her to get accustomed to it.

"Second, do not ask me to read or write," she continued. "I'll need a secretary to help me with that."

He wrote quickly, noting all her requests. Most were related to household affairs, and as he wrote, he noticed that none were about their marriage. After he had written down six conditions, he said, "My turn."

She paused, and he read aloud as he wrote. "You will do your best to willingly give me an heir as quickly as possible. There can be no delay."

Though he knew it was quite a lot to ask of her, it was his reality. In another few weeks, he might not have the strength to sire a child.

Her face turned crimson, and she glanced downward. "I—I will try."

He saw the shyness in her expression, but he sensed that she wasn't repulsed by him, which was a benefit. Then he added his next condition.

"Next, you will tell me if something is bothering you. I am terrible at reading the minds of women. I know I've offended many during the past year, though I don't know why."

"Asking a woman to wed you ten minutes after you met her might have something to do with it."

In her voice, he heard a light teasing, but he didn't take offense. Instead, he pushed back and replied, "You're right. I probably waited too long."

At that, her face lightened with amusement, though she said nothing. Cormac picked up the pen again. "My last condition is that I want you to experience anything and everything you could not do because of your blindness. Whether it's reading, painting, dancing—anything you ever wanted to try, we will do."

She fell silent, not at all enthusiastic, as he'd hoped. "Lord Dunmeath—"

"Cormac," he corrected. "When we are alone, I'm wanting to hear you say my name, *a chroí*."

"Cormac, shouldn't we . . . do the things *you* want to do?" she ventured. "If you're dying?"

Her words stopped him all of a sudden. He'd been so focused on getting her to agree to the marriage, he hadn't truly stopped to think of what he wanted. Because in all honesty, he didn't think the marriage would last very long.

But her words struck him with a thoughtfulness he hadn't considered. A heaviness caught his heart that she would consider him when all he wanted was a few months of happiness with her.

"We will," he said. "We'll do them together."

"ARE YOU READY?"

Emma's heart was pounding as she rested her hand upon her

father's arm. "I am." She'd returned home three days ago, and since then, she'd been caught up in a whirlwind of wedding plans. Cormac had made most of the arrangements, asking her about flowers and what she wanted for a wedding gown. Because there was no time for something new, she wore the blue ballgown with the raised embroidery. Lucy had helped her with her hair, and strangely enough, her stepmother had been kinder than usual—almost as if she felt guilty for what she'd done.

But Emma wasn't ready to forgive her for the auction, despite it being her wedding day.

"Are you pleased with the man you've chosen to marry, Emma?" her father asked. "I know he's helped me with my debts, for which I'm grateful. But if you do not like him, we can find another way."

"No, I do like Lord Dunmeath," Emma admitted, "but I am nervous about living so far away from home." The thought of being in another country, with strangers who probably wouldn't want her to be the lady of their household, terrified her.

Her father began walking with her the sixteen steps that remained before the doorway to the drawing room. They would be married by special license. The one Lucy had claimed to have had apparently been false, but Cormac had managed to acquire the real one that was necessary for the wedding.

When they reached the door to the drawing room, someone pressed a bouquet of flowers into her hands. The fragrant scent of lilies and roses made her smile, and as they continued into the room, the aroma seemed to surround the room.

Cormac had done this for her, she realized. Though she could barely see anything, the floral fragrance was a gift she'd never anticipated. Within her heart, she felt an unexpected tug of gratitude.

And then, there was music. She heard the sound of violins, and the beauty of it filled her heart. It was a second gift she'd never expected.

This was more dangerous than she'd realized. The earl had

done everything in his power to give her an unforgettable wedding day, but the fact remained that he was going to die. She didn't know how much longer he had or what would happen, but an invisible pang struck her like a physical blow.

We cannot fall in love.

It was one of the most fundamental rules they'd agreed upon. And despite the swell of happiness that threatened her, she forced herself to put an invisible wall around her heart. She would not let herself feel anything beyond friendship. She simply couldn't. But even then, the thought of losing Cormac brought an ache to her chest.

Her father stopped walking, and a moment later, he gave her to Cormac. Her bridegroom took her hand and gave it a light squeeze, just as the musicians ended their song.

"You look beautiful, Emma," he murmured.

"Thank you." After a slight pause, she added, "And thank you for the flowers and music. They are lovely."

After that, they spoke their vows and were married. Cormac brushed a light kiss upon her lips and then she heard the applause of the guests. She guessed there were perhaps a dozen people, and soon enough, she heard the congratulations of Lady Ashleigh and her husband, along with Lord and Lady Scarsdale.

Mrs. Harding and Mr. Gregor were also there, but it occurred to her that no one from Cormac's family was here. Did that bother him? She didn't know what to think.

The rest of the morning and afternoon blurred into a celebration with good food and more music. Then her new husband asked her to dance.

A refusal came to her lips, but then she realized there were only friends and family here. What did it matter if she stumbled? He'd given her so much, and this was what he wanted in return. It wasn't right to say no to such a small request.

"All right," she agreed.

But to her surprise, Cormac guided her outside. He let go of her hand for a moment, closing the door behind him.

"Can you still hear the music?" he asked, as he took her hands.

And she could. He rested his hands upon her waist, and as they waltzed, she could feel the sunlight on her face. Though the air was cool and autumn was swiftly approaching, she would remember this day's warmth and sunshine.

She reached up to his face, and it was then that she felt the coolness of his skin. She touched his forehead and his cheeks, and though he was forcing a smile, she sensed he was not feeling well.

"How much pain are you in?" she asked.

"It doesn't matter. This is our wedding day, and I'll not be letting anything get in the way of that."

Which meant he was putting on a brave face for her sake. And it made her wonder how many days he'd had to endure pain and suffering while trying to appear as if nothing was wrong. It must be exhausting.

"Is there anything I can get for you?" she asked. "Food or something to drink, perhaps? Or should we leave early so you can rest?"

He shook his head. "It wouldn't make a difference, Emma. I will stay as long as you want me to." And before she could voice another protest, he leaned in and stole a kiss.

This one was far different from the kiss that sealed their wedding vows. He kissed her like a man who knew he had only a little time left in the world. She clung to him, yielding as he laid siege to her defenses.

Her body came alive at his touch, awakening to more. Against the juncture of her hips she could feel his desire, and an echoing ache answered within her. The pine scent of his skin allured her, and she broke away from the kiss, resting her face against his throat to inhale.

He let out a shaky breath and admitted, "I've changed my mind. Let's go home now."

Emma didn't quite know how to respond to that, but beneath her fingertips, the pulse at his throat was as wild as her own.

She couldn't deny her own fears of what was to come on their wedding night. Her stepmother had told her nothing at all, and the only knowledge she had of conceiving children was from gossip and whispers she wasn't meant to overhear in the ballroom.

"Could we stay just a little longer?" she asked. "W-we still have the wedding cake," she said. "And our guests will be waiting."

He stopped and rested his forehead against hers. Though he acceded to her wishes, she sensed that he wanted to distract himself from his pain. She rested her hands on each side of his face for a moment before pulling back.

"I haven't forgotten our agreement," she said. And although she was frightened, she told herself that Cormac Ormond, the Earl of Dunmeath, had done everything to help her. All he wanted in return was a child. Surely, she could set aside her fears and give him what he needed.

Chapter Seven

I T WAS LATER in the afternoon before they left the celebration, and Cormac could barely remember anything about the wedding. His stomach was killing him, though he'd drunk medicines Hawkins had found for him in the hope that he could dull the pain. But at last, he was married. And if he could somehow get through the vicious pain, he would share Emma's bed and perhaps attempt to conceive his heir.

The carriage continued on through the cobbled streets, and he took slow breaths, trying not to think of his illness. His wife was seated across from him, her mood pensive.

"What are you thinking?" he asked.

"I'm trying not to be terrified," she admitted. "I know my responsibilities, but I don't know what to do."

He reached out to take her gloved hand. "It's grateful I am that you've agreed to this marriage. And I swear I will not hurt you. I hope to bring you naught but pleasure."

He could hear her shallow breathing, though she gripped his hand in return. "I—I'll try."

It had been a long time since he'd been with a virgin or any woman at all. Even then, he'd been a green lad himself, knowing nothing except a quick tumble. He wanted this to be good for Emma, for her to take joy in their union.

"It will be all right," he swore. After a while, the carriage came to a stop in front of his townhouse. Cormac escorted her from the vehicle, and as they walked toward the entrance, he murmured, "Eleven steps."

Her hand tightened on his arm, and the look in her eyes held a startled expression. But he paused in front of the first step and then walked with her to the front door. Under his breath, he murmured, "Two more and then the threshold."

The footman held the door open for them and then his secretary Hawkins stepped forward with a smile. "May I be the first to welcome you, Lady Dunmeath?"

"Thank you," Emma answered, braving an answering smile.

Then Hawkins added to Cormac, "All the arrangements you requested have been made, my lord."

"Very good." He turned to Emma and asked, "Would you like a tour of the house? Or would you rather rest first?"

Her cheeks flushed, and she answered, "A tour, if you don't mind."

She was stalling—he could see it in her face. But it was still early enough. His wife removed her bonnet and he helped her with her cloak, handing them both to a footman. "Allen will take these."

Two other servants waited nearby, and Cormac introduced them as well. "Lady Dunmeath, may I present our butler, Graham, and our housekeeper, Mrs. Foster? I'm certain you will want to meet with her later."

"I am pleased to meet you both," Emma said. Then she asked Cormac, "How long will we remain in London before we travel to meet your family?"

"A few more days," he answered. He hoped that he could manage to push aside his illness a little longer. "But I thought we would travel to the seaside first. For our honeymoon."

He felt her grip loosen on his arm, revealing her tension.

"All right," she answered.

"Mrs. Foster, we won't be eating our supper until later tonight. I'll ring for food when we're wanting it." After the feast from their wedding celebration, there was no need to eat just yet. Then, to Emma, he said, "I'll show you around the house." He dismissed the servants, and then turned her toward the left. They took slow steps down the hall, and he counted along with her.

"This is our library," he said, guiding her through the doorway.

"Nineteen steps," she said quietly. For a moment, she breathed in deeply. "Are there roses here?"

"There's a vase of them on the other side of the room."

"I can smell them." She let go of his hand, and he sat while she explored the drawing room, counting steps and touching the bookcases. "It's a lovely room."

But as she traced her fingers across the book titles, he realized she had never known the joy of reading the stories. Perhaps he could give her that gift and calm her nerves about the wedding night at the same time.

"Will you sit down for a moment?" he asked. "There's something I'm wanting to give to you. A different sort of wedding gift."

He led her to the settee, and after she sat down, he searched through the books to find a book of fairytales. Then he flipped through the pages, searching for a good story. It was in German, but he translated as he read aloud.

"There once was a widow who lived in a small cottage, deep in the forest, with her two daughters. Every day, she bade her eldest daughter to go out and spin thread by the well."

"Cormac, what are you doing?" Her voice held amusement, and he caught her hand and sat beside her.

"Telling you a fairy story, if you'd like to hear it."

"A fairy story? I thought you were giving me a tour of the house."

"I realized that you've never known the joy of reading stories. And I thought you might enjoy it."

Her face flushed, and she looked away. "I'm not a child,

Cormac. You don't need to read to me."

She had misunderstood his intentions. "Oh, you needn't worry, *a stór*. I'm fully aware that you're not a child." His hand moved to her waist, and he drew her to sit on his lap. He couldn't stop his rigid arousal, but having her so near was a welcome balm to the illness he was fighting.

For a moment, he breathed in the scent of her throat. Her pulse was racing, and he reached up to touch her hair. He drew her hands to his face and turned his mouth to kiss her palm. He could feel her body trembling, but he didn't know if it was fear or the echo of his own desire. "I've never wanted anyone more in my entire life."

"It doesn't seem real that you're my husband now," she murmured.

He wanted to press her back against the settee and learn the shape of her mouth by kissing her, tracing every part of her lips. The wedding gown she wore skimmed the edges of her figure, baring her shoulders and revealing every curve. He wanted to unfasten those buttons to see more of her lovely skin.

Instead, he asked, "I am grateful that you're my wife now, Emma. But don't be thinking that I'm reading a story because I feel pity for you. It's my way of courting you. If you're willing to listen."

"You don't have to court me," she said softly. "We're already married."

He opened the book, returning to where he'd left off. While she remained in his arms, he read her the story of Mother Holle. Throughout the tale, he watched her face. There was a softness in her countenance, as if she'd hungered for such stories.

And it was the beginning of her seduction.

EMMA LOST TRACK of time as he read to her. Lord Dunmeath's voice was a rich baritone with an Irish lilt that made the fairy story come to life. She'd never heard the tale before, and it was as if another world had opened up to her. She was fully conscious of his body beneath hers, his arms around her as he read.

And she began to feel an aching yearning inside her, the need to touch this man. She shifted against him, and the ridge of his erection made her go breathless. He tensed but finished the story.

"Did you like it?" he asked.

"Very much."

He set the book aside, and she kept her hands in her lap, not knowing what to do now. Cormac answered her unspoken question when his arms circled her waist. He touched his forehead to hers, and she could feel the warmth of his breath against her lips and the burning heat of his skin.

Without understanding why, she leaned in close and kissed him. The gesture seemed to awaken a storm within him, and he captured her mouth, sliding his tongue against the seam of her lips. She didn't know what he wanted, but when she opened her mouth slightly, his tongue entered.

The kiss deepened, and she moved in his lap until he groaned. "You're killing me, Emma."

She didn't know what he meant by that but wound her arms around his neck. The kiss gave her a sense of power, and when she imitated him, sliding her own tongue against his, he adjusted her position until his shaft rested between her legs.

She could feel the length of him pressing against her, and it shocked her to realize how good it felt. He was kissing her hard, and the motion of his body made her grow wet between her legs. Even her breasts seemed to tighten beneath her gown.

When he started to lay her down on the settee, she suddenly came to her senses. "Cormac," she whispered, breaking from the kiss. "Someone could see us."

He cursed softly in Irish and then moved her from his lap. "Let's go upstairs, *a stór*."

Her breathing was unsteady, and she knew the fateful moment was coming. He would remove her wedding gown and consummate the marriage. She was torn between fear of the unknown and the desire she now felt.

She barely knew Lord Dunmeath, and the thought of being intimate with him scattered her thoughts. She lost track of the steps as they walked upstairs and down the hallway to his bedchamber.

Cormac led her into the room and closed the door behind him. To her surprise, she saw a bright fire burning on the hearth. The room was warm, and everywhere, she could smell flowers.

He'd done this for her—just as he'd brought the wedding flowers. It was a thoughtful gift, and she gathered courage from his kindness.

Cormac caught her hand in his, and she pulled him to stand close to the fire. "Are you cold?" he asked.

Emma shook her head, but she couldn't suppress a nervous shiver. Or was it anticipation? She couldn't deny that Cormac tempted her with his kisses. She'd been overwhelmed by the mere sensation of sitting in his lap, and the story that he'd read to her had crumbled her defenses. Now it was time to surrender to that temptation.

"I'm not cold now, no," she answered. Then she rested her hands upon his chest, feeling the warmth of his muscles beneath her palms. He wouldn't hurt her; she believed that. But what startled her most was her own response to him—the yearning he'd awakened. And she dared to add, "I might be cold, after you remove my gown." Then she turned her back to him in a silent invitation to undress her. She shivered again when his hands rested against her buttons. One by one he opened them, baring her skin. Then his mouth descended to her nape, and he kissed a path lower as he unfastened each button. Soon enough, her gown slid to the floor, and she stood in her corset, chemise, and petticoats.

Emma closed her eyes, transfixed by the touch of his mouth against her skin. She listened to the sound of Cormac's unsteady breathing, and it made her wonder how he was feeling. Even now there was a sadness about him, the sadness of a man who knew his time was running out. He touched her shoulders and arms so carefully, as if trying to memorize her body.

Slowly, he loosened the laces of her corset, until he could remove the garment. Clad only in her chemise and petticoats, Emma felt completely exposed. She started to turn to him, but Cormac shocked her when he drew her hips against his. She could feel his rigid erection against her spine, and a moment later, his warm hands cupped her breasts through the cotton chemise. Her nipples hardened at his touch, and she was overwhelmed by the sudden rush of sensation. He bent to kiss her nape while his hands explored her breasts. Between her legs, she felt a warmth, almost as if he were touching her there.

And suddenly, she realized that she didn't want to simply stand here and let him do as he wished. She wanted to learn about him as well, to know his body in the same way.

She turned to him and helped him remove his jacket, then his waistcoat. Last came his cravat and shirt. When his chest was before her, she traced his skin with her sensitive fingertips. She closed her eyes, learning his muscles and the hard planes of his ribs and chest. In her mind, she formed a picture of him, one conjured from her touch.

He, in turn, untied her petticoats and her chemise. The rest of her undergarments fell away until she was completely exposed. He removed the rest of his own clothing until there were no boundaries between them.

"You're exquisite," he said roughly, kissing her again. He guided her to the bed, and she grew lightheaded, nervously imagining what came next. Her stepmother had told her nothing except to submit to her husband's wishes.

And it seemed that her husband wished to explore her body with his mouth. He covered one nipple with a kiss, and a bolt of desire shot through her. His hands were everywhere, moving against her ribs, down to her hips, gently nudging her open.

This was it, then. The moment when she would give him her

virginity. She braced herself, waiting for him to enter her body and take her innocence.

But he suddenly stopped. His entire body had gone rigid, and he lowered his head to the coverlet.

"Damn it," he cursed softly.

Had she done something wrong? Emma reached out to touch him, and then realized that the heat she'd felt from his face wasn't from desire—he was burning up with fever. Oh God.

"Lie down," she ordered. She rested her hand against his heart and felt it beating rapidly. "You're still feeling ill, aren't you?"

He closed his eyes and shook his head. "Unfortunately."

She'd known it from the time they'd danced together at their wedding celebration, but she'd hoped the pain had begun to ease. Instead, it seemed that he'd tried to suppress it.

"I didn't want to ruin our wedding day," he said quietly. "Or our wedding night. But it seems I've done that already."

"How bad is your pain?" She touched his forehead and face. Both were hot to the touch, but as she moved her hands down to his shoulders, they seemed rather cold.

"My stomach feels like I'm being stabbed," he admitted. She thought back to their wedding feast and wondered if he'd eaten anything. She'd been so distracted with the guests and the celebration she'd not noticed until now. Even the cake—he'd fed her a piece, and then he'd kissed her before she could offer one back to him.

"When did you eat last?" she asked. "Have you had anything today?"

He shook his head. "Hurts too much. I didn't want to be sick on our day. So I didn't risk it."

"I'm going to get some food and medicine for you. Lie down and rest for now."

"I'm sorry," he apologized. "This wasn't at all the night I was wanting to spend with you."

Emma pulled the coverlet over him and adjusted a pillow

beneath his head. "Let me take care of you." She smoothed his brow, suddenly aware of how much he'd been hiding from her. He'd pushed aside his own pain and suffering, trying to give her the wedding of her dreams. And her heart simply broke at the thought of it.

She stood from the bed and saw a blurred shape on the opposite side of the room. When she approached it, she touched the trunk of her belongings. After rummaging around, she found a dressing gown and donned it.

It took some time to find the bell pull, but she rang for a servant. Within a few minutes, a knock sounded at the door, and Emma answered it.

"Lord Dunmeath needs broth, bread, and medicine," she ordered. "Bring them immediately, along with a basin of water and linen." She wanted something to cool down his fever, and the maid readily agreed.

It might not have been the wedding night Cormac had wanted, but she had vowed to take care of him in sickness and in health. Emma steeled herself, uncertain of how much time they had left together.

And despite his insistence that they could not have feelings for one another, she worried that she was already losing her heart to this man.

CORMAC COULDN'T TELL how many days had passed, but he remembered Emma feeding him soup and dry bread. A physician had come once, but the man had given him sleeping potions. He could barely recall anything since their wedding night.

He heard a slight noise and when he opened his eyes, he saw Emma on the far side of his bedchamber, surrounded by trunks.

"Good morning," he managed weakly.

She turned and smiled at him. "How are you feeling?"

"A bit rough," he admitted, "but somewhat better. I'd rather not drink any more sleeping potions." He didn't like the feeling of being unaware of his surroundings. "How long have I been asleep?"

"Two days, off and on."

It seemed that he'd already begun their marriage on poor footing. "It's sorry I am," he said quietly. "I had hoped to offer you a better honeymoon than this."

"It's not your fault." She came and sat beside him on the bed. "But it did take me by surprise. Please don't hide your suffering from me. Let me try to help you."

He reached out and took her hand. "I wanted more for you than to become a nursemaid." And it was true. He'd never wanted to become an invalid, with Emma forced to feed him or wipe his brow. It burned his pride that he'd made such a mess of his own wedding night.

Slowly, he sat up. "I think we should leave for Ireland today. It will be a long journey for us, but we can stop along the way. I still want to spend a few days by the sea before we make the crossing."

The expression on her face revealed that she didn't believe him capable of making such a journey, though she didn't say it.

"Perhaps we should wait another fortnight."

He swung his leg to the side of the mattress, ignoring her suggestion. Though he still felt impossibly weak, he couldn't simply lie in bed waiting to die. He realized that he was fully naked still, and he eyed Emma, wondering if it would embarrass her.

But then he remembered that she couldn't truly see him this close. He flipped the coverlet back and eased to his feet.

"Cormac, be careful," she urged. "You shouldn't be up and walking this soon."

"I'm fine," he said. "But very hungry."

"I'll ring for food," she said and turned to pull the bell.

"You may want to be finding some clothes for me, *a stór.* Else, I'll be quite naked when the footman arrives with breakfast."

She blinked a moment and then a sheepish smile slid over her face. "Oh. I'd forgotten about that."

"Here I am, wearing the clothes God gave me, and my wife can't even appreciate it," he teased. "'Tis a blow to my pride, indeed."

"I don't even know where your clothes are." She started to laugh. "I think you'd better get back into bed before—" A knock sounded at the door, and she blurted out, "Cormac, hide!"

Instead, he stood behind a wingback chair. "Come in," he called out. Quite honestly, he was enjoying Emma's mortification. He paid the servants well enough that they would never dare to say a word.

"My lord, my lady," the footman said. "How can I be of service?"

"We'd like to have breakfast here, John," he told the footman. "Could you have Cook prepare our food?"

"Right away, my lord." He inclined his head and closed the door.

"Cormac, you—you can't—"

"Be naked when my servants bring me breakfast?" he questioned. "I do pay them quite well."

"What if a maid had answered the door?" She seemed to bemoan his unclothed state. "If you won't get back into bed, then we'll have to find you some clothes quickly."

He moved across the room and caught her by the waist, pulling her close. Her face flamed, but she didn't move. "Will you help dress me?"

"I—well, if you need my assistance, I suppose I could try—"

He cut off her words with a kiss. The honeysuckle scent of her skin and the taste of her lips made him want to drag her back into bed. He remembered the delicate feeling of her own naked body against his own, and his desire flared.

She kissed him back, but her hands rested between them like a shield. Despite his efforts to seduce her, she pulled back. "Clothes first. Then kissing."

He gave a slow smile. "Do you promise?"

"Where are your small clothes? And your trousers?"

"I don't know if I remember," he hedged. "My valet usually takes care of them."

She started opening drawers and then let out a frustrated sigh. "I can't tell what any of these are." Then she turned back to him and demanded, "I need your help."

He decided to stop his teasing and instead went to find undergarments and trousers. After he dressed, he pulled out a shirt and handed it to Emma.

"Will you help me put this on, *a stór?*"

She lifted it over his head, which put her arms around him, as he'd wanted. "What does that mean?"

"It's Irish for my treasure or my darling." He put his arms into the sleeves and then drew her hands to the buttons. She fastened them one by one, and the touch of her hands on his chest only deepened his desire.

Then he went to sit in the chair and pulled her into his lap. "Time for more kissing."

Her day dress was made of thin muslin, and he could feel the curves of her body against the fabric. She did kiss him back, and when her tongue threaded with his, he murmured against her lips, "I don't think I'm wanting breakfast anymore."

"Are you feeling unwell again?" she whispered.

"Nay. I'm wanting to feast upon you instead," he answered. "I want to taste every inch of your skin."

She exhaled sharply, and it was then that two footmen arrived with their food and tea. Emma instructed him to place the trays on a small table, and Cormac could smell the delicious aroma of eggs, sausage, and what appeared to be scones and jam.

His stomach growled with hunger, and after the footmen had gone, he took a plate and loaded it with food. Emma didn't do the same, but she instructed, "Come and sit beside me. We'll share."

"You do seem to feel a little better," she offered. "But shouldn't you start with toast?"

He patted the seat beside him. "I'm feeding you. We're sharing a plate."

She joined him, but he could see that she was starting to turn shy again. "Oh. I don't know if I'm feeling very hungry."

"Are you nervous?"

She glanced down at her lap. "Given what you just said about wanting to taste every inch of me? Of course, I am."

He guessed that she was probably still afraid of being hurt. "I want you to feel wonderful when I touch you," he said. "I want you to crave me as much as I want you." He spread jam upon a piece of toast. "I know you promised to share my bed as part of our marriage agreement. And I intend for you to enjoy it." Gently, he touched the toast to her lips in silent invitation.

She took a bite of the toast and then confessed, "I don't know anything about what's expected of me."

His earlier idea of spending the rest of the day in bed with her was now sounding like her greatest fear. He *was* feeling better today. And if he could simply show Emma what it could be like between them, he felt confident that their marriage would be a good one, even if it wouldn't last long.

Though he would have preferred to consummate the marriage right now, she still appeared terrified. And he didn't want her to be afraid—not at all.

"What would you like to do today?" he asked. "More reading? Or something else?"

"I want you to feel well again," she said. This time, she reached for the sausage and fed him pieces of that. "I think part of me didn't truly believe you were this ill. You hid it from everyone so well."

"It was a necessity. No one wants to wed a dying man."

"I don't want you to die," she said gently. "You don't deserve that fate. We should try other physicians. Someone might know a way to stop this from happening." In her voice, he heard a softness, as if she cared about him beyond companionship. But he didn't want her to have those feelings. They needed to maintain the boundary of friendship, nothing more.

Before he could speak, she continued, "But in the meantime, I should fulfill my part in this marriage. If you truly wish to conceive a child, we cannot wait any longer."

Chapter Eight

FROM HIS SILENCE, Emma wondered if she'd made a mistake. Wasn't this what Cormac wanted from her? It was her duty to conceive an heir. And from his kisses, she'd believed that he desired her—but more than that, she'd enjoyed the breathless feelings he'd evoked.

"Or, if you'd rather not . . ."

He reached for her hand. "No, it's what I want very much. I didn't want to frighten you."

Emma finished off the toast and rose to her feet. She walked the seven steps to the bedroom door and turned the key in the lock. Though her hands were trembling, she told herself to be sensible.

"It will be all right," she said. "As your wife, it's expected of me." Her face was burning with embarrassment, but she went to go sit at the bedside. She began to untie her stockings, but then Cormac was standing in front of her.

"Allow me," he said. His voice was deep, resonant, and it reached inside her to kindle something unfamiliar. When his hands moved beneath her skirts to the ribbons holding her stockings, she felt completely vulnerable to him. His hands upon her inner thighs were dangerously close, and when he began to remove her stockings, his warm hands slid down her thighs.

To her shock, he followed his hands with his mouth, kissing her legs. She was stunned by the sensation, and her hands gripped the coverlet. It seemed he'd been serious about kissing every inch of her body. The thought was dizzying.

When her legs were bare, he reached behind to unbutton her gown. Although he'd done it before, this time, she was more conscious of his touch. And she didn't want to remain passive; instead, she felt her own urge to touch him again.

After he removed her gown and stays, she turned around in his embrace. Without asking, she unbuttoned his shirt and lifted it up and over his head. "I suppose I needn't have dressed you."

"I rather enjoyed your hands on me." He loosened her chemise, baring her breasts. In the cool morning air, her nipples tightened into hard buds, and his mouth moved over her neck.

Soon enough, he removed the last layer of clothing, and Emma was fully naked before him. She felt so exposed, and yet, she couldn't deny the rise of anticipation. He would join his body with hers, and though there might be pain, somehow she believed it could also be something more.

Cormac knelt down before her at the edge of the bed. Her heart was pounding, but she grew distracted when his hands moved to her breasts, sweetly stroking the nipples. She bit back a moan, and he guided her to lie back. Another pulse of fear rippled through her, but she pushed it away. She heard the sound of him removing his clothes, and then he hesitated. Somehow that slight pause aroused her more, for she didn't know where he would touch her next. Her body ached for more, and she couldn't deny that he fascinated her.

But then his mouth moved to her inner thigh. She gasped at the wicked sensation, and before she could breathe, he lifted her legs to rest on his shoulders. Then he bent and tasted her intimately.

Molten heat washed over her, and she went utterly liquid. Never in her life had anyone kissed her there, and she arched her back, crying out when his tongue stroked her. A thousand starry lights seemed to explode within her head, and when he began to torment her with his mouth, she could scarcely breathe.

Never had she imagined that anything like this existed. He slid a finger inside her easily while his mouth continued to stroke the flesh above her entrance. She was falling apart, breaking into pieces. He seemed to know just when to push her further, and she strained, fighting against the wave that threatened to drown her.

But his gentle invasion suddenly crested in a shimmering eruption of pleasure so fierce, she shuddered at the sensations. His hands reached up to touch her bare breasts, gently caressing her nipples as his mouth feasted.

And she came apart a second time, crying out as her body released.

Emma didn't know what was happening, but a moment later, he reversed their positions. Her body was still quaking, but now she was lying on top of him. He guided the tip of his rigid manhood to her wet entrance, and the sensation was not painful—instead, it made her crave more. She wanted him inside her, needed him.

She rose up to her knees, guiding him inside, but he didn't move. It was then that she realized he was allowing her to take control. He'd shown her the mind-searing pleasure that could be between them, and he didn't want to hurt her now.

Her breathing was unsteady, but she tried to take more of him inside.

"Easy," he said. "Just do what feels good, Emma."

She realized then that he would not force their joining—instead, he'd empowered her to reach for what she wanted. He kept his hands upon her hips and raised up slightly. When his mouth covered one of her nipples, the aching between her legs made her want more, and she pressed against him. He lifted her hips once again, and she pressed down. The rhythm of taking him inside and then rising up was starting to bring back the sensations of pleasure she remembered.

He continued suckling at her breast, and she pushed back, no longer caring what happened. And then abruptly, she pushed past the barrier of her own innocence, until he was fully embedded inside her. There was a slight pain, but not nearly as bad as she'd imagined. Her knees rested on either side of him, and he held her in his arms.

"Is it . . . over?" she ventured. Now that they were joined, was that all there was?

"Not yet." There was a strain in his own voice, but he asked, "Did I hurt you?"

"I'm a little sore, but no. I don't think so." She didn't know what he meant when he said it wasn't over yet, but she moved slightly against him, and he groaned.

"I'm sorry," she murmured. "I didn't mean to hurt you. I should stop."

"Don't," he said in a husky voice. "Emma, will you let me continue?"

She didn't know what else was going to happen, but she said, "Yes, of course."

Gently, he moved her to her back, his body still inside hers. Slowly, he started to withdraw, but then he slid in deep. The motion startled her, but it evoked the same delicious feelings she'd known before. Cormac began to penetrate in a slow rhythm that seemed to caress her deep inside. She dug her fists into the coverlet again, overwhelmed by the sensations pouring over her. Once again, he pushed her over an invisible edge, and her body seized up with tremors, squeezing around him as he thrust.

He continued on, and she met his rhythm, arching her back and gripping his backside.

She felt the moment his body tensed, and he drove hard against her, finding his own release. Skin to skin, she welcomed his embrace, and he collapsed against her, sweaty and hot.

She'd never known that lovemaking was like this, and a part of her heart broke away at the thought of losing this man. He'd warned her not to fall in love with him, but it would take every defense she had to shield her heart. Even then, it might already be too late.

CORMAC STARED OUT at the sea, watching the waves slide across the sand in a soft motion. Emma had insisted that they leave everything behind and travel with only a few bundles of clothing, a coach, and money. Over the past week, they had stayed at traveling inns with a coachman and a single footman until now they were a short distance from the crossing. His wife had ordered the servants to travel separately and to send all their belongings to his home in Ireland.

Something had shifted in Emma's demeanor since they'd left London. He didn't know what it was, but he suspected she was on her own personal quest to help him heal.

Cormac knew better than to give himself false hope. Time and again, he'd started to improve, only for the symptoms to return. But he couldn't deny that ever since they'd arrived by the sea yesterday evening, he was starting to feel stronger again. He didn't know whether it was because they'd left London or whether it was the fresh air, but he intended to savor the time with Emma.

He had brought her to a more isolated part of the strand, and there were fewer people here now that the sun was setting.

She appeared enchanted by the view and smiled at him. "Is it terrible that I want to walk along the edge of the sea in my bare feet?"

"It's going to be cold," he warned.

"I know. But I want to feel the sand and what it's like to have the waves wash over my feet." The wistful expression on her face could not be denied.

"I'll help you with your stockings," he offered.

Emma flushed and answered, "No need. I can manage." She sat down in the sand and removed her shoes. Cormac caught a glimpse of her bare legs before she rolled down her stockings, one at a time. Then she stood in her bare feet, a smile spreading over her face. "I've never stood in sand before."

He gave in to impulse and removed his own shoes and stockings. The sand was cool beneath his feet, and he took her hand in his. "Do you want to walk in the waves?"

She nodded, and he guided her to the water's edge. Emma held her skirts in her hands, and he kept his arm around her waist as they walked. The sand was wet, and their footprints made imprints behind them. The first wave washed over the sand, and he winced at the frigid cold. His wife gasped and laughed at the same time. "It's like ice."

"It's nearly autumn," he reminded her. "But even in summer, the water is cold."

"It takes your breath away," she admitted, moving back to the sand and out of the freezing seawater.

"It does," he agreed. But he never took his eyes from her when he spoke. Her expression shifted, as if she'd sensed that he wasn't talking about the water.

"Are we alone?" she whispered.

"We are." Sand coated his bare feet as he walked away from the water. He kept his hands at her waist, and she rested her palms against his chest.

"Good." She reached up to his face and pulled it down to hers. He kissed her hard, and she met his tongue with her own. The embrace was as wild as the sea waves, desperate and unyielding. He went rigid at her touch, and he wanted nothing more than to be with her.

"We'll make the crossing soon," she said against his lips. "And in a few days, I'll be at your home in Ireland."

"In another week," he corrected. "We'll cross the sea after a few more days here. I'm not finished with you yet." He nipped at her lower lip, his hands moving over the curve of her breast.

"And what do you plan to do with me?" she teased.

"Mrs. Harding sent a few more lessons for you. I wouldn't

want to neglect your education." He continued stroking her breasts, and she moaned at his touch. But the truth was, he wanted more time with her before leaving for Dunmeath.

"Will your family like me, do you think?" she mused aloud as he raised her skirt, touching her bare legs.

"I think the more important question is whether you like them," he admitted. He caressed her thigh, and she shuddered against him. "And how soon I can bring you back to our cottage tonight, so I can spend the next few hours making love to you."

"That does sound appealing." She reached up to touch his face. "I worry about you, Cormac. And I can't help but wonder if something in the house—or someone—was making you sick. You do seem to be better since we left everything behind."

"I'm enjoying these days with you, *a stór*. But I've had spells like this before. They come and go." Though he understood her veiled hope, he didn't want her to imagine it would last. He drew her between his legs, pressing her body close. "We can only savor the time we have left."

"I want more time," she admitted. "And I don't want to waste any of it. You should do all the things you've ever wanted."

"And so I will." He fully intended to begin by laying her down on a bed and exploring every part of her body.

"Cormac," she asked as they began to walk back together, "What will it be like in Ireland?"

Though he understood her fears, he didn't want her to imagine he would make any demands of her. "You'll be my wife, just as you are now. I have no expectations of you to become the countess."

"But there are responsibilities," she insisted. "I don't know what they are. I'll need help in the beginning."

"My mother can continue in that role," he answered. "There's no need for you to worry about it."

"And what about years from now?" she asked. "When your mother is gone?"

"Or when I'm gone?" he dared to ask. Her face fell, and he

regretted what he'd said. He shouldn't have ruined the moment by mentioning his own death.

"What will happen to me if I become your widow?" she asked softly. "Am I to stay in Ireland? Or do I return to England?"

"If you are pregnant with our child, then you must stay at Dunmeath. I will see to it that you have everything you need."

But in her voice, he heard the uncertainty. And though he wanted to shield her from it, he knew he could not.

"And if there is no child?" she murmured.

There was no answer he could give her. His cousin would inherit, and there was nothing he could do to stop it.

"We'll worry about that later," was all he could say.

"YOU HAVE A caller."

Rachel glanced up from her papers and saw Cedric Gregor standing at the doorway. From the enigmatic look on his face, she suspected she wouldn't like his answer. Before she could ask who it was, he gave the answer.

"Sir Brian Lucas is here."

She closed her eyes and set down his pen. "Cedric, why? You know I am not interested in being courted."

"He is here because I asked him to come. You are aware that after Emma Bartholomew's hasty departure we still have expenses to pay."

"We will find another student." Their improved reputation after finding good marriages for Lady Ashleigh and Lady Scarsdale had resulted in many young ladies showing interest. She wasn't at all concerned about their finances.

Cedric paused and added, "Although I know how you love to help young wallflowers find husbands, we don't have enough students to make this into a true school, Rachel. We haven't the money or the ability to hire more teachers. And one spinster at a time is not enough to run a business."

"We've always had one student at a time, and it has worked for us," she argued. "That way, we can give her the attention she needs."

"But we've paid for gowns and dancing lessons with very little profit for ourselves. Servants are leaving, and our costs have risen. If Sir Brian could be a potential investor, we should listen to him."

The thought didn't appeal to her, but she could see his point. "I will see him, but it must be very clear that I do not intend to allow him to court me, regardless of whatever past he thinks we might have."

She had never answered his letters, though she had read them several times. The last thing she wanted was a man's interest. Rachel set her papers aside and steeled herself for a call she didn't want.

A few minutes later, Sir Brian entered the room. He was as she remembered from his last call—tall with dark brown hair and kindly brown eyes. Though he had a friendly demeanor, she hadn't forgotten the strength that he hid beneath his clothing. During their last meeting, he'd defended her from an irate marquess who had barged in, furious at his daughter's disappearance. Sir Brian had kept the man away from her, and she'd been grateful for his help.

She kept her expression neutral and remained seated at her desk, wanting the physical distance between them.

"Good morning, Mrs. Harding," he greeted her. "It's been several months since I've had the pleasure. Are you well?"

His last question was a subtle reminder that she hadn't answered any of his notes.

"Sir Brian," she greeted the baronet. "It's nice to see you again." She gestured for him to have a seat. "I am well, indeed, thank you for asking. What can I do for you today?"

He took a seat across from her. At this close distance, she noticed a pleasant aroma of shaving soap. He didn't look at all to be seven-and-thirty, as he'd told her during a previous visit.

"I spoke with Cedric Gregor not long ago about your school," he began.

"Yes, I believe he mentioned something like that. Were you wanting our help in finding a young lady to marry?" She swallowed her pride and added, "Or did you wish to become an investor?"

"I have come to enroll myself as a student," he said.

Rachel blinked at that, and for a long moment, she had no idea how to respond. He wanted to what?

"I'm sorry, but we are a school for young ladies, not gentlemen," she managed to say. "We could try to find candidates for marriage, if that's what you are looking for."

He ignored her remark and continued. "Mr. Gregor informed me that you only take one student at a time, and you give lessons on how to help a young lady find her confidence, as well as a marital match. I don't see how this would be any different for me."

Though his voice sounded pleasant enough, she was dumbfounded by the prospect. "But I don't see how we could possibly help you. You don't need lessons."

"I've never been married," he said. "Clearly, I *do* need lessons. Though I will leave it to your expertise to determine what they are."

She couldn't believe he was serious. "But during their schooling, my students live in the house," she protested. "That way they can attend all their lessons without interruption. You—you couldn't—"

"Mr. Gregor has apartments next door to your house, I believe. I could rent a room from him if he is amenable."

Everything within her turned to ice at the thought of him living so close by. She couldn't imagine creating lessons for a gentleman—much less one who was handsome and had made no secret of his interest in her. It was impossible.

"I am sorry, but I still do not think we could accommodate you."

In response, he slid a large bank note toward her. "Mr. Gregor has already agreed that since your previous student is now married, I could become your next prospect." He stood from his chair and reached for his hat.

With a light bow, he smiled. "I will see you next week to discuss this further."

WHEN EMMA AWAKENED in the cottage, she reached over for Cormac and found him gone. She sat up and picked up her discarded chemise from the floor, pulling it over her head. The morning sunlight streamed through the window, and she was about to go look for him, when the door suddenly opened.

"Good morning, *a stór*. I've brought you breakfast."

She heard him set down the tray and walked toward him. He caught her in his arms and kissed her, and she surrendered to the now-familiar touch of her husband. But she saw him carrying a brown paper parcel under his other arm.

"What is that you're carrying?"

"Part of your lessons, as I promised."

She had no idea what he meant by that. Her lessons at Mrs. Harding's School for Young Ladies were over. "But we're already married. I thought—"

"Lessons for the things you missed out on when you were a child," he added. "Painting, books, cards. Perhaps archery." The enthusiasm in his voice brought a pang to her heart. Although she knew he'd made these arrangements in an effort to please her, she couldn't deny that it felt like pity. No, she hadn't experienced any of these things. But there wasn't truly a reason for them now. Even if she did try painting, she wouldn't be able to see the results. She would never be able to read on her own. And as for archery . . .

"No one should let me near a bow and arrows," she warned.

"Not alone, no. But we could practice together. I've made

arrangements with the innkeeper who owns our cottage. I just need to know what you'd like to try first."

His enthusiasm was endearing, but she took his hand in hers. "Cormac, as I said before, I don't really need to experience those things. It's all right if we do the things *you* want to do."

He stroked her hair back and admitted, "This is the first time in almost a year that I've felt as good as I do now. And while I'd be glad enough to spend that time trying for our heir, I don't know when I'll feel this way again. I'd rather take advantage while I can."

At that, she gave a nod. "All right. But you choose."

The excitement in his voice reminded her of a young boy with a bowl of candy. "Archery contest it is."

She sensed that he had a competitive spirit, but there truly was no chance of her even striking the target without him helping her aim. "I think you're going to win."

"I might." He reached for her stays and handed them to her. "Do you want me to send a maid to help you dress?"

"You can help me," she said with a smile.

"I'd rather undress you, *a stór*, but I suppose if I'm wanting to teach you archery, I should be on better behavior."

"Perhaps later you'll get that chance," she said.

Half an hour later, Emma found herself outside where a straw target was set up a good distance away. She could only see the blurred straw and what might have been paint in the center. Beside her, Cormac held something that she assumed was a bow.

"Are you ready to learn archery?" he asked. There was an edge of eagerness to his voice, and although she knew she would fail miserably at it, she would never dream of ruining his enjoyment.

"I suppose," she answered. "I would ask you to demonstrate, except you could tell me that you hit the center, and I wouldn't know any differently."

"I'll be honest," he promised. "Here, take the bow."

She did, and the wood felt smooth and polished against her

fingertips. The bowstring was taut, and she experimented with pulling it back. "It's not as easy to draw the bowstring as I thought it would be."

"It takes a bit of strength," he agreed. "I'll help you." He helped her grasp the center of the wood in one hand, and he nocked an arrow to the bowstring, guiding her fingers into position. "Hold it like this."

As he helped her, his body was pressed close to hers. She could smell the scent of his skin, and his arms surrounded her as he guided her into position.

"Cormac, you're trying to distract me," she teased. "Which isn't really necessary when you know you're going to win this contest."

"But I can't be knowing that, *a stór*. If you set the arrow and aim it as you wish, once you let it loose, you could very well beat me."

"I would be fortunate to even hit the target," she said. But he helped her pull back the bowstring and aim the arrow.

"Can you hold the bowstring if I let go?"

"I think so." But the moment he released his hands, the arrow shot from her bowstring and hit the ground. Or at least that's where she thought it went.

"I suppose I underestimated my lack of strength."

He was about to give her another arrow, but she handed him the bow. "Your turn." She wanted him to enjoy the sport since the day was unseasonably warm for August. There wouldn't be many days left like this before autumn came. And somehow, she imagined that her husband would think of other ways to keep each other warm. She couldn't stop her smile at the thought.

"Put your arm on mine," he said. His voice was deep and seductive. "I'm still teaching you how to shoot."

She took a breath and put her arms around him, resting her left arm atop his as he held the bow. Then she touched his right wrist as he pulled it back. Beneath her fingertips, she could feel the lean muscles of his arm. It suddenly evoked the memory of him balanced on those arms while he made love to her.

She had started to grow acquainted with his body, and her new husband was insatiable each night. The memory brought a warmth to her body, kindling the familiar desire.

The problem was, she was finding it more and more difficult to keep her heart at a distance, though it was one of their rules. *Don't fall in love.*

So she pushed back the unwanted feelings, reminding herself of the boundaries. Cormac had brought her here because he enjoyed archery, and he'd wanted to share it with her, like any friend would.

She felt the power release in his forearm when he shot the arrow, and the soft thunk in the straw told her that he'd hit the target.

"Well done."

"You don't even know if I've hit the target," he said. But she could hear the smile in his voice.

"I'm confident you did. Or at least you hit something made of straw."

"I hit the target to the right of the center," he said. "Now it's your turn again."

He brought her another arrow and helped her pull back the bowstring. Now that she knew how much harder she would have to hold it, she prepared herself for when he let go. She kept her arms rigid, fighting against the tension of the bow and the arrow that trembled in her fingers. She couldn't see the target, but she trusted Cormac to help her aim. He seemed eager to give her these new experiences, and his faith in her was such a change from the others in the past who had ridiculed her or spoken cruel words about all the things she couldn't do.

"Are you ready?" he asked.

"Yes."

This time, when he let go, she held the arrow steady. Her arm tightened with effort, but she held steady.

"Release the arrow," he said.

When she did, the bowstring snapped against her forearm. "Ouch." Her skin was already swelling from where it had struck. She rubbed it lightly, and then he raised the spot to his lips, kissing it gently.

"All of us have been struck by the bowstring before, *a chroí.* Shall I tell you where your arrow landed?"

She lowered the bow and turned in his arms. "It doesn't matter." Even now, her sensitive skin longed for his touch.

"You hit the target," he told her.

"This is the only target I care about." And with that, she brought his mouth down to hers, kissing him. His arms came around her, and he pulled her body close. She opened to him, feeling the slide of his tongue against hers, and she surrendered to the dark pleasure.

They had their rules, true enough. But if she was not allowed to fall in love, at least she could enjoy the pleasure of being in his arms.

At least, for a little while longer.

Ireland

AN INVISIBLE HAND seemed to grip Emma's stomach as the carriage pulled to a stop in front of Dunmeath. She'd mistakenly believed it would be a manor house—but no. It seemed that Dunmeath was a castle off the coast of southwest Ireland. Dear God, he might as well have been a duke, given the size of the estate. Even so, she could see little more than vague shapes and colors. Very *large* shapes. Her stomach twisted up with fear of what lay ahead. The very thought of such a place filled her with terror.

You're going to fail, a silent voice warned. No matter what she tried, she was going to get hopelessly lost. The servants would lose all respect for her the moment they learned of her blindness.

And as for his family . . . her stomach lurched with more knots.

"Are you ready?" he asked in a low voice, taking her hand.

"Not in the slightest," Emma answered. "I'm terrified."

She would give anything if she could push the fear aside. She wanted to take his hand, walk inside as the new Countess of Dunmeath, and be a wife he could be proud of.

Even so, they both knew it was a role to play. She was pretending to be like any other lady, a bride filled with excitement to be at her new home, yet she couldn't even see the dwelling. She didn't know the voices of the servants or how many steps took her to each room.

Her heart was pounding as the footman opened the carriage door, and Cormac reached for her hand and gave it a squeeze. Part of her wished she could remain inside the vehicle while he greeted everyone, but she couldn't. She'd made a promise to be his wife and live in Ireland at his family home. That meant setting aside her fear and learning to live here.

Cormac escorted her from the carriage, and he murmured, "Twelve steps, I think." She counted along the way, and he was right.

A footman opened the door and greeted him with a warm voice. "Welcome home, my lord. It's so very good to see you again."

"And you, Stephens," he answered. To Emma, he said, "Stephens is one of our footmen, and behind him is Barton, my butler." Then he introduced her to the servants, saying, "Your new countess, Lady Dunmeath."

They murmured words of congratulations and welcome. Emma turned in the direction of the servants and said, "I'm glad to meet you."

She took a deep breath, trying to learn this space. There were familiar scents, of flowers, fresh air, and the faint traces of tea. Beneath her feet, she thought it might be a marble floor.

"Have our belongings arrived from England?" Cormac asked.

"They have, my lord. But only a few hours ago. We didn't

know when you'd be coming home, and we've not had time to unpack."

"We'll handle the matter later," he said. "For now, I want to introduce my wife to her new home."

Emma tried to brave a smile, but as she took Cormac's arm, she had to push back her nerves. She'd been so accustomed to remaining in the shadows, being overlooked. Now, she had to face the prospect of becoming a true countess. For some young ladies, it would be a dream fulfilled. For her, it was the beginning of a nightmare.

One step at a time, she told herself.

Before she could take her bearings, she heard footsteps hurrying toward them. Then a woman blurted out, "Cormac, why did you come back?" Her voice sounded as if she were aghast at what he'd done.

"Mother, allow me to introduce you to my wife." Cormac held her hand in his and said, "This is Emma. Emma, may I present my mother Josephine Ormond, the Dowager Countess of Dunmeath."

She extended out her hand to Cormac's mother, but instead of greeting her, the woman seemed to take a step backward.

"No. I sent you away to get well. You weren't supposed to come back. It's not safe."

The woman's words held a dire warning—and Emma recalled Cormac saying that Lady Dunmeath believed he was being poisoned. And although it was a morbid thought, she rather hoped it was true—because then there was a chance it could be stopped and he could be well again.

She sensed that his illness was not what he thought it was, but she had no proof one way or the other. She'd had a few blissful weeks of traveling with him. He'd not been ill once, and seeing him grow strong, eating well, and using up his energy at night loving her had been a welcome respite of healing—for both of them.

"You know I had to return," he said to his mother. "I have

responsibilities here."

"It's too soon."

Emma was starting to feel as if she ought to say something, so she greeted the dowager, extending her hand again. "I'm very glad to meet you, Lady Dunmeath."

Josephine ignored the greeting and Emma faltered, uncertain of what to do next. Instead, she lowered her hand and fell silent. But she caught the faint scent of verbena from the older woman as she took another step away.

"Well, it seems you've gone and disrupted all our plans by getting married, Cormac." The dowager sighed. "Why would you do such a thing?"

Emma could feel the tension tightening within her husband, and he spoke to his mother with coolness. "We both know I need an heir."

"We could have made other arrangements," she said. It made Emma wonder if Cormac had been betrothed to someone else. Had he left Ireland for another reason?

"It's sorry I am if I've inconvenienced you by returning," he said. "I suppose you were hoping I would die instead?"

Emma heard Josephine's sharp intake of breath. "Don't be saying such things, Cormac. It's bad luck."

Emma itched to say something, but she worried that anything she said would only make this first meeting even worse. Better to hold her silence until later.

"We've been traveling for a long while," Cormac said. "I think it's best if I take Emma to our room to rest. We'll see you at supper time."

He escorted her away from his family, and Emma added, "It was nice meeting you."

Her husband's hand tightened upon her waist, and she knew he wanted nothing more than to escape. She wanted to say something to him, but he was walking too quickly.

"Seventeen steps and maybe thirty stairs," he muttered beneath his breath. She was grateful that he continued estimating the distance for her sake. And when they reached the foot of the staircase, he guided her hand to the banister and walked beside her while she counted the remaining steps.

"Thirty-two," she corrected. "A good guess."

He didn't answer, and she took his arm as he escorted her down another hallway. Beneath her hand, she could feel his tension and the unspoken anger. "Are you all right, Cormac?"

He took a deep breath. "I never imagined she wouldn't want to see me. It wasn't at all what I expected."

"She sounded overprotective," Emma responded. Beneath the woman's words, there had been a strong note of worry. And she suspected that he'd neglected to tell his mother he'd been searching for a wife. "I suppose you never wrote to her to tell her about our marriage."

"No, I didn't." There was a heaviness to his voice, and she couldn't tell if he'd avoided the news on purpose. "I'm sorry she didn't welcome you the way she should have."

"I imagine our arrival was a surprise," Emma answered. But she couldn't deny her discomfort that Lady Dunmeath wouldn't even speak to her. She'd always been uneasy about coming to Ireland, but now there was not only the challenge of behaving like a countess but also gaining his mother's approval.

Every fear she'd pushed back during these weeks seemed to return. She still didn't know what her responsibilities would be. Nor did she know anyone here, save Cormac. Part of her wanted to simply ignore this new life and isolate herself. It was clear that no one had been expecting him to marry. And the thought of being countess of such a vast household overwhelmed her.

But a voice inside her warned that it wasn't right to give up without a single attempt. She could do *some* things, even if it wasn't everything. She had to try, and she believed that Cormac would help her if she asked. Already they were friends, so he would want her to succeed. And if she somehow managed to be the wife he needed her to be, perhaps their marriage might shift into something more. Which was a secret hope she didn't dare to voice or even fully imagine.

Cormac had made her promise not to fall in love. And yet, with every day at his side, she found another reason to smile or laugh. He'd given her so much—not only saving her father, but perhaps even saving *her* from the life she'd known.

If he died . . .

Emma closed her eyes, pushing back the thought. No. She couldn't think of that right now or else she might start crying.

Instead, she would focus on the task at hand and ask him for assistance. "Now that I'm here, I'm going to need your help," she confessed. "As your countess, I want to manage the household. If you could—"

"No," he cut her off gently. "That's not what I want. I wouldn't ask that of you."

His words caught her like an invisible blow she hadn't been expecting. Although he probably thought he was easing her burden, instead it suggested that he didn't think she was capable. It was the first time he'd refused to help her—and she hid the hurt it caused.

Confusion caught up within her while she walked alongside him to their room, and she ventured again. "Cormac, I really do want to try." She needed to learn what was expected of her and the sooner, the better.

"It's not necessary," was his answer.

She didn't understand why he would try to keep her from learning how to be his countess. It wasn't like him at all. Cormac had always been supportive of teaching her. Whether it was dancing or archery, he'd never treated her as if she were helpless. But now that she was at his home, she wondered if all that was about to change. Already she could see him behaving like a different man, and the thought troubled her.

After twelve more steps, he opened the door to their bed-chamber. The drapes were drawn, and sunlight filled the room with bright patches and shadows. The hearth was cold, but there was a coal hod nearby. The air smelled faintly stale, as if no one had opened the room in many months.

"Do you wish we hadn't returned?" she asked. "Should we have stayed in London a little longer?"

"I would have preferred staying by the sea," he admitted. "I enjoyed our holiday there together."

She had to agree. During the past week, her new husband had drawn her into the center of his life. He'd made love to her at night as if he couldn't get enough. He'd worshipped her body, giving her such fierce pleasure until she no longer knew where his body left off and hers began.

But a darker fear made her wonder if that had become her only role now. To share his bed and give him an heir—nothing more.

"I've duties to attend at Dunmeath that I've neglected," he continued. "I won't be able to spend as much time with you as I'd like."

"I understand." But she could tell that he was shouldering the burden alone. He likely didn't have time to read ledgers to her or explain how to run the estate. Whether he knew it or not, she could feel the distance widening between them.

After a pause, he added, "I'll arrange for you to meet the staff later when you've had the chance to rest."

She wasn't at all tired but recognized that he was trying to avoid facing his family. Or perhaps he wanted to give her an escape. For a moment, she hesitated—but then, he pulled her into his arms and embraced her tightly, offering silent comfort. And something within her wanted to prove to him that she was more capable than he knew.

"What do you think of Dunmeath?" he asked.

"Your home is much larger than I imagined," she admitted. Though she kept her tone bright, inwardly, she knew it would take days—possibly weeks—to learn where everything was. It might be better to explore later at night after most of the household was asleep. Then, at least, she could practice with no fear of anyone learning about her blindness.

"You'll get used to it." Cormac smoothed her hair back and leaned down to brush a soft kiss against her lips. She savored the affection, but there was another challenge that lay ahead, besides that of learning her way around. She needed to navigate her relationship with his mother and learn how to make an ally of the dowager.

She broached the subject by remarking, "I didn't expect your mother to be so disappointed in our marriage. When she mentioned that you had ruined their plans, it almost sounded as if . . ." She took a moment to choose her words carefully and a wild thought occurred to her. "Cormac, before you left for England, were you betrothed to someone else?"

He pulled her into his arms. "Let's not talk of anything else now except how I'm going to lay you down on that bed."

But she put her hand between them, not allowing him to distract her. "You haven't answered my question."

It wouldn't surprise her if his mother had meant to play matchmaker. Though she'd sent him away to England, surely Josephine would want her son to marry a local heiress.

Cormac pressed her body close to his. "In the past, my mother did introduce me to several young ladies, hoping I would wed one of them. But they knew of my family's curse, and they didn't want to wed me. It didn't matter."

"Did you want to wed any of them?"

He reached back to unbutton her gown. "There's no need to worry about the past, *a stór*. I am wedded to you now, and that's all that matters."

Was there something his mother had planned, a future that they'd somehow disrupted? It might be yet another reason why Josephine was so furious with him—for marrying without inviting or consulting his family.

As he laid her back against the bed, uneasiness tightened within her. And despite their agreement, she was starting to question what sort of marriage this would be. Worse, she'd learned only today that there was no child. She'd begun spotting this morning, and a bleak sadness washed over her. Still, she understood the truth of her situation. Unless she learned how to cast aside her fear and become a countess, this might be all she had.

And she simply could not return to the shadows and become a wallflower once more.

Chapter Nine

I T WAS LATE at night when Cormac reached over and found Emma gone from the bed. She'd been quiet ever since they'd arrived in Ireland, and he'd sensed her discomfort at being the new Countess of Dunmeath. Even during their lovemaking earlier, she'd seemed less responsive, as if her mind were caught up in the confusion of being here.

He lit a candle and put on a dressing gown before he slowly walked downstairs. The household was quiet, but he listened intently. He stopped in each room on the first floor to look for Emma. But she was nowhere to be found.

He continued all the way down the main hallway, but there was no light, save his candle. As he passed a grandfather clock, it chimed three o'clock. He continued down the hall and around the corner, and then at last he saw her walking toward another staircase. She held no candle and made no sound at all, but he could tell she was counting steps.

He was careful to be quiet as he approached, and when he drew near, she froze. "It's only me."

"I'm sorry," she whispered. "I didn't mean to disturb you. It's so late."

Cormac took her hand in his. "You couldn't sleep?"

In the faint light of the candle, he saw the worry in her eyes.

"No. There's too much for me to learn."

Although he understood her desire to know her way around the house, he didn't want her wandering the halls in the middle of the night simply to hide her vision difficulties from the servants. She could explore the house as much as she liked, all day long if she wanted.

Cormac put his arm around her and guided her down the dark hallway. "Come back to bed with me," he suggested. When she hesitated, he offered, "Or if you're wanting me to, I could read you a story. We could go into the library."

The candlelight illuminated her face. "You don't have to do that. You can go back to bed, and I'll join you soon enough."

Cormac wasn't about to be deterred. "But this way, I can be alone with you sitting on my lap."

"Somehow, I don't think you want to read to me at all," she murmured.

He ignored her speculation and said, "We'll go into the library, and you can count our steps on the way there. I'll see if I can find a book on farming or fertilizer to put you to sleep, *a stór.*"

She put her arm around his waist, and they walked together down the hallway, counting in whispers. When he brought her into the library, he set the candle down on the desk and saw the stack of books that he'd packed from the townhouse in England. The footmen must have begun unpacking and sorting through their belongings.

His grandfather's familiar diary called to him like an old friend, and he touched the broken cover before flipping through some of the pages. Their stories were memories he wished he could have been a part of. And now, it was all he had left of them.

"What book is that?" Emma asked.

"It was my grandfather's diary. It's falling apart, it's so old." He held up the green cover, and it seemed that flecks of paint were falling off it. "My father continued his own notes in the diary. It makes me feel close to them whenever I read it."

He flipped through a few pages before he set it aside. Then he lit a lamp with the candle and walked over to the bookshelf. "Now let me see what I can find to help you sleep."

He studied the titles in the dim light while Emma took a seat on the settee. In her nightgown, she looked beautiful. And yet, he could see the exhaustion in her eyes. He pulled a book off the shelf and came to sit beside her. Then he lifted her legs across his lap and put his arms around her.

"What book did you choose?"

"I've no idea." He glanced at the title and opened the book. "I believe it's about law. Something about the brehons."

"That sounds as dull as dust," she remarked. But she snuggled in and rested her head against his heartbeat.

He started reading to her, not understanding half of what he was reading. But Emma slid her hands beneath his dressing gown and began caressing his chest. Her fingertips were soft, and he went rigid at her touch.

"You're distracting me from our book," he accused.

"I am, aren't I?" She straddled him with her knees on either side of his lap. "But I suppose I have your full attention now."

"You do, *a chroí.*" He fumbled with his clothing, but she stopped him.

"Not yet. We need to talk."

"I am listening." But when she reached down to take him into her hand, his thoughts scattered apart.

"Go on." Her warm hand stroked him, and he let out a shuddering gasp. "Whatever you're wanting, Emma, you've only to ask."

"I need your help here at Dunmeath," she said. "I can't do this alone."

"Do what?" He was so caught up in her touch, he couldn't grasp what it was she wanted. At the moment, he would give her anything she desired.

"I want to be your countess." Before he could say a word, she lowered herself onto his shaft, taking him in deep. The sudden warmth of her body stunned him, and he bit back a gasp. Emma rocked against him and continued, "But that's not what you want from me, is it?"

There was an edge to her voice, a warning that he didn't understand. "You don't have to be anything except my wife," he murmured, as she began to move. Cormac palmed her hips, groaning as she squeezed him within her depths. "It's enough."

She rose slowly, and he began to push aside her dressing gown, needing to touch her. He wanted her to be happy at Dunmeath, unbothered by any sort of duties.

"I want to be more," she insisted. "I'm tired of always standing in the shadows, always being a wallflower. I want to be better than I was in the past."

"You can do as you please," he said. "Do everything or do nothing." He didn't understand what she was talking about. The freedom was hers, and he'd thought that having no responsibilities would make it easier on her.

She was tormenting him with the slow strokes, and finally, Cormac could bear it no longer. He gripped her bottom, standing up from the settee and walking toward the wall.

"What are you doing?" she asked.

"Making you into my own wallflower," he answered. And with that, he released all his control, taking her hard. He invaded and withdrew, tasting her breast through the linen of her nightgown. She cried out, gripping his hair as she wrapped her legs around his waist.

He surrendered to the storm of need and emotion swirling through him. Every moment had to count, every fragile minute fading. This marriage was his last and only chance to have a child, and he poured himself into loving her. Emma arched her back as he penetrated hard, and when she found her release, he reveled in her body quaking around him. He thrust a few more times before his own body surrendered, and he filled her with his seed.

For a moment, he rested, still holding her against the wall. And then, when he withdrew, he saw the traces of her blood on him.

Disappointment weighed upon him when he cleaned himself. Now, he was starting to understand the other reason for her despondency—and he felt the same way. "There's no child this month, is there?"

"Not yet," she admitted.

And though he'd known it would take time for her to conceive, he couldn't deny the feeling of sadness. "We'll keep trying."

But although she nodded, the shadow of failure seemed to slide between them.

THE MORNING SUNLIGHT speared her eyes, and Emma sat up from their bed. Cormac was still sleeping, but she thought his face might be flushed again. She decided it was better if she gave him more time to sleep.

After she took a moment to gather her courage, it was time to face the duties she dreaded. Emma donned her dressing gown and went through the doorway to the adjoining bedchamber. After she closed the door behind her, she rang for a maid to help her dress. She still felt tired, but it was time to face the household.

When the maid arrived, Emma learned that her name was Darcy. Though Darcy seemed to be quite young, she insisted, "It's glad I am to be your lady's maid. I've been working nigh on two years at Dunmeath, and I'd much rather be here than a scullery maid."

She helped Emma choose a day dress and remarked on the fabric. "Ooh, this is lovely, it is. The violet color will look well with your hair. And I know just the way to fix it for you." Darcy helped Emma with her dress and then picked up a hairbrush. "We were all so surprised to learn of your marriage. Her ladyship, especially."

"Lady Dunmeath didn't seem very happy about it," Emma admitted. She hoped Darcy would tell her more, and asked, "Had she chosen another bride for him?"

"Nay. His lordship has a curse upon him." The maid paused, and from her motion, it appeared that she crossed herself. "Has he told you?"

"I know a little," Emma answered. "But I should like to know more."

"A terrible curse it is," Darcy insisted. "One that ends in death. And some of the ladies around here were afraid they would die too if they married him, along with any babes they might conceive." She paused a moment and asked, "Am I talking too much? Da says I do."

"No, I want to know more about my husband," Emma insisted. "Was he ever betrothed?"

"Lady Dunmeath was hoping that his lordship would be cured in London and would come back to wed Lady Eileen," Darcy answered. "It would've been a good match."

"But he wasn't cured," Emma admitted. "We still don't know what's causing his illness."

"Oh, it's the curse, to be sure. But no one knows how to break it. It could be that the faeries cursed his grandfather to lose all his sons and grandsons." Darcy's voice grew darker. "Every firstborn son has died. And it may be that you should wear an iron bracelet to protect you from the faeries. I'll ask Cook to find you something."

Though it was only superstition, Emma gave a nod, realizing that the maid truly believed this. "And you don't think it's an illness . . . or worse?" She didn't want to mention the possibility of poison for fear of offending her.

Darcy continued brushing Emma's hair and divided it into sections to braid. "Nay. But we all pray that the curse will be broken one day." She moved the brush to her other hand and crossed herself again. "Lord Dunmeath is good to all of us. None wish him ill, and he takes care of everyone."

"What about his cousin?" Emma ventured. "If something were to happen to the earl, he stands to inherit, does he not?"

Darcy laughed. "Lorcan could never manage Dunmeath, and well he knows it. Afraid of his own shadow, he is, along with the curse. And he does everything his wife wants."

Though Darcy's description didn't make it sound as if Lorcan was a threat to Cormac, Emma couldn't rule it out just yet. Nor even his wife. At the moment, she had to consider every threat.

Darcy finished with her hair and said, "There. You look beautiful, Lady Dunmeath."

Though Emma couldn't see her appearance, when she reached up to her hair, it seemed that the maid had pinned it up in a braided arrangement. She thanked Darcy and said, "I think I'll go down for breakfast. Would you like to walk with me?" It was entirely a means of having a guide to the dining room, but she added, "I'd like to know more about you."

Darcy seemed to brighten, and she readily agreed. "I'd be glad to tell you, my lady. I've six brothers and four sisters. The youngest was born last year..." She continued chattering on, making it easy for Emma to follow her down the hallway to the stairs.

Just as they reached the dining room, she could smell the delicious scent of eggs and sausage. But mingled in with the scent was the faint aroma of verbena.

Cormac's mother was already there. Emma forced a smile on her face. "Good morning, Lady Dunmeath. May I join you?"

The dowager made a noncommittal sound, and the footman pulled out a chair for her before he brought Emma eggs, blood pudding, roasted tomatoes, and sausage. She helped herself, grateful that she managed to select food she couldn't see without spilling it all over the floor. Then she asked the footman, "Could you have breakfast sent upstairs to Lord Dunmeath a little later?" She was about to mention that he was still asleep but then thought better of it.

"Cormac can ring for food himself when he's wanting it," the dowager remarked. Her tone made it clear that she didn't approve of Emma's suggestion.

A moment later, footsteps approached, and another woman entered the dining room. Her perfume smelled of lilacs, and she greeted Emma warmly. "Good morning. You must be Cormac's new wife. I am Nuala Ó Falvey, Josephine's sister."

"It's good to meet you, Mrs. Ó Falvey," she answered. "Do you live nearby?"

"Oh, you may call me Nuala, or Aunt Nuala," she offered. "And I live here. Or, at least, I have since my husband died years ago."

It made Emma wonder if the woman's husband had also been a victim of the same illness or whether it was an unrelated ailment.

"You'll have to come and see my gardens after breakfast," Nuala continued. "It's late in the season, but I do have some flowers still blooming. Chrysanthemums and some late roses. I like to bring them into the house for some color."

"I would enjoy that."

Josephine only sniffed with disapproval. Emma tried to eat, but despite Nuala's attempts at cheerful conversation, she could feel her mother-in-law's invisible anger.

"Would you like to come with us to the gardens, Lady Dunmeath?" Emma asked the dowager.

"I have enough to do," she answered. "As you will soon learn when you begin to take up your duties."

There was no denying the slight prickle in the dowager's voice. Emma tried again. "Perhaps later you can show me. I would like that very much."

"I imagine you would." The woman's tone suggested she believed Emma was nothing more than a fortune hunter.

Her cheeks burned, and she tried again. "I would also like to become better acquainted with you, Lady Dunmeath."

The dowager said nothing, which only heightened the awkwardness between them. Emma was torn between disappointment and embarrassment.

"Oh, do give the girl a chance to settle in, Josephine," Nuala chided. To Emma, she added, "Don't be minding my sister. Always in a bad mood, is Josie," Nuala chided.

"If you'd lost your husband and oldest son, you'd be in a mood, too," Josephine said. "Now, if you'll excuse me, I have duties to attend."

After she'd gone, Nuala said softly, "But I *did* lose my husband, too." Her voice held a note of sadness that made Emma sympathize.

"Was it the same illness as Lord Dunmeath?"

"I don't know what it was," she answered. "His heart, I suppose. One morning, I thought he was asleep. But by nightfall, he was simply gone."

"I'm sorry." Emma picked at the food on her plate, but Nuala reached out to pat her hand.

"It was two years ago. And though I miss him every day, at least I had twenty good years with Orlan."

The warmth in her voice made it sound like a love match. "I'm glad."

Emma reached for her teacup and realized no one had filled it. She set it down, but Nuala said, "Oh, let me pour you a cup of tea. It's my own special blend. Chamomile, mint, and a bit of this and that."

She tasted the tea and found it pleasant. "Thank you." For a little while, they both sat and ate, and eventually Emma asked, "Did I do something to offend Lady Dunmeath? She seems so angry with me."

"You married her son," Nuala answered.

But Emma sensed it was more than that. There was resentment there, true, but it seemed as if Lady Dunmeath considered her to be a threat to her son. Perhaps they could talk alone later, and she could ease the dowager's suspicions.

They finished eating, and Nuala led her along the hallway to another doorway that opened up into the gardens. Outside, the sunlight gleamed, and the matron guided her to a gravel pathway. "I usually come into my garden every morning after breakfast,"

Nuala said. "You are always welcome to join me."

Emma thanked her, and she shielded her eyes against the sun as she followed. The hedges were cut into what appeared to be a maze, and the woman took her deeper into the garden where there were splashes of color from the roses.

"Josephine gave me this plot of land for my garden," Nuala explained. "It gives me a way of occupying my time."

"It's lovely," Emma said, admiring the neat rows of green and the deep fragrance of roses. She walked around the garden, keeping on the pathway to guide her. "What are your favorite plants to grow?"

"Oh, everything," the matron answered. "Sometimes I grow herbs for my tea. Cook often uses basil or mint from the garden." She reached out and used a pair of gardening shears to cut a rose. "Here. It's a welcome gift for you."

"Thank you. I can't say as I've felt very welcome until now," Emma admitted as she took the deep red rose. No, the dowager didn't want her here. But more than that, she didn't know how to begin making a place for herself—especially when Cormac seemed unwilling to help.

"You're the countess now," Nuala said quietly. "Josie has no choice but to accept you."

But that wasn't true at all—especially if the dowager learned that Emma couldn't read. It would only make matters worse.

Emma breathed in the scent of the rose and asked, "Is there anything I can do to gain her approval?"

"It's unlikely," Nuala said. "My sister has always been diffi-cult. And even more so after Cormac became sick. She doesn't want to lose another son." Her voice softened, and she took a deep breath. "I'm sorry. I hope, for your sake—" Her words broke off when footsteps approached on the gravel path.

"There you are, Emma." Cormac leaned in and rested his hand on her spine in a silent greeting. Then he added, "Good morning, Aunt Nuala."

"Good morning," she answered in a cheerful voice. "It's very glad we are to have you home, Cormac. How are you feeling?"

"I am well, thank you." But Emma detected a note of caution in his words, as if it weren't entirely true. "I've been wanting to speak with Cousin Lorcan," he said. "Have you seen him?"

"Oh, my son is out and about somewhere," Nuala answered. "He may be riding at the moment. If you go toward his house, you might see him."

"Thank you," Cormac answered before he turned back to Emma. "I'd like to show you the grounds of Dunmeath. Will you join me?"

"Of course." She bid farewell to Nuala and followed him down the pathway. To her surprise, she found horses waiting for them.

"Have you ever been riding before?" he asked.

"Not since I was a little girl." The idea was both thrilling and frightening. Cormac brought her close to the animal and let her rest her hand upon the mare's face. The horse sniffed at her, and when she scratched her ears, the mare leaned in closer.

"She likes that a lot, does Flora," he said. "Now that you're acquainted, I'll help you up." He helped her find the stirrup and then lifted her on sidesaddle. Emma felt awkward about the position, but she rested her hands upon the mare and found her balance. She was sensitive to the movement, but Cormac kept the horses at a gentle walk.

Only after they were a short distance away did she ask, "How are you truly feeling?"

He was silent for a little while, then admitted, "It's coming back. This morning, the sickness was like a blade in my stomach."

"I'm sorry." But an apology would do nothing to help. "Did you eat anything?"

"Not yet."

Emma tried to remember what they'd eaten last night, but it had only been light fare, a supper tray sent to their room. They had shared the food, and she felt well enough.

Cormac took the reins of her horse and continued their path

toward the edge of Dunmeath. The color green stretched out over the land as far as she could see, while blurry gray stone walls divided the plots for farming.

For a long time, they rode alongside one another. He brought her farther and then stopped the horses. "I hate being ill. I was enjoying our time by the sea. But I should have expected that it would come back."

She reached out for his hand and took it. His skin felt cool, but when she reached out to touch his forehead, it seemed clammy. "We should return to the house, Cormac."

Though she kept her voice calm, inwardly, she was frightened that his time was running out.

"Aye," he answered. But when he gazed off into the distance, he said, "I'm sorry I brought you to Ireland, Emma. It wasn't fair to you."

"What do you mean?"

"I took you away from your home and family for my own selfish reasons. And if you do conceive an heir and I die, I'll be leaving you behind for my mother to torment." His face twisted with frustration.

"I know she doesn't like me," Emma agreed. "But we both want you to be well. Surely, we can find common ground somehow."

He released her hand. "Promise me something, Emma."

"What is it?" She didn't like the grim tone of his voice.

"I don't want you to stay and watch me die," he said quietly. "I never wanted that." His voice sounded as if he were in pain. "If the worst happens, I want you to go back to England—even if somehow there's a child. It's not right that I asked you to stay here."

She'd never heard such bleakness in Cormac's tone, and it bothered her deeply. And whether the cause was the pain of his illness or the fact that she was not yet with child, she couldn't simply stand aside and let him give up. He needed her to fight for him, even if he didn't know it. She had no intention of leaving him to die in such pain.

A pang caught her heart, and she straightened. "We've only been here one day, and I am going nowhere, Cormac." When he didn't speak, she continued. "You bought my hand in marriage in the auction, and I won't let you give it back."

He leaned in to kiss her, and she met his lips softly, savoring his touch. With a heavy sigh, he cupped the back of her nape. "You are a stubborn wife, *a chroí*."

"I am. We're going to see new doctors and find the reason for your illness."

And even if he didn't believe she could ever be his countess, she would find a way. Even if it took months of counting steps in the hallways in the middle of the night, or if she had to hire someone to read to her—somehow, she would make a place for herself here, for his sake.

Cormac had gone silent, which sent a dark wave of foreboding over her. They started riding back to the castle, but he struggled to keep his seat on the horse. She was careful to stay beside him, more afraid with every moment that he might fall off.

When at last they were nearly there, Cormac said quietly, "Emma, I'm going to need help getting to my room. I'm feeling even worse."

"I'll get a footman to help," she said.

When they reached the gravel near the entrance, Emma stopped their horses and awkwardly dismounted first, not waiting for anyone to help her. She hurried to his side, but after he swung his leg over, he seemed unsteady.

"Cormac!" Emma called out, struggling to catch him when his knees buckled. "Help!"

But as he lost consciousness, she held him in her arms with the very real fear of losing him.

London

"THIS IS A terrible idea," Rachel warned Cedric. "I cannot take a male student in our school—especially not Sir Brian."

"We have expenses and bills to pay," he reminded her. "Taking him as a student will easily cover those. And since he is our only student, why does it matter?"

It mattered because she didn't want to spend time alone with a man who had previously expressed interest in her. She'd already escaped a terrible marriage and had a thousand invisible scars to prove it. Nothing he could say or do would heal those wounds, and she'd already given up any thoughts of ever marrying again.

"I might assign *you* to give him lessons," she began.

Cedric ignored her and said, "I've already given him a room. He's unpacking now, and I've asked him to come over for tea as soon as he's finished. Treat him as you would any other student. Find out why he's unmarried."

I don't want to, she thought. And yet, they did have more expenses they needed to cover. Emma Bartholomew's father had been unable to pay the rest of her fees, and the school's bill had apparently not been among those given to Lord Dunmeath as he settled the man's debts. And the gowns they'd given Emma had been costly.

She didn't harbor regret for it. Seeing Emma married to Lord Dunmeath had made it worthwhile. Although she would probably ask the earl to pay for the remainder and the gowns in due course, it would still take time for her letter to arrive. And Cedric had a point—they needed money now.

"Very well," she said. "I will meet with Sir Brian in the drawing room for tea." And in the meantime, she would begin creating his first lessons.

Rachel spent the next half hour making lists that made little sense to her. She needed to ask questions, to steel herself against the insecurities that rose up like a vicious wave. He was no different than any other student. It was best to remember that and to treat him the same as the young ladies she met with.

One of the footmen alerted her that Sir Brian was waiting, so she picked up her lists and tried to assume an air of calm. She walked into the drawing room, and the moment she did, the clean scent of his shaving soap allured her.

Do not be weak, she warned herself. *He is like everyone else.*

He stood and greeted her, "Good afternoon, Mrs. Harding." Then he inclined his head and gestured for her to take a seat across from him where tea and refreshments were waiting.

"Good afternoon." She took her place and studied him. His brown hair was slightly overlong, in need of a trim. But those blue eyes stared into hers as if he had missed her desperately. And the unexpected stare rattled her senses.

"Would you care for tea?" she asked.

"Yes, please."

Before she could take the teapot, Sir Brian poured a cup for her. "Oh, you didn't need to do that," Rachel said. "Normally, the mistress of the household will pour the tea."

"I thought I'd make myself useful," he remarked. He held up the tongs and asked, "Milk or sugar?"

She nodded and reached for the creamer while he broke off a piece of sugar with the tongs and set it in her tea. She stirred it, trying not to be so conscious of his nearness. It was unnerving to be so close to Sir Brian again, especially since he continued to make no secret of his interest in her.

Despite her efforts to keep a distance between them, his kindness utterly disarmed her.

Rachel sipped the tea to help gather her thoughts and said, "I've begun making a list for your lessons. Before we begin, I usually assign my students a small task. I do not accept every student, and if you cannot complete this task, we will, of course, return your tuition."

His eyes seemed to sparkle with interest. "What sort of task?"

She struggled to think and stalled a moment. "Before I tell you that, I would like to know how many balls you've attended this past Season."

He shrugged. "I don't remember. Many, I suppose."

"And how many young ladies did you ask to dance?

"I don't recall." But from his amused tone, she suspected he knew exactly how many. Sir Brian struck her as an observant sort, one who was probably shy as a younger man and now had set aside any concerns about what society might think of him. He didn't have a fortune, and his title of baronet was so small, the more superficial debutantes might overlook him.

Still, some of the wallflowers or shyer ladies might do well enough.

"I have the notes I took during our last meeting a few months ago when you told me your requirements for a wife." She unfolded the paper and read aloud, "You said you wanted someone mature. You do not mind if she has children. And you'd prefer someone who knows her own mind."

He inclined his head. "Those are still my wishes, yes."

"And what if she is a younger lady who is still mature for her years? Would you consider her?"

"I might." But in his tone, there was a sudden intensity. And when she glanced up from the paper, she saw those blue eyes staring into hers. A slow smile spread over his face, but she couldn't answer it.

He was plotting something, and she suspected it had everything to do with her. But she had no intention of being matched up herself.

Rachel straightened and set down her papers. "Your task, Sir Brian, is to attend a ball and dance with six unmarried ladies of all ages." That in itself would be a challenge since the Season was over. But it was a means of buying time and perhaps dissuading him. "You will return with the names of these women and tell me which ones interest you. We will meet again after you have completed this task."

His eyes gleamed with amusement. "So, we'll meet again in September, is that it?"

"After you attend your next ball," she corrected.

"You mean Lady Scarsdale's birthday ball, don't you? I understand we are both attending."

"And how do you know that?" Her words were sharp, and she made no effort to hide her annoyance.

"Mr. Gregor told me of your plans," he answered. "He suggested we could go together and share a carriage."

Of course, Cedric would join in on the plotting. She tightened her mouth and stated, "I don't see a reason to share a vehicle. I'm certain you have your own."

"Are you afraid of me?" he asked softly.

"No," she lied. But inwardly, she couldn't deny that his presence made her uneasy, his kind demeanor notwithstanding. If he did become a student, the idea of seeing Sir Brian every day felt like a blatant interference with her privacy.

He seemed to read her expression and asked, "Will it be a problem if I attend the birthday ball, Mrs. Harding?"

Rachel wanted to say yes, but she shook her head. "Of course not." She could not let the baronet get under her skin or interfere in any way with her business. And perhaps the unwanted, nervous feelings of attraction would disappear once she began treating him like any other student.

They simply had to.

Chapter Ten

Ireland

"DRINK THIS." EMMA guided Cormac's hands to hold a mug that contained broth. "See if it eases your pain."

Ever since they'd managed to get him back to his bedchamber, she'd been forced to face a truth she didn't want to acknowledge. His sickness was real, and even now, she hated how helpless she was.

"Thank you," he said.

She waited until he'd finished and then took the mug. "Do you want something else? Bread, perhaps?"

"A little later."

But the weariness in his voice suggested it wouldn't happen. She'd asked a footman to summon a physician, and while she waited, the dowager entered the room.

"I want to speak with you, Emma." Josephine's voice held a rigid anger. "Alone."

She tried not to jolt at the acerbic tone. Before she could answer, her husband intervened. "Hello, Mother. Would you care to sit down and join us? I would stand, except that I'm not feeling as well as I might." His voice held a trace of irony, and she sensed that he meant to defend her.

"I told you this would happen if you returned, Cormac." Her voice was crisp, filled with an air of no nonsense. "And now I wish to speak with your wife."

Emma reached for his hand, uncertain of what the matron wanted, other than to berate her. She wasn't so certain she wanted to go with Josephine. "What would you like to talk about?" she asked, not looking at the woman.

"Your marriage and your future here."

Well, that wasn't exactly the sort of conversation she wanted to have at this moment. Especially since Cormac had endured several days of sickness. She wanted to remain at his side to ensure that he was feeling better.

"Perhaps in the morning," she hedged. "I don't want to leave my husband."

But the dowager would not be dissuaded. "It won't take very long."

Although Emma thought of refusing, she sensed that it might make matters worse. She had to face Josephine sooner or later.

"Don't let her bark frighten you," Cormac said, squeezing her hand. "She's more worried than angry."

"Mind your tongue, lad. I can bark if I wish." The dowager's tone remained sharp, and Emma held his hand a moment longer before she released it.

She already knew Josephine didn't like her, and the dowager probably thought she was only after Cormac's fortune. Perhaps this might be an opportunity to be frank and possibly make an ally. They both had the same goal, she felt certain.

"Where would you like to converse?" she asked calmly.

"Downstairs in the library. That way, we won't be interrupted."

Emma rose from the bed and walked toward the door. It was only eight steps, so she counted as she made her way toward the earlier sound of the dowager's voice. She'd nearly made it across the room when her foot caught on an armchair that had apparently been moved since yesterday. Just as she was about to lose her balance, Emma seized the arm and caught herself.

"Sorry," she apologized.

Not that she *was* apologetic about being unable to see, but she was rewarded when the dowager called out, "Walk with me."

Now that she had Josephine's location, she crossed through the doorway. "I'll return shortly," she said in Cormac's direction. "Try to rest."

"I'll be waiting right here," he assured her with a teasing lilt to his voice. But beneath his humor, she didn't miss the tinge of pain.

Emma turned to follow the blur of the dowager's black dress. Josephine's silence suggested that she fully intended to wait until they were completely alone before they had their discussion.

She counted the stairs, and from their direction, she could tell the dowager was indeed leading her to the library. She was glad it was one of the rooms she knew. Once they reached the doorway, Emma entered and the dowager ordered her, "Sit down, girl."

She bristled at the woman's words but decided that now was not the time to antagonize her mother-in-law. Instead, she felt around discreetly for the chair and then sat down. It reminded her of the many times her teachers had scolded her after her lessons, telling her how stupid she was.

Josephine took the seat opposite Emma. "Now that you've seen my son's illness, I suppose you're hoping to become a widow soon."

Though the matron's words were quiet, Emma was aghast. She sat up in her chair and turned toward the older woman. "Why would you say something so terrible?"

"There are several who are wanting to see him dead," she responded. "Perhaps even you." Her voice was thin, filled with accusation.

"No," she shot back. "Never me." The woman's words infuriated her, shattering any thoughts she had of them becoming friends, much less allies.

"Then why else would you marry him?" Josephine asked. "The only reason would be that you're wanting his fortune. Perhaps you discovered his illness while you were in London." She moved closer and said, "And we both know that if you bear a son, this castle and all the lands become his inheritance. You would live like a queen."

Although the woman spoke matter-of-factly, Emma intended to set her straight. "I am not a fortune-hunter. And the last thing I want is for Cormac to die." She stiffened and added, "My husband is a good man, and he doesn't deserve this."

His mother fell silent. "You've the right of that. Which is why I won't be standing back and letting an English debutante wait like a vulture for him to die."

An unexpected laugh broke forth from her at the accusation. "I am not at all a debutante, Lady Dunmeath. Much less a vulture." A wallflower, yes. But she was nothing like Lady Persephone or any of the other London heiresses who cared only for a man's title and wealth.

And yet, Emma knew she was the very worst sort of lady Cormac could have wed. She was barely hiding her blindness, and once the dowager learned she could not read or write, Josephine would do everything in her power to keep her from becoming a true countess.

She took a steadying breath, feeling her insecurities rising higher, despite every effort to push them back.

"Then why did you marry my son, if not for his fortune?" Josephine demanded.

Emma didn't quite know how to answer that. But she sensed that full honesty was best, despite how bad it sounded. She took a breath and steeled herself. It didn't truly matter what the dowager thought, but she did want the woman to know that they were on the same side.

"At first, I told Lord Dunmeath I wasn't going to marry him. I didn't think he wanted a wife like me. I thought he should have one of those lovely heiresses you seem to think I am."

Josephine didn't respond, so Emma continued. "But he was persistent and kept asking." An ache caught her heart as she thought of it.

"Why did he choose *you* for a wife?" Her tone remained

harsh, and she added, "Surely everyone knew of his title, and he has a fair face."

The invisible barb stung, but Emma answered, "Because I was the only one who said yes."

"Idiots," Josephine remarked.

"They were," she agreed. "But he never told them of his fortune or the castle. He asked young ladies to marry him within a few minutes of meeting them. No one took him seriously." It was strange to remember Cormac's easy, blithe demeanor in London before his illness had stolen the smile from his face.

"And you? Did he ask you to wed after meeting you for the first time?"

Emma shook her head. "I was a wallflower, too afraid to speak to anyone. Lord Dunmeath was curious and came to my side."

Lady Dunmeath paused a moment before she remarked, "You don't have a title of your own, do you?"

"No." She could almost sense the calculating tone in her words, along with the disapproval. Emma straightened. "My stepmother has friends who invited us to balls and gatherings. But I was only Miss Bartholomew, never Lady Emma." A memory caught her unexpectedly. "After we first met, Lord Dunmeath could never quite remember my name."

"So, Cormac picked the only young lady in London who would marry him," Lady Dunmeath remarked. "And you never suspected he was a man of wealth?"

"Not until later when he paid off my father's debts," she corrected. "I knew nothing of his fortune. Just as I never knew he was ill until a few weeks ago."

Josephine muttered what sounded like a curse in Irish, her voice was edged with fear. Emma recalled Cormac saying that his mother had sent him away to London because she feared he was being poisoned.

"I thought, if he left, he might . . . be well again," Josephine said. Emma heard the bleakness within her voice.

"The only time he felt truly better was when we spent a few days by the sea before we made the crossing to Ireland." Emma's voice turned wistful at the memory. Cormac had been healthy and smiling, and their nights had been nothing but pleasure. "I wish I could take him back there." A surge of emotion caught her throat, but she held back the tears.

"But instead, you returned here, and whoever is poisoning him now has a second chance." Josephine stood from her chair and began pacing.

"Then we need to stop it from happening," Emma said. Though she knew it would dredge up terrible memories, she forced herself to ask, "What happened to your husband and older son? Was it the same? Or was anything different?"

"Cormac has lasted longer than either of them. But the sickness was the same."

The information didn't tell her anything that she didn't know already. "Should I take him away from here again?" Emma suggested. "Do you think it would help?"

"I don't know." Josephine's voice hardened. "If he didn't improve while he was in London, then I fear there's nothing we can do. And if this is the end, I would rather have Cormac here, to say my goodbyes."

She sounded as if she were giving up, but Emma wasn't ready for that yet. There had to be something causing the episodes. If only she could discover what it was.

"I want to hear what a physician has to say." She stood from her own chair. "But regardless, I'll do everything I can to help him get well."

Josephine walked to the door first and turned slightly. "A shame, it is, that I don't believe you."

IT WAS THREE miserable days before Cormac started to feel like himself again. He despised his own weakness, but Emma had remained at his side, giving him food and tea. Exhaustion lined her face, and he hated that her life had become this.

Abruptly, his bedroom door burst open, and his sisters came inside. Their voices collided in a cacophony of exclamations.

"Cormac! I've missed you so much."

"Are you very ill? Have you seen a doctor yet?"

"Did you really get married? Mother said—"

"I've been so worried about you."

He accepted their hugs and good wishes, but he noticed that Emma was slowly backing away to let the girls visit.

"This is my wife Emma," he said to them. Then to Emma, he added, "This is Nora. She's fifteen. And this is Maire. She's twelve."

Emma murmured greetings to them, but although they echoed the hellos, Cormac didn't miss the suspicion on Nora's face. His sister had always been overprotective.

"I thought you would both still be at school," he said. But he didn't have to ask why they had returned. His mother had probably brought them home again for fear that this was the end.

Maire's face turned fearful. "How sick are you, Cormac? Is it the curse again?"

He took her hand in his. "There's no curse, and you know this. It's just an illness, and we've no way of knowing the cause. But I am feeling a little better today."

There was a slight relief in his sister's face. "That's good."

Nora glanced over at Emma, and he could read the suspicion in her eyes. "Mother said you're English."

Emma nodded. "I am, yes."

"Why did you marry our brother? He's only been gone a few months."

Cormac interrupted his sister, not wanting Nora to draw the wrong conclusion. "I married Emma because I thought she would make an excellent wife. And so she has. Perhaps the three of you can get better acquainted today."

Emma stepped forward and regarded the girls. "I married

Cormac because he is my friend." Before his sisters could say anything, she added, "I know he's been ill, I want to find the cause of his illness. Would you be willing to help?"

Maire brightened, and she studied Emma. "I'll help you." His youngest sister had always been hopeful, and of the two of them, he suspected she would warm up to Emma first.

His wife thanked her and said, "I want to know everything that happened to your father and your older brother. How they got sick, how long they were sick, what their symptoms were. We need to gather information."

Nora stared at her. "Do you think he's being poisoned, like Mother does?"

"I don't know. But I do think there's a way to help him get well, if we can find out what is making him ill. Whether it's food or an illness, we need to find the reason."

Her determination startled him, for he'd never seen Emma this way before. She appeared resolute to find the answers, and it warmed him to hear it.

"The physicians couldn't save our father or Finn," Nora argued. "None of the medicines worked." Her voice held a hopeless tone.

"I won't stand by and do nothing," Emma insisted. "There has to be a way."

Maire offered, "I'll go fetch a pen and paper. We'll write down everything we know." There was a note of lightness in her voice, and Cormac was glad to hear it.

After his youngest sister left the room, Nora turned back to Emma. "My sister always sees the good in everyone. But I see the truth, not what everyone wants me to hear."

"Nora," Cormac warned. The last thing he wanted was his sister attacking his wife. And it was clear that she was echoing their mother's suspicions.

"No, let her speak," Emma said. "There is no harm in honesty."

"Our mother brought us home from school because she

believes Cormac will die soon. And I don't believe that you want to save him."

"Why wouldn't I want my husband to be well?" Emma asked quietly.

Cormac wanted to intervene, but he sensed that if he did, it would only cause more trouble between them. He sent Nora a warning look that she was ignoring.

"Because you'll gain more if he's dead," Nora said. "Mother says you don't have a title. But you are a countess here. If Cormac is gone, you'll inherit everything."

"I don't want him to die," Emma argued. "I care very much for your brother."

Her words slipped within his heart, and when Cormac studied her, he saw the shadow of emotion in her eyes. If he were a better man, he would try to keep more distance to avoid breaking her heart. Already the boundaries of friendship were shifting. And God help him, he didn't know if he had the willpower to keep his own feelings at bay.

"I don't believe you," Nora said. "You don't even know him. And if you did, you would find him *terribly* annoying."

He almost smiled at his sister's obvious attempt to dissuade Emma from wanting to remain married to him. When he glanced over at his wife, he saw that she was hiding her own amusement.

"We are getting to know each other better," she said simply, refusing to take the bait.

"He leaves cups everywhere," Nora insisted. "If you walk into a room, you can be sure that if you find a cup of tea, it was Cormac's. And he forgets everything. He'll forget your birthday," she predicted.

He decided to tease Nora. To Emma, he said, "I'm sorry, *a stór*. When *is* your birthday?"

"December," she answered. "You haven't missed it yet."

"But he will forget," Nora insisted. "One year, he forgot his own birthday."

"How awful," Emma said, but he could see the sparkle in her

eyes. "When is *your* birthday, my lord? I don't think you ever told me."

"I don't remember," he teased. "I suppose we'll have to simply choose a date."

Nora grimaced and rolled her eyes, as if she couldn't stand listening to them. But he had to admit, he was rather enjoying himself. He was reminded of more playful times with Emma in London and at the seaside.

His bedroom door swung open at that moment, and Maire returned. "I've brought paper, a pen, and ink. Shall we begin?"

"Yes, let's," Emma answered. "We'll start with what you remember of your father's illness."

Though Cormac doubted they would come to any sort of conclusion, he was glad to see his younger sister trying to help. But Nora rose from his beside and turned away. It was clear that she wanted no part of their discussion. Instead, she shook her head and walked to the door, closing it behind her.

He caught Emma's look of disappointment, but then she listened to Maire as his sister started writing down her memories. His wife also offered her own thoughts as Maire wrote, and as they spoke, it occurred to Cormac that Emma truly needed someone trustworthy to help her write letters and read correspondence back to her. He'd forgotten about it since he'd become ill again, but now, it could not wait.

He'd initially planned to hire someone in his household or perhaps someone from the village. But the more he thought of it, the more he wondered if he could hire his secretary Hawkins to come and live in Ireland—particularly since the man did not have a wife or children of his own. Hawkins could handle Emma's correspondence, and he believed his wife needed an ally—especially since his mother seemed unwilling to help.

He decided to write the letter today. And with any luck, Hawkins would arrive within a few weeks.

AFTER A FEW hours, Emma left Cormac to rest. She kept a warm smile on her face, but the truth was, the façade was beginning to exhaust her. It was clear enough that the dowager didn't want her here, and Josephine had refused to even speak with her since their conversation in the drawing room.

Although Maire might become an ally, she was still so very young. The girl had pressed her list into Emma's hands eagerly, promising to add more to it later. A list that Emma couldn't read. She let out a sigh and decided to take it to the study where it could remain on Cormac's desk.

Before she got very far down the hallway, she heard an unfamiliar woman's voice ahead of her saying, "Thank you, Stephens."

The footman must have taken the woman's bonnet and cloak, Emma guessed. Then he asked, "Are you here to pay a call upon the dowager Lady Dunmeath, Mrs. MacPherson?"

"Actually, I am here to meet Lord Dunmeath's new countess."

Emma barely had time to turn around before the woman hurried forward. "Oh, you must be Cormac's bride, aren't you?" she gushed. "Allow me to introduce myself. I am Moreen MacPherson. It's pleased I am to meet you at last. I've been asking Lorcan to bring me to the castle, but you know men. Always too busy, they are."

She extended a gloved hand, and Emma took it, feeling rather bewildered. "Good afternoon, Mrs. MacPherson."

"Oh, you simply must call me Moreen." Her laughter tinkled, and she drew Emma's hand to her arm. "I've come for tea and to get acquainted with you. I know we will be wonderful friends, Lady Dunmeath."

The woman reminded her of Lady Persephone with her false enthusiasm, but Emma tried not to make too swift a judgment. It was entirely possible that Nuala or Josephine had not been fair in their view of Moreen.

"I will ring for tea," she said.

"Oh, you needn't bother. I told Stephens to make the arrangements." Moreen guided her down the hall to the drawing room. Maire and Nora were already there. The younger sister was writing a letter—Emma could hear the scratching of her pen—while Nora seemed to be reading a book. "Hello, there," Moreen greeted the girls. "I heard the two of you were back from school."

Nora glanced up from her book and appeared to shrug before turning another page. Maire answered, "Yes, we returned last night."

"It's so dreadful about your brother." Then she seemed to catch herself and added, "Forgive me, Lady Dunmeath. I spoke without thinking. We are all praying for your husband."

Emma wasn't so certain, but she didn't reveal her thoughts. "Lord Dunmeath is improving," she answered. "I feel confident that he will be feeling better by morning."

"I do hope you are right," Moreen answered. Even so, her voice held a touch of insincerity.

Emma turned to Cormac's sisters and said, "Mrs. MacPherson came for tea. Would you both care to join us?"

Before either could answer, Moreen said, "Oh, I'm certain the girls have their lessons, or their mother will be wanting them to join her for tea."

Emma was taken aback by the woman's remark, and she felt the need to correct her. "Actually, Lady Nora and Lady Maire are more than welcome. I've not had the chance to get to know them very well."

"No, thank you, Lady Dunmeath," Maire answered. "We— we ought to be going."

"You needn't be so formal," Emma said. "You may call me Emma."

But neither answered. Instead, Nora closed her book loudly

and followed her sister from the drawing room. Their reluctance made it all too evident that they, too, were less than fond of Moreen. And although the woman might be nothing more than an envious wife, Emma decided that it might be best to learn what she could about Moreen.

"I suppose it's just us now," Emma said. "I'd like to hear all about you and how you met Lorcan."

Moreen launched into a tale of how she'd been swept away by Lorcan, enchanted by the castle at Dunmeath, and sorely disappointed when she learned that her husband had no desire to live there. Throughout the conversation, Emma smiled and nodded, but her thoughts drifted back to Cormac. Did he know of Moreen's ambitions? Was Lorcan's wife greedy enough to plot his death? Her blood grew cold at the thought.

But again, she needed to learn more.

"Have you ever been to England?" Emma asked. "Or have you lived in Ireland all your life?"

"No, I've never been to England," Moreen admitted. "But Lorcan's grandmother was English, so I believe he visited, years ago." She paused when the tea arrived and asked, "Would you like to pour out, or should I?"

"I'm happy to let you pour," Emma answered. She was grateful for the offer since she was fearful of spilling the tea whenever she was forced into the role.

But although Moreen had no connection to England, Emma found it interesting that Lorcan did. She wondered about Cormac's cousin, for neither she nor Cormac had seen him since they'd arrived.

After she poured the tea, Moreen sighed. "Oh, this is good. Much better than the herbal teas Nuala tries to make. Sometimes it seems as if she's brewing blades of grass."

Emma hadn't minded it, but she said nothing and sipped at her own tea. "Why have I not met your husband yet? Has he been very busy?"

Moreen set her cup down. "No. It's only that Lorcan is a very superstitious man. When he heard that Cormac had grown ill again, he stayed far away. If you ask me, it's very heartless. He said it's because he wants to protect me from the curse, but I think he ought to be more supportive of his cousin."

Or it might be that he stayed away to avoid being blamed, Emma thought.

Moreen brought her hands to her waist. "We're expecting a child of our own in the spring. Lorcan's hoping for a boy."

"Congratulations." Emma tried to smile for her, although she couldn't tell whether or not Moreen was pregnant. Even so, the woman's news brought a pang of remorse at the reminder that she'd been unable to conceive a child right away. Although she and Cormac had only been married a few weeks, it felt as if time were moving faster. Perhaps one day she and Cormac would have a baby of their own, but part of her worried it wouldn't happen.

She heard footsteps approaching from behind, and Moreen called out, "Lord Dunmeath! Oh, you must join us. I'm simply delighted to see that you're feeling better."

Emma worried that Cormac was pushing his strength too soon. But when he came to sit beside her on the settee, she felt her own surge of gratitude that he was here. His shoulders brushed against hers, and he accepted a cup of tea from Moreen.

"Thank you, Moreen." He stirred the tea and asked, "How have you and Lorcan been these days?"

"Oh, well enough. I was just telling your wife of our happy news. Lorcan is so worried about the baby, but I simply had to come and meet Lady Dunmeath. It's glad I am to see your health has improved," she gushed.

Emma reached out to Cormac's hand and gave it a light squeeze. He spoke with Moreen about Dunmeath and news of the local folk, but amid their conversation about people she didn't know, Emma let herself daydream, wondering what she could do to help him. *Was* there something else causing the illness? It seemed as if every time Cormac was at home—both here and in

London—he grew ill. When he'd gone on holiday with her by the seaside, he'd been quite well for days.

The thought took root, making her consider it. What if she tried it again, taking Cormac away from Dunmeath Castle and spending a week away from everyone? If his strength and health improved, then they would know for certain.

She smiled to herself and decided to start making her plans today.

CORMAC HAD BARELY seen his wife the remainder of the day, and she'd fallen into bed exhausted that night. The next morning, she was up before dawn, and he wondered what she was planning.

"Emma, come back to bed," he murmured. "It's too early."

"I have something I have to finish," she argued. "You can go back to sleep, and we'll talk later."

"What are you up to?" he asked. He flipped back the coverlet and walked over to her. "Come to bed."

"I have a surprise that I'm planning for you," she said. "I'm not quite ready with the arrangements."

She'd piqued his curiosity, and it was then that he noticed a traveling trunk beside the window. "Are we going somewhere?"

His wife nodded. "We are."

"Where are we going?" He slid his hands around her waist and bent to kiss the curve of her neck.

She shivered and turned in his arms. "I'm kidnapping you."

Her statement was spoken with such nonchalance, he had to hold back a laugh. "Are you now, *a stór*? But is it really kidnapping if I'm your willing prisoner?" He moved his hands to her backside and pulled her close. Right now, he wanted nothing more than to press her against the mattress for he ached to be inside her.

"How long will we be gone?" he asked, kissing her again to remind Emma just how badly he wanted her.

"One week," she answered. "There's a small cottage just on—

on the edge of Dunmeath." She caught her breath when he drew his hands to cup her breasts through her nightgown. Her nipples were tight, and she gave him a light push. "Let me finish, Cormac. There will be time for this later."

He was disappointed but let her go. "The roof leaks in that cottage, so I'm told. Are you certain you're wanting to go there?"

"We'll try it and see if the weather holds," she said. Then, in all seriousness, she said, "We were alone by the sea, and your health improved with every day we were there. I want to see if it happens again."

"We could also try again for a child," he said, reaching to touch her face.

She blushed but nodded. "We could. If you're feeling strong enough."

"Before we go, I should meet with Lorcan to ensure that all is well with Dunmeath," he said.

"No, your mother took care of everything. I told her I was kidnapping you."

"And she didn't protest?" He raised an eyebrow at that. While he knew his mother wanted his health to improve, he wondered whether the pair of them had plotted this together or whether his mother still resented Emma's presence.

"I . . . didn't exactly ask her permission." She ventured a smile. "I have plans for you."

He returned her smile. "I like the sound of that."

"I'll ring for your valet, and I'll go to the adjoining room to have my maid help me dress," Emma said. She turned away and added as she reached the connecting door, "And while we're away, we're going to find out why you're becoming ill."

He knew she was hoping to find answers, but he didn't truly understand why he'd only begun to get sick after his brother Finn had passed away and not before. While it was entirely possible that someone was poisoning him, there were an equal number of reasons why it could simply be an illness.

But he wasn't about to argue with his wife about spending

time alone with her for a week. The responsibilities of Dunmeath would still be here when he returned, none the worse for waiting. And it was a better—and more pleasurable—use of his time to try again for an heir.

After he was dressed and came downstairs, he found Emma directing servants to load several hampers of food into a carriage. "We aren't going to ride?" he asked.

She shook her head. "The carriage will drop us off, and the footmen will unload the food. They'll return by the end of the week to fetch us."

"So, you truly are kidnapping me," he mused. "Lead on."

His mother was nowhere to be seen, but he wondered how she and Emma had gotten on while he'd been recovering.

In a low voice, she murmured to him, "Actually, I need *you* to lead the way to the carriage." He offered his arm, and she took it while they walked outside. "Are you feeling all right?"

"Weak," he admitted. "But a little better."

He walked alongside Emma, noticing her slight awkwardness around the servants. Even as they asked her where to put the hampers, she seemed uncomfortable giving orders. But he said nothing and let her continue.

Throughout the short carriage ride to the cottage, he studied his wife. Her dark hair was pulled up, and she wore a green morning gown. He hadn't seen this one before, but it was plain and serviceable. Her face was pale, her eyes lined with such weariness, he wondered how much she had endured during the past few days.

The last thing he wanted was for her to be his nursemaid while he lay dying. It wasn't fair to ask that of her. Although he knew she wanted to find reasons for his illness, he hated the fact that he could not control his body's weaknesses.

After half an hour of traveling, the carriage stopped in front of the cottage. Cormac helped Emma out while the footmen unloaded their food into the tiny dwelling. The leaves were beginning to fall to the ground, and the air was so chilly, he could see his breath. Cormac studied the thatched roof, wondering if the weather truly would remain fine or whether they would find themselves huddled together during a downpour. And despite the sunshine, it was indeed quite cool, even when he followed his wife inside.

One of the footmen built a peat fire in the hearth, and Emma thanked him before she went to stand by it. Then, a few moments later, they were alone.

She was rubbing her arms, and the expression on her face held nervousness. Though it had been only days since she'd shared his bed, something between them had changed. His wife almost seemed uneasy.

"Are you hungry?" he asked.

She shook her head. But neither did she offer conversation. It was almost as if she was starting to doubt the plans she'd made, and he wanted to set her at ease.

"Are you regretting your decision to kidnap me?" he teased. "Should I call the coachman back?"

That earned him a smile at least. "No. I just . . . suddenly feel uncertain. And I don't even know why."

He decided to offer a distraction. "Do you want to take a walk?"

She gave him a grateful smile. "That would be nice. But it's colder than I thought it would be. Let me get my pelisse from the trunk. And will you be warm enough in your coat?"

He gave a nod. After she finished buttoning up the wool, he led her to walk outside, resting his hand against her spine. "Are you nervous around me, Emma?"

Her face turned crimson, but she put her arm in his. "No, not really. It's just that . . . I—I'm not very good at kidnapping, I suppose."

That wasn't the reason at all, but it didn't seem that she was ready to share whatever was bothering her. He decided to bide his time and wait for the answers.

They started walking along a woodland path. Old leaves

crunched beneath their feet, and he admired the reds and yellows of the ones that were on the trees. It occurred to him that, although she had arranged this time together, she might mistakenly believe that lovemaking was all he wanted from her. He'd been honest in his desire for an heir, and though he'd been disappointed that their first efforts hadn't worked, it wasn't the only thing between them.

"I enjoyed our time together when we were by the sea," he said.

"So did I."

He slid his arm around her waist. "And it will be the same here. Unless it rains through the roof, perhaps."

That coaxed a slight smile at least. "That would make this week less comfortable, I agree." She leaned against him, but a moment later, her smile faded, replaced by an emotion that knotted her face.

"Emma, tell me what you're thinking. For someone who went to a lot of trouble to plan this kidnapping, you seem as if you have regrets."

She slowed her pace and said, "No, that's not true. I did want to spend this time with you."

"Then why are you so upset? Have I done something to make you angry?"

"No." But she pulled her hand from his arm and stopped walking. "It's just that . . . whenever I think about you becoming ill, it terrifies me." Before he could try to soothe her fears with words, she added, "I'm afraid of losing you. You nearly died a few days ago. And I couldn't do anything to stop it."

He stopped walking and reached out to trace the outline of her face. "I never wanted you to see me like that."

"I know. But I need to do something, to help you fight this. And this was the only thing I could think of. Spending time alone with you." She covered his hand with her own. "I know my duty is to bear you a son. I know that's why you married me. But if I can't give you that, and if you die . . ."

Her words broke off, and he saw her tears slide down her cheeks. "That's not the only reason I married you, Emma."

He leaned in to kiss her, and she answered it, wrapping her arms around him. He pulled her body to fit against his, soothing her with his mouth. But when he ended the kiss, Emma stared back at him. "There's also something else bothering me."

He waited for her to continue and stroked her spine. She took a deep breath and added, "I don't like the person I'm becoming around your mother. Helpless. Unable to do the things I need to do." She closed her eyes, taking a breath. "I know you say that she can help me with my duties or the other servants can—but I hate it that I cannot be the countess you need. And if I cannot give you a child, what purpose do I even have?"

He didn't know what to tell her without sounding patronizing. And so, he answered, "We'll keep trying." He took her hand in his as they walked along the edge of a stream. But as they continued in silence, he didn't know what he could do to help her rebuild her courage.

He might not be alive within a few more months. Empty words and false reassurances wouldn't change that. It was better to face what lay ahead with honesty. He had no idea how much time he had left.

But he'd be lying to himself if he didn't admit that he wanted to spend the remainder of that time with Emma.

Chapter Eleven

EMMA WISHED SHE'D never confessed her true feelings. Although Cormac had tried to be kind, she didn't want him to pity her. But she'd blurted out everything without thinking, and now she wished she'd said nothing at all.

After they arrived back at the cottage, the space had warmed from the peat fire. She removed her pelisse and set it aside. Her mood had grown somber, and she stared into the flames. She'd allowed her near-blindness to interfere with her life in the past. Instead of reaching for what she wanted, she'd remained in the shadows, letting others decide the course of her life. And now, she was letting the shadows win once again. It wasn't who she wanted to be anymore.

The melancholy was a wave that threatened to drown her. But then, Cormac's hands moved to the buttons of her gown. He stood behind her, and his mouth lowered to the soft place between her throat and shoulder.

A thousand shivers erupted over her body, and she felt his hands against her skin as he unfastened the buttons, one by one.

What purpose do I even have? She wanted—no, *needed* to change. Although Cormac might say that being his wife was purpose enough, she wanted more. She wanted to cast aside the woman she'd been, the woman who couldn't manage any of the responsibilities of a countess. And somehow, she wanted to find a way to be Lady of Dunmeath. To be the woman no one thought she could become.

The thought was a single thread that spun through her mind. Was it even possible to earn their respect, to transform herself?

Her gown fell away, and her husband began unlacing her stays. She grew distracted by his touch, and soon enough, she stood only in her chemise. Emma turned to face him, and she removed his coat and waistcoat. He cupped her breasts, stroking her nipples through the thin linen, and the familiar warmth of desire flooded through her. She suddenly craved her husband's touch.

And instead of remaining passive, she reached for him. She undressed him, lifting his shirt away, and traced the outline of his chest. Cormac had lost weight during the past few days, but she still loved touching him. Her heart softened, and she pushed away the emotions she didn't want to face. Better to lock it all away and simply live in the moment right now.

She explored his skin with her hands, the familiar strength of his shoulders. When she drew her hands down his ribs toward his waist, she heard the catch of his breath. Then when she touched his arms, her fingertips grazed a slight scar on his right wrist.

"What happened to you here?" she asked, bringing the scar to her mouth.

He froze a moment and then told her, "It's a scar from when I was a boy. I was beaten by my tutor almost every day."

Her words startled her, and she asked, "Why? Why would your father allow such a thing?" Something in his demeanor made her realize that they were more alike than he knew. She took a breath and admitted, "My governess struck me, too."

"I couldn't read until I was nearly ten," Cormac said. "I hated every moment of it. And every time the words got mixed up or I lost my place, my tutor struck me."

She drew his wrist to her mouth and kissed the scar again. "But you did learn."

"In time. With the right tutor who read me stories I wanted to hear." He expelled a half-laugh. "He would always stop at the most exciting part and close the book. I got so angry that after he left, I tried to read it myself. I didn't realize at the time that he was doing it for that very reason."

Emma smiled. "My governess gave up on me, eventually."

He leaned in to steal a kiss and rested his forehead against hers. "It's sorry I am that you had to endure that, *a stór.*"

"It doesn't matter now."

"You won't need to worry about reading," he said. "I've sent for Hawkins. If he agrees to come, he'll handle your correspondence."

"I wish I could manage it myself," she confessed. "I knew coming to Ireland would be hard, but I didn't realize how difficult it would be. I know nothing about how to command an estate, much less where everything is."

"You don't have to worry about any of it," he said. He removed her chemise and guided her to sit on the bed while he knelt before her. "Be a countess or don't. Get to know my household or leave them alone. It's your choice."

Beneath his words, she heard his hidden message—*Because it won't last.*

And something within her grew angry that he would give up like this. All her life, she'd had to fight to do the things others took for granted. How could he expect her not to fight now?

"I'm going to find out what's happening to you," she swore. "And I'm going to find a way to stop it. I promise you that."

He touched her chin softly. "If there *are* any answers to be had."

"Don't ask me to stand aside and let you die." Emma's hands curled into his hair. "I won't do it."

He rested his hands on her waist and faced her. "And what if we cannot stop it? What if there is no one trying to harm me and it's just an illness?"

"I don't believe that." She couldn't. Giving up on Cormac

wasn't something she could do. Though she lacked the answers, or even the right questions to ask, they had to start fighting. Or else there would be no future at all. "It's why I brought you here with me. We'll stay here for seven days with no one else. If you don't get sick, we'll know that it's not a true illness."

She took his hands and pulled him up to the bed, guiding him to lie on top of her. Between her legs, she could feel the heated length of him, and she wanted to feel his body moving inside hers.

Cormac kissed her deeply, his hands stroking her body with such tenderness, she wanted to weep. For despite all the ways she'd tried to hold up the boundaries, with a single touch he shattered them all.

And nothing would stop her from trying to save his life.

EMMA WAS RIGHT.

Cormac hadn't wanted to admit it, but after nearly four days of spending time together, his strength was improving, day by day. They ate the food she'd packed, spent their hours making love or taking long walks. At night, he read stories to her by candlelight.

Only once did it rain, and they'd laughed and moved closer to the fire, finding other ways to get warm.

Although he should have been heartened at his change in health, Cormac's suspicions darkened. If he were indeed being poisoned, he had no idea how. There was no way to know for certain who was responsible. It might be his cousin Lorcan, whom Cormac hadn't seen since his return. Or perhaps his wife Moreen. Both were logical possibilities, for each stood to inherit a great sum if he were to die.

But how had the threat continued in England?

"Is something bothering you, Cormac?" Emma asked. "How are you feeling?" Her arms slid around his waist, and he leaned in to kiss her cheek.

"I'm feeling fine."

"You don't sound fine."

He let out a sigh. "It's because you were right, *a stór*. Somehow, I suspect that if we stayed in this cottage forever, I would never become sick."

"Just like the seaside," she said. She reached out to touch his hair and rested her hand there a moment. "So, I was right. Someone is causing your illness."

"Aye. And now, we must decide what to do about it." He took her hands in his. "We'll have to find out who is responsible."

"Cormac," she said softly. "I think you should stay here and send me back to Dunmeath on my own to learn what I can. If you're there, your illness will only return."

"But then that puts you at risk." He drew her into his embrace. "I won't allow that."

"We'll make a plan together," she suggested. "Tell me who might want to harm you, and I'll investigate."

"I don't want to leave you alone." The thought of her facing danger while he remained here wasn't an acceptable choice to him.

"I won't be alone. If I ask her, I believe your mother will help me," Emma insisted. "Neither of us wants you to die. So, we'll work together."

"She's . . . difficult," he admitted. Ever since she'd lost her husband and eldest son, bitterness had become his mother's invisible cloak. She'd let it sink into her skin, transforming her into a woman with little hope.

"I won't let that stop us from finding our answers," she said. "Now tell me whom you suspect." With a chagrined smile, she added, "I would ask you to make a list of names, except I couldn't read it."

"It's probably better if we don't write it down." He began to pace across the small cottage while Emma sat on the bed.

"Lorcan and his wife," he began. "Possibly Aunt Nuala or the servants."

"I'm not certain it *is* the servants," she countered. "I watched them pack our food myself. Or, at least, I let them think I could see what they were doing."

He shrugged, not knowing who else it could be. "What do you think?"

She was hesitant, and he saw that she was reluctant to add another opinion. "Go on and say it, Emma."

"I don't want to offend you, but we have to consider everyone," she began. "Could your sisters have anything to do with it? Even unknowingly?"

"I don't think so, no. Nora and Maire have always been dear to me." Though he understood that Emma was only contemplating all possibilities, he couldn't imagine any circumstances under which his sisters would or could cause him harm.

"Then perhaps they can help us find something we haven't considered."

His mood grew somber. "Although I want to know who's behind this . . . in some ways, I don't really want to know." The thought of a close family member wanting him dead wasn't at all something he wanted to face. And yet, it now seemed quite likely.

Emma took his hand in hers. "We're going to find our answers. I promise you that."

EMMA ARRIVED BACK at Dunmeath after one of the tenants gave her a ride in his wagon. Though Cormac didn't like it, she'd left him behind in the cottage. It was far too dangerous for him to return. No one particularly cared about her, so it was hardly a risk at all.

But she was determined to succeed in finding out who was trying to harm her husband. Although she was nervous about it, she couldn't help but think that she had her own advantage. All her life, she'd gone unnoticed, a wallflower who had faded into the background. She truly believed that if she used her senses and opened her ears, she would discover what she needed to know.

Emma was careful to count her steps as she walked to the main doors of the castle. Though her insecurities were rising again, this time she told herself that the earl's life depended on her ability to work with his mother.

She gave her bonnet and pelisse to Stephens, the footman, and asked, "Where can I find the dowager Lady Dunmeath?"

"She's not here at the moment," he answered. "But she should return by luncheon."

"If you see her, please tell her that I would like to speak with her."

Emma started to walk toward the stairs but stopped and changed her mind. This might be a good opportunity to get better acquainted with Dunmeath without the countess's disapproval. At first, she thought about asking a servant to guide her . . . but then, how else could she find out the secrets no one wanted her to hear?

She decided to start in the kitchens. Though she didn't truly know where they were, besides being down on the lower level, she decided to follow the scent of food.

Emma pretended to be studying the hallway and taking a slow walk. She rather hoped there was art on the walls, for otherwise she might look very foolish indeed.

But soon enough, it did seem that the staff members paid her little heed. She started to walk down the stairs but paused when she heard voices.

"Do you think Lady Dunmeath was right?" a maid asked. Then their voices dropped lower, and Emma couldn't hear what they were talking about. She took a few steps down the stairs, hoping no one could see her. She was careful to keep her back against the wall, and then she heard the maids again.

"Will his lordship be all right? He's been gone for days," a young woman said.

"Aye, he will. I'm certain of it."

"But Lady Dunmeath thinks—"

"Now, don't be telling stories," came the voice of an older woman. "'Tis the curse, and everyone knows it. Nuala has been trying to break it. I've seen her tying off charms and making those teas of hers. But she's had no luck yet."

Emma remembered that Cormac's aunt had been on his list of possible suspects. And it was quite possible that a woman with such a garden and knowledge of herbs might be willing to use the plants for harm rather than good—especially if she wanted her son to inherit.

She was trying to decide whether to continue down the stairs, but a moment later, one of the servants nearly collided with her.

"Lady Dunmeath!" The maid stumbled and caught herself. "I—what are you—are you hungry?" she finished.

"No, thank you." Emma thought quickly, fumbling for a reason she could be downstairs. "I am still getting acquainted with the staff," she said at last. "I thought I'd come and meet everyone in the kitchens."

"Oh." The maid seemed somewhat confused on what to do. "Would you . . . like me to introduce the others to you, Lady Dunmeath?"

"Yes, please." Emma counted her remaining steps down the stairs and followed the maid toward the kitchen. The sounds of pots bubbling and knives chopping were familiar, and for a moment, she savored the delicious aromas.

When the sounds ceased, she could feel the eyes of the servants on her. "Good morning," Emma said at last. "I wanted to meet all of you and say hello."

There was an awkward silence among them, and she felt her cheeks burn with embarrassment. "Or is that . . . not something a countess should do?"

"Lady Dunmeath, you may do anything you like," a matron said. Emma guessed she might be the cook but couldn't tell for certain. "I am Mrs. Ó Neill. And this is Florence, Molly, and Eithna. They help me in the kitchen and in the scullery. Can I be getting you anything to eat?" the woman asked.

There was a warm welcome in her voice, and Emma said, "Oh, I didn't want to trouble you for anything. You're busy enough. I only wanted to say hello." And find out all the information she could about any threats to her husband.

"Well, you're here now, and it's very welcome you are," Mrs. Ó Neill said. "Here. Try one of these." She held out what looked like a plate, and Emma took it. She couldn't quite tell what was on it but removed her glove and reached for the blurry object. It turned out to be a sweet bun, covered in what seemed like honey and nuts. "Thank you."

"Come and sit," the cook offered, pulling out a stool. "Would you like tea?"

"Oh no, thank you. I wouldn't want you to go to any trouble." The moment the words left her mouth, she realized that the dowager would never have said such a thing. Weakly, she added, "Or, if you need to continue cooking, please do."

The cook pulled up a stool beside her. "Flo, see to the roast. Molly, the bread wants kneading. Eithna, finish the spice cake."

The kitchen maids went about their tasks, and Mrs. Ó Neill said gently, "I suppose you must be missing your family."

Emma gave a nod. "But I am happy to be here with my husband. I only wish—"

"You're wishing he didn't get so sick, aye?"

"I know his father and brother suffered the same, but I don't want it to happen to Lord Dunmeath."

The cook gave a heavy sigh. "I didn't want to speak of it, but we all know of the curse." She stood and went over to a drawer. A moment later, she held out something that clinked in her palm. "Take these. It may help him."

Emma held out her hand, and the cook gave her two pieces of metal. From the shape of them, she guessed, "Nails?"

"*Iron* nails," Mrs. Ó Neill said. "To keep away the faerie folk who are trying to destroy us."

Emma took the nails and tucked them away in her pocket. It

was clear that the cook truly believed in such things, and she didn't want to offend her. Instead, she simply thanked the cook. "What can you tell me about Cormac's cousin?"

"Afraid of everyone and everything, Lorcan is," the cook answered. "He stays as far away from Dunmeath as he can, so the curse won't touch him."

"I thought he lived here with his mother?" Emma guessed.

"Nay. Lorcan has a small house near the river. He lives there with his wife Moreen. She's expecting their first child, so he wants naught to do with Dunmeath."

Emma remembered Moreen's triumph and pushed aside her own regrets. "Then you don't think Lorcan wishes he were the earl?"

"Not in a thousand years," Mrs. Ó Duinne said. "He's spoken of traveling toward Dublin, to get as far away from us as he can. It's my fondest hope that someone will break the curse, so Lord Dunmeath gets well again."

Emma took a bite of the sticky bun. Though she knew it was a risk to confront the cook openly, she asked, "Do you think there's anyone—anyone besides the faeries, that is—who could want to hurt Cormac? Have you heard or seen anything?"

"Nay." Mrs. Ó Duinne's voice turned softer. "He's a good soul, is Lord Dunmeath. There's no one here who wants to harm him. Takes care of everyone, he does."

And it was time that someone took care of him, Emma thought. She thanked the cook for the sweet bun and rose from her chair. "It was very nice meeting you."

"And you, my lady," Mrs. Ó Duinne answered.

But even as she left, Emma felt as if she was nowhere near the answers she needed. She doubted if the servants had anything to do with Cormac's illness. She decided to go into his study, to take a few moments to think.

After walking up the stairs and down to the end of the hall, she opened the door that she thought was the study. The moment she entered, she detected the familiar scent of her husband. The hint of pine allured her, and she went to sit at Cormac's desk.

Clearly, he'd spent time here after he'd arrived, for ledgers and books covered every surface of the desk. He had stacks of papers that she couldn't possibly read, but she moved them aside, along with the books and another book that was so old, the binding had cracked, and it was falling apart. She didn't know if it was anything important, but she was careful to close it and stack it neatly with the others. There was a layer of dust on it, and she brushed it off her hands.

After she'd cleared Cormac's desk, she searched the drawers, not even knowing what she was looking for. There were only pens and inkwells on one side of the desk, along with stacks of paper. Her fingers bumped against a single teacup, and she smiled, remembering Nora's remark about Cormac's habit of leaving them behind. The room was an utter mess, but Emma supposed her husband had his own way of keeping track of the estate.

She decided to speak with his Aunt Nuala next. Though she didn't want to imagine that the kindly woman was poisoning her nephew, Emma couldn't deny that she had a strong knowledge of plants. And though it frightened her, she couldn't shy away from what she had to do.

She rose from the desk and walked toward the door. A grandfather clock chimed in the hallway, and Emma decided to see if Nuala wanted to join her for tea. She needed answers, and Cormac's aunt might let something accidentally slip.

It was the best she could hope for.

London

LADY SCARSDALE'S BIRTHDAY ball had an autumn theme. The decorations included colorful foliage, harvest turnips and pumpkins, and the countess served hot spiced wine along with delicious cakes and biscuits. But Sir Brian was there for his own purpose—to dance with Rachel Harding and learn more about why she had retreated from the world with her infamous school.

She'd given him a task—to dance with six ladies—in order to earn a place at her school. After one country dance with at least seven other women and men, he could safely say that he'd satisfied the requirement. He had no intention of finding a bride among them—not when he'd set his hopes on Rachel.

He saw her enter the ballroom with Cedric Gregor, her business partner. Brian was grateful to the man for his assistance in helping him become a student at the school. They had both suspected that Rachel would refuse, but Brian was willing to pay any price.

He understood that this was a Herculean task. He'd been helpless, years ago, to help Rachel when she'd been married to that monster. Now, he had the second chance he'd been waiting for—but he had to be so very careful not to frighten her. She'd been hurt so badly she might refuse him entirely.

Rachel wore a demure gown of dove gray, one that covered her arms. She wore another shawl over her shoulders, and she remained firmly in the background, watching over everyone. He could almost imagine her silently making lists of young ladies, just as Cedric was finding gentlemen who would become their future husbands.

He'd intended to ask her to dance, but when he saw the way she held herself back, remaining in the shadows, he sensed that she would say no. Breaking down the walls of pain and healing her invisible wounds would take time. And he didn't know if she would grant him that time.

But when he looked at her, he saw more than a woman who had been hurt for so many years. He saw a survivor, someone who created happy endings for so many young women—the happy ending she'd never had for herself.

He walked through the ballroom and went to stand near her.

"Are you enjoying yourself, Mrs. Harding?"

She appeared startled that he was speaking to her. "Aren't you supposed to be speaking with six different young ladies?"

"And so I have. You are the seventh."

"Have you found anyone who has caught your interest?" she asked.

He let his gaze meet hers. "I might." Though he kept his expression vague, he was already looking at the object of his interest.

He admired how Rachel had transformed her life, seizing control and finding her path. All he wanted now was the chance to show her that he cared. And perhaps this time, she wouldn't turn him away.

"Good," she said. "We will speak of the young ladies in the morning. If you are fortunate, perhaps I can set up a way for you to pay a call upon them." She stared straight ahead with a silent message for him to go away.

Instead, he remained at her side, surreptitiously studying the flushed curve of her cheek, the mahogany hair that was pulled up in a soft knot. Her eyes were a blend of gray and green, almost like the river on a foggy day. Those eyes held the weariness of a woman whose dreams had faded, one who had known only suffering for years. But there was also the strength of one who had endured and rebuilt a life for herself from the ashes.

She guarded her heart fiercely, and he didn't know if he would ever win it. But he wanted to try.

Ireland

IT WAS THE next afternoon before Emma was able to meet Nuala for tea. Yesterday, the older woman had been out shopping with Moreen, and she'd only returned this morning.

"Good afternoon, Emma." Nuala's voice was warm and

welcoming when she joined her in the parlor for tea. "You look very well. How is Cormac faring?"

Although the matron's words were friendly and held a note of concern, Emma remained cautious about believing the woman truly cared for her nephew. She didn't know whether Nuala's warmth was genuine or whether she viewed Cormac as an obstacle in the way of Lorcan's inheriting the estate. She reminded herself that the purpose of having tea with Nuala was to learn what she could about Lorcan and the woman's ambitions.

Emma rose from her seat and extended her hand to greet Cormac's aunt. "He's much better, thank you."

"Will he be joining us for tea?"

"No, he is visiting some of the tenants, I believe." Emma didn't want to reveal his real location yet, especially when she wasn't certain about Nuala's intentions.

"Then perhaps I'll see him tonight at supper," his aunt said. They sat, and a moment later, a footman brought out the tea and refreshments. "Shall I pour?"

"Please," she agreed. While Nuala poured, Emma chose a sandwich from the tray. Her stomach had been unsettled since this morning, and she'd slept poorly last night. The thought of breakfast had brought a wave of nausea, but she would force herself to eat something now. "How is your garden faring?"

Nuala took a sip of her tea. "Some of the cooler morning weather has threatened many of the plants. But I've transferred some into pots and have brought them inside for the autumn. There's a great deal of light in the conservatory, so I tend them there." She offered milk and sugar, and Emma took both.

The tea was warm and comforting, and she tasted peppermint that did soothe her stomach. When she nibbled at the sandwich bread, it did little to ease the ache. She forced herself to eat.

Nuala asked, "Will we be welcoming a new heir in the spring or early summer, perhaps?"

The direct words startled her. "No. Why would you ask?"

The woman gave a soft laugh. "Forgive me. I'm just overly inquisitive. I do love babies."

"I understand Moreen is expecting," Emma said, hoping to divert the conversation.

"Yes, so she says." Oddly enough, the tone of Nuala's voice revealed her doubts, along with the slight sigh. "But we shall see. You, on the other hand—I believe there *will* be a new heir soon. You have that look about you." The prospect seemed to please her.

"What look?" Emma took another sandwich, feeling unsettled.

"That look as if you're experiencing sickness right now, but you also have a glow of happiness about you."

Her words struck Emma with surprise. Was that what was causing her sickness? She'd believed she wasn't expecting a child, but then again, her menses had only lasted a day. Was it possible that she *could* be pregnant? The thought sent a flush through her cheeks, along with a surge of hope.

"And I know Cormac desperately wants an heir, so I'm certain he's made every effort," Nuala continued. She took food from the tray and added, "I suspected he might try to find a bride when he went to London."

The mention of London pulled Emma's thoughts back to the present. She needed to find out how Cormac was being harmed in England, and this was the best opening she could hope for.

"Moreen said your son Lorcan has been to London, years ago," Emma said. "Did you go with him?"

"No, but I went with my mother a time or two." Nuala's voice grew guarded. "She hated it in England and was only too glad to remain in Ireland with my father." She sipped at her tea and added, "After she died, she left the house to Finn, and then it became Cormac's. Josie and I wanted nothing to do with London."

The anger in her voice startled Emma, but Nuala quickly

masked it. "But let's not talk of that. How are you liking Ireland?"

"It's beautiful," she answered. "Though I've only seen some of the country when we sailed here. Perhaps we'll travel later, if Cormac is feeling better."

"That is my dearest hope," Nuala said. The sorrow in her voice sounded genuine, and Emma didn't know what to think of it. "Lorcan loves Killarney and Dingle. Perhaps you'll have the chance to see them one day."

"I hope so," she said. The thought of eating more of the sandwich bothered her, so she set it aside and reached for the tea. Her face was also feeling flushed, and she couldn't understand why.

"Is it warm in here?" she asked Nuala.

"No, but when I was pregnant with Lorcan, I would often feel moments of hot and cold. There were days when I had to keep fanning myself. It might be the same for you."

Emma still wasn't convinced of pregnancy, but she gratefully accepted a fan from Nuala. The cool air did make her feel better.

"Were Lorcan and Cormac friends when they were growing up?"

"Oh, my son tried," Nuala said. "He was always wanting to play with Finn and Cormac. But they were both older and didn't want a lad of five years following them when they went fishing or hunting."

Emma detected a slight note of sadness in her voice. "Lorcan and Cormac became friends later, after Finn died. And then Lorcan married Moreen last year and . . ." Her words drifted off, revealing her disapproval of the match.

"Is there something you don't like about her?"

"She's one of those women you can never please. Always wants more than she has." Nuala poured herself another cup of tea and added more to Emma's. "She's angry with Lorcan because they live on a house at the edge of Cormac's lands. It's a very good house, and they have a footman and a maid to tend it. But she thinks she should be living here."

"And what does your son think?"

"Lorcan is happy to stay far away from Dunmeath. As I said, he's listened to the stories of the curse upon Cormac." She released a sigh. "It's nonsense, of course."

"What do you believe it is?" Emma tried to drink more tea, but the twisting sensation in her gut tightened even more.

"It's an unfortunate illness, passed down from father to son," Nuala answered. "Cormac has lasted longer than the others. And my sister thought that by sending him away, she could save him."

"But you don't think it will work, do you?" Whether it was Nuala who was responsible for harming Cormac or another reason, Emma didn't know. The woman's revelation about Lorcan's wife Moreen made her even more wary of the woman—especially if Moreen believed she ought to live at Dunmeath.

"I would do everything in my power to save my nephew, were it possible," Nuala said. "He's a good lad, and he genuinely cares for the people here. Everyone knows it. And we pray that somehow, we'll find a way to help him live as long as he can." The solemnity in the woman's voice was nearly believable.

Before Emma could answer, Nuala added, "I am very happy he found a woman like you to marry, Emma. And I pray that your marriage is indeed blessed with a child."

Heavy footsteps approached at that moment, and Nuala said, "Hello, Josephine. Won't you join us?"

"No. I've come to speak with my daughter-in-law. Alone," she added. To Emma, she said, "Meet me in Cormac's study. We need to talk."

Without waiting for an answer, she strode away. Nuala set down her teacup and said, "I see Josie's in one of her moods again. I'll bid you good luck with her. You're going to need it."

Chapter Twelve

CORMAC DIDN'T LIKE the thought of Emma returning to Dunmeath alone. But he couldn't deny that his wife was right—something or someone was causing his illness. And now that he was here alone, each day he could feel himself getting stronger. The only problem was that he was going to run out of food soon. Emma had promised to bring back supplies, but he would need more by the morning. It was as if his body craved food, and he suddenly couldn't get enough.

He left the cottage, feeling the urge for fresh air and sunshine. It was late in the afternoon, and he began walking along the edge of his lands, moving toward a main road. Before long, he found himself near Lorcan's house.

He thought of turning back but decided against it. Emma was searching for answers at Dunmeath. And despite what others might believe, he didn't think his cousin had anything to do with his illness.

Cormac was about to knock on the door, when he heard the sound of his cousin cursing in the stables. He walked around to the back of the house and found Lorcan struggling with one of the horses.

"Need a hand?" he asked.

Lorcan spun, and his face lit up. "I'd be glad of one, cousin."

He grasped the reins while the horse struggled to pull away from him. "This fine lad is being difficult."

Cormac went to join him and ran his hands over the horse's mane. As he did, he noticed that the horse wasn't putting his full weight on one of his back legs. "Lorcan, have a look at his foot."

He held the reins steady while his cousin went to check. "Looks like he's stepped on some brambles." He pulled away a thorny twig that was embedded in the horse's foot. "There you are, lad. Does that feel better to you?"

The horse tossed its head and gingerly stepped on it. Then Lorcan led him toward the pasture, and Cormac opened the gate.

"It's glad I am to see you're looking better," his cousin said. "What brings you to the house?"

"I was taking a walk," Cormac answered. "I've not seen you since I returned to Dunmeath and thought I'd say hello."

Lorcan's face turned frustrated. "I've been wanting to. But I heard you were ill again, and I didn't want to get in the way. And then—Moreen has been . . . unhappy."

"Would you like to join me on my walk?" Cormac offered. "We could talk about it."

His cousin gave a nod. "I'd be glad to."

They continued along the edge of the pasture, watching the horses graze, and Lorcan continued. "She says I haven't given her the life she was wanting. She thought we would be living at Dunmeath."

Cormac paused a moment. "And what of you? Is that what you're wanting?"

Lorcan shook his head. "I am content to be where I am. We've a house of our own, plenty of land, and I enjoy being your land steward. But I don't like that Moreen is angry with me."

His cousin's wife reminded him of Lady Persephone. "Is there anything I can do to help?"

"Nay. I'd rather she grew accustomed to the life we have instead of one that will never happen."

Something turned cold within Cormac. "How badly is she

wanting to live at Dunmeath?"

His cousin's mood darkened. "It doesn't matter what she's wanting or how badly. She'll learn to be content, and that's the end of it."

But Cormac wasn't so certain. An envious woman—one who knew her husband was the heir—might turn to desperate means. Was she desperate enough to threaten his life?

"And what of you?" Lorcan asked. "Are you happy in your marriage?"

The question only made him smile. "Emma is everything I'd ever hoped for." The only shadow was his illness and how to discover its cause.

"I am glad for you, truly," Lorcan said. They continued walking back toward the house, and his cousin invited him to stay for supper.

The thought of a hot meal was inviting, and he readily agreed. "I'd be glad of it." He also wanted to speak with Moreen and determine whether she was a threat.

But even as they continued back, he thought of Emma and wondered when she would return. And more than all else, he hoped she would be safe.

"WHERE IS MY SON?" the dowager said when they were alone in the study. Emma took a few steps toward Cormac's desk and found a chair. She nearly knocked over a stack of books but managed to set them right. The broken book fell into her hands, and she caught it before it hit the floor. Some of the cover crumbled again, and she brushed off her fingers after she set it on top.

"Cormac is still at the cottage," she said, taking a seat. Her nerves mingled with the pain in her stomach, for the dowager still made her anxious.

"You left him there alone?" Josephine's voice held the invisible weight of a mother's worry.

"I did, but you needn't worry. He's fine," Emma reassured her. "In fact, within a day of leaving Dunmeath, his health took a turn for the better, as I suspected it would." The relief that flooded through her at seeing him well again had only deepened her resolve to find out what was preventing it.

She paused and said to his mother, "Someone is causing his illness. Someone here, at Dunmeath. Which means if we can find the cause, we can save him."

The dowager remained silent for a time. "So, you do want to save him, then?" The words were soft, almost disbelieving.

"I *will* save him." And somehow, speaking the words seemed to make them real. No, she wasn't the sort of wife Cormac needed. But she could learn every inch of this castle, get acquainted with every servant, and one day, she might be enough. She did believe that he cared for her, even if it was only rooted in pity.

Her own feelings for him were deepening with every day, until she was afraid to face them fully. They had made the rule not to fall in love. And though she'd tried to keep that rule, part of her knew it was already too late. If Cormac died, it would cleave her heart in half, making her into a shell of a woman. She simply couldn't imagine waking up without hearing the smile in his voice or feeling the touch of his hand against hers.

"I've written a list of possibilities," the dowager said. "Have a look and tell me your thoughts."

She held out what appeared to be a piece of paper, and Emma felt a wave of uneasiness. It mingled again with her nausea, and she tried to calm her nerves. She wasn't ready to reveal her inability to read to Lady Dunmeath. To avoid it, she said, "Pardon me," and pretended to sneeze. She reached for her handkerchief and wiped her nose.

"Could you read it aloud?" She dabbed with her handkerchief a little more. "I fear some of the dust is affecting me."

The dowager paused a moment and said nothing. For a moment, Emma wondered if she suspected anything. But then she asked, "How long was my son ill in London?"

"Most of the time, from the moment I met him—though he tried to hide it from me. There were good days and bad days. Whenever we were alone together, away from everyone and everything, his illness disappeared."

The dowager fell silent again before she finally spoke. "What is it you're wanting from my son?"

A heavy emotion filled her heart and throat. "I want him to live," she said honestly. "I want to grow old with Cormac and have children."

"Do you think you could be pregnant now?" Josephine asked. There was an edge to her voice, one Emma didn't understand.

But she remained honest. "No. Not yet."

"My sister thinks you could be."

Emma shrugged. "I had my menses a little over a week ago. Only a day, but I don't think it's possible." Her face felt like it was on fire again, and her stomach pain twisted in her gut. "It's so hot in here, isn't it? I think I need some air."

Her earlier decision to try eating a sandwich had been a terrible idea. Her nausea had grown so bad, she felt like the slightest motion would send her stumbling toward a chamber pot to empty her stomach. Even her hands felt rather itchy, which was odd.

"Are you all right?" Josephine asked. "You look peaked."

"I'm just feeling hot. I think if I go outside for a moment, it would be best."

But when she stood from her chair, the room seemed to sway. The warmth of the room combined with a roaring noise in her ears, and she felt faint. The pain in her stomach sharpened, and she brought her hands to her waist, terrified of what it could mean.

"Emma, sit down," her mother-in-law ordered.

She was dimly aware of the dowager ringing for a servant, but it seemed best to lay her head down for a moment. She rested it upon the desk, and once again, the pain in her stomach rippled until it felt as though she were being stabbed.

Dear God . . . what if she *was* pregnant? Was that even possible? What if this pain was not nausea—but instead her worst nightmare of a miscarriage? The thought brought a wave of anguish within her, and Emma tried to slow her breathing, tried to calm down. But a moment later, she lost all awareness of anything except the vicious pain in her gut.

"I think I need to lie down," she murmured. She staggered from the chair but tripped over a small stool she hadn't seen.

And dimly, as she started to feel even more faint, she wondered if whoever was trying to harm Cormac had now done the same to her.

CORMAC WAS SITTING by the fire in the cottage when he heard the sound of voices shouting. "Lord Dunmeath! We've come to bring you home. It's her ladyship. She's very ill."

He threw the door open and saw Stephens on horseback, along with another servant. Both held torches, and they had a horse saddled and waiting for him.

"Please, my lord. The dowager Lady Dunmeath is with her now. We've sent for the doctor."

Fear iced through him at the thought of Emma becoming sick. He'd been afraid of this, despite Emma's insistence that nothing would happen to her. And now, the danger was clearly for both of them.

Cormac didn't bother taking his cloak, but mounted the animal and spurred his horse as fast as he could, galloping hard toward the castle. It was already dark, and Stephens led the way. The frigid air tore through him, but he felt none of it. The flare of orange against the darkness was the only light, and with every mile, Cormac's fear shifted into rage.

How could anyone want to harm Emma? His wife was kind,

and she deserved none of this. She'd left England for him, traveling to his home and giving up everything to live at his side. He'd known that this was hard for her, and his mother had not made it any easier.

A sudden hardness caught at his gut as he wondered whether Josephine had anything to do with Emma's sudden illness. His mother wouldn't do such a thing, would she? Or had Nuala given her a tea that caused it?

When the towers of Dunmeath emerged, he continued riding swiftly until he reached the entrance. He swung down, not even bothering to hand off his horse to the stable lads. Instead, he took the stairs two at a time, hurrying toward the front door and throwing it open.

"Where is Lady Dunmeath?" he demanded of the first footman he saw.

"In her bedchamber," the man answered. "We've sent for the physician, but—"

Cormac didn't wait for him to finish but instead raced up the stairs. His legs were burning, and he'd lost his breath, but he could only think of reaching Emma in time.

When he turned down the hall, he saw his aunt Nuala waiting outside.

"Oh good, Cormac, you're here," she said. But before he could go inside, she barred his path. "Wait, lad."

"I'm going to see her," he insisted, fully prepared to shove her aside.

"And so you shall," Nuala answered. "But she's fighting to keep her baby. Do nothing to upset her. Keep her calm and lift her spirits. I will continue praying for you both."

"A baby?" The words were both a prayer and a heartbreak. "But she's not—"

"Women *can* bleed and still be pregnant," Nuala said. "And I think she is, though it may be too soon to know for certain." She stepped away from the door and added, "She needs you, Cormac. Go and be with her."

He pushed open the door, and his heart nearly stopped when he saw Emma lying down, her face ghostly pale. His mother's expression was grim, but she sat beside his wife.

"Emma, I'm here," he said, reaching for her hand. Her skin was cool, and she opened her eyes.

"You were supposed to stay at the cottage," she said weakly.

"They told me you were ill. I wasn't about to stay behind." He squeezed her hand, but she didn't return the gesture. Cormac hated being so helpless. He now understood the way she'd felt at his bedside, and he was determined that it would never happen again.

"I'll let you rest for a while, *a stór*," he told Emma. "I need to speak with my mother." He beckoned for Josephine to follow him, and they stood closer to the door.

"How did this happen?" he demanded of his mother. "She was in perfect health two days ago when I saw her last."

"Nuala thinks she's pregnant," Josephine answered. "She was feeling nauseous and warm yesterday."

But he didn't believe her illness was from pregnancy. This was clearly far too serious for that, and he knew the familiar symptoms of weakness and nausea.

"Tell me what she ate and who she saw," he ordered.

"She ate in the kitchen with the cook and then had tea with Nuala the next day," Josephine began.

Neither seemed likely, so he pressed further. "Was Moreen here?"

"I don't think so," Josephine answered. "But she and Nuala went out together the first day Emma arrived back. I think they were out shopping."

He believed now that Moreen was the greatest threat to Emma. The woman's ambitions were clear, and if anyone wanted to hurt his wife, it had to be her.

"Send word to Moreen and Lorcan," he said firmly. "It's not a request—it's an order. I want to question both of them."

His mother reached out to touch his shoulder. "It's good to

see you well again, Cormac. Emma was right. You do look better."

But it wasn't about him anymore. Whoever had been harming his family had gone too far when they'd hurt Emma. The thought of her suffering, fighting for her life, enraged him. No longer would he stand aside and accept that he was going to die. He would find the culprit and bring them to justice.

Abruptly, he realized that she had endured exactly the same thing, watching him grow ill while struggling to survive. But he'd accepted the inevitability of his own death. She hadn't. His brave Emma was determined to fight for him. He could do no less for her.

He returned to her bedside, and seeing her so pale, so sick, only heightened his worry. Cormac leaned down and pressed a kiss to her forehead, but she didn't awaken. For a moment, he studied his wife, suddenly realizing how much he needed her. He'd once believed that he could wed any woman, and it would be enough, so long as she could provide him with an heir.

But right now, an heir was the furthest thing from his mind. He only wanted his wife whole and well again. He wanted her to awaken beside him each morning, to hear her laughter and feel her touch upon his skin.

His mother was standing at the doorway, and Cormac said, "I want you to take her back to the cottage. Would you do that for me? Tend her and make certain she gets well again."

Josephine nodded. Her eyes held a softness he'd not seen in a long time. "You're in love with her, aren't you?"

The words seemed to unlock a dormant part of him. This marriage was always meant to be an arrangement, and he'd never imagined that it could become something more. But he realized now how much he admired Emma's courage and her determination to overcome challenges. He wanted to share new experiences with her and spend the rest of his days at her side. Even if she never had a child, it didn't matter to him anymore.

"She is everything to me." He couldn't imagine losing her,

and the attack had sparked his own determination to find out who was trying to poison both of them.

But more than that, it gave him hope that—if they did find the answers—he might live. And a lifetime with Emma was worth fighting for.

"I'll go with her after the physician looks at her," Josephine promised. "I'll have a footman bring us there. She will get better," his mother insisted. "I promise you."

He crossed the room and embraced her. "Thank you."

Cormac went to a small escritoire and pulled out paper, pen, and ink. His mind was roiling with distractions, and he stared at the paper, trying to think. What had he planned to write down? Was it a list? What good would that do? He closed his eyes and set down the pen. It had only been a means of occupying his time to prevent him from thinking about what could happen to his wife while they waited for the physician.

He shut down the thought immediately and tried to focus on what lay ahead. His mind drifted to thoughts of Hawkins. He hoped his secretary would agree to take the position here to help Emma. He'd been so grateful for Hawkins's strong sense of organization. The man was constantly writing things down.

Abruptly, a thought struck him like a bullet from a gun.

There were others who had always been writing—first his grandfather, then his father, and finally, his brother. All had died from the same illness, and all had written their stories in the diary.

His grandfather's book was crumbling apart, but Cormac planned to search through it for answers. There had to be something in the pages that he hadn't thought of before. A name that was mentioned or perhaps something that connected the three men.

With one last look at his wife, he left to find out who the true threat was.

EMMA AWAKENED LATER that night to find a physician poking and prodding at her. She was exhausted, but when she looked for Cormac, he was not there. Only her mother-in-law Josephine stood in the corner.

"I understand you think you've been poisoned," the physician said. "What makes you believe that?"

Emma blinked at the man. "I—I don't know what caused my illness. I just felt sick to my stomach."

"I've a purgative for you," the physician said. "Drink this, and it will empty the contents of your stomach. If there is any bad food or something causing you to be sick, that should help."

The idea of spending the next hour bringing up the contents of her stomach sounded awful, and Emma turned her face away from the man.

"Is it possible . . . that she could be pregnant?" Josephine asked. "Could this be a miscarriage?"

The physician turned back to her and then shook his head. "No, I don't think so. If it were a miscarriage, we'd know with certainty. This does seem to be a malady related to food."

Relief flowed through her, and Emma took a breath. "Where is Cormac?" She wanted to see him again to ensure that he was all right.

"He sent for Lorcan and Moreen and plans to question both of them in the library, I believe." Josephine took the vial from the physician and said, "Thank you, that will be all."

Just as he was leaving, Nuala came to the door with another footman. "I've brought tea. How are you feeling, Emma?"

"Weak and tired," she admitted. "The physician thinks I need to purge my stomach."

Cormac's aunt rolled her eyes. "I'm not fond of Dr. Ó Neill. He thinks the cure for everything is vomiting." She came closer and said, "I've made you some ginger tea. It should help settle your stomach for now."

But Josephine stepped in front of the footman and ordered him to put down the tea service. "Not now. Let her rest."

"She'll rest easier with the ginger," Nuala argued. "And don't be giving her that purgative. It's the last thing she needs."

Although Emma was grateful for Nuala's offer of tea, she was startled by the dowager's sudden shift in mood. She'd become defensive, which startled her.

"You've made many teas for Cormac, haven't you?" Josephine said. "I think you even sent some to England, did you not?"

"Well, of course," Nuala said. "I wanted to ease his sickness. With the right blend of tea and herbs, it would help him."

"You made those teas for my husband and Finn, too, didn't you?" Josephine's tone turned darker, and Emma suddenly realized what she was implying.

Dear God. She didn't want to believe such a thing. Nuala had been nothing but kind. Was it possible that she had used her knowledge of herbal teas to harm all of them? The thought didn't seem plausible.

Nuala stood from her chair and inhaled sharply, as if horrified. "Josie, you can't think that I'm the cause of their illness. I would never harm anyone! I was trying to stop them from getting sicker."

"Cormac is downstairs questioning Lorcan and Moreen. I wonder what he'll learn from them?" Her voice turned dangerous. "Perhaps that you've always been ambitious." A hard tone lined her words. "Perhaps Lorcan was my husband's bastard son because Orlan was incapable of fathering a child."

"You're wrong, Josie." Nuala's voice held the weight of grief with a trace of anger. "Aye, Brandan flirted with me, but I never returned his attentions. Nor did I *ever* share his bed." Without a word, she turned her back and started to leave.

"Seize her," Josephine ordered the footman. "I want her locked away until I have my answers."

Emma was reeling from what she'd learned. But more than that, she found it difficult to believe that Nuala meant any harm.

"Josie, you're wrong," Nuala said softly. "I swear to you, Lorcan was Orlan's son. And I never, *never* wanted anyone to die."

"Take her to her room," Josephine ordered the footman. "And she is not to leave Dunmeath under any circumstances."

"I did nothing wrong," Nuala said quietly. But she went with the footman without argument.

After she was gone, Emma struggled to sit up. It felt as if there had been a terrible mistake.

"Lady Dunmeath—"

"Shh." Josephine bade her to sit back. "It's going to be all right. Nuala can't hurt you, or anyone else anymore." But despite her words of reassurance, Emma could hear the heavy emotions in her voice.

"I need to see Cormac," Emma insisted. "Please."

"I will send him to you soon. After he's finished speaking with Lorcan and Moreen." Josephine gave a heavy sigh. "I never wanted to believe my own sister could do such a thing."

"Are you certain that she did?" Emma ventured.

The dowager shrugged. "I don't know. But . . . it's possible. Even if I'm wrong about her and Brandan, she might have been resentful of Finn and Cormac for taking what she believed should have been Lorcan's birthright. I can't be sure."

The dowager walked to the door and said, "Rest now. I'll bring Cormac to you after he's spoken with them. We'll leave for the cottage in the morning." Just as she was leaving, she picked up the pot of tea and took it with her.

Emma took a few deep breaths, trying to gather what was left of her strength. Although the pieces did fit, she couldn't quite believe that Nuala would do something like this. The woman had been kind and caring, doing whatever she could to help.

But what if Moreen had added something to Nuala's teas? What if *she* had been the one to cause their suffering? To Emma, that made far more sense.

And lying in this bed was accomplishing nothing at all, except heightening her worries.

Emma pulled back the coverlet and slid her feet off the bed.

Though she was exhausted and weak, she managed to stand and reach for her dressing gown. She took a few faltering steps and had nearly reached the door when it swung open, and she saw Nora and Maire.

"Lady Dunmeath," Maire said, rushing toward her. "You must go back to bed."

"No. I need to speak with Cormac." She glanced over at Nora. "Is he downstairs with Moreen and Lorcan?"

"I don't know," Nora said. "I haven't seen him. And I don't think Moreen or Lorcan are here."

"Will you help me find my husband?"

"I can try to bring him to you," Maire offered. "Please lie down. You don't look well."

Emma knew it, but an unspoken need pulled at her, a visceral fear she couldn't explain. "We have to find Cormac. Now. I'm not going back to bed until I know he's safe."

Nora surprised her when she came to Emma's side and put an arm around her. "All right. I'll help you."

Maire joined the other side, and the two of them guided her outside her bedchamber and toward the stairs.

Her mind was spinning, but as the girls helped her toward the library, her sense of dread deepened. It was as if instinct pulled her to him, along with the fear that something wasn't right.

When they reached the library, there was only silence. Emma turned to Nora. "Is anyone inside?"

"I don't think so," Nora answered. She left her side and asked a footman, "Where is my brother? Is he with our cousin?"

"I haven't seen Lord Dunmeath," the servant answered. "And we've had no visitors yet today."

"Open the door to the library," Emma insisted. "He said he was going to meet Lorcan and Moreen there." Her heart was pounding with unspoken fear, and she dreaded what they would find inside.

Nora opened the door, and Emma saw the faint glow of the fire hearth. It had died down to glowing coals, and the rest of the room was dark.

Maire went to draw the drapes, and the moment she did, she let out a cry of alarm. "Cormac!"

Emma hurried forward and realized her husband was lying across the desk unconscious. She could see very little, other than a stack of books and what looked like paper. She knelt before him, pulling him off the desk. It did seem that he was breathing—barely. "Cormac, look at me," she pleaded. Tears flooded her eyes, and she didn't care about holding them back. All that mattered was her husband. "Who's done this to you?"

"He made a list of names," Maire said. "Grandfather, our father, Finn. I've not heard of any of the others."

"He was reading grandfather's diary," Nora said. "Searching for answers, it looks like. But it's completely fallen apart. The binding is broken, and the paint on the cover is everywhere."

The answer came to her in a flash of understanding. The book. It had been with Cormac both in Ireland and in London. She knew he'd been reading it regularly, enjoying the stories his grandfather had written. It had been passed down to his father, who had also read it faithfully. And Finn, his older brother. It had been their prized possession—a deadly one.

During the times they'd spent together by the sea and at the cottage, he hadn't been near the diary. But after she'd touched it the other day, she had fallen ill within hours. Although she'd only touched it once, it had made her skin itch. She thought she'd inhaled some of the dust on it—or was it crumbling paint?—and later, her stomach had twisted with nausea. Had someone added poison to the binding or even the paint itself?

"It's the book," Emma blurted out to his sisters. "I think the painted cover contains poison."

"Oh no," Maire whispered. "What should we do?"

"We should burn it," Nora suggested. "Then no one will be hurt by it again."

Although Emma was inclined to agree, they had to be cautious. "Not yet. We need to know what kind of poison, if any, was in it to help Cormac. Cover it with a handkerchief so no one else will touch it." Nora obeyed and then Emma ordered, "Maire, please go and find some footmen who can help me bring Cormac upstairs."

The young girl hurried out, but before Nora could follow her, Emma called her back. "Nora, will you ask someone to bring back the physician? And tell your mother what's happened. Your Aunt Nuala might be able to help." The orders came pouring out—she was determined to save Cormac. She felt the strangest sense of relief, even though she was still worried about him. It felt as if they finally had the answers it would take to help him.

After the girls had gone, she knelt beside her husband. "Can you hear me, Cormac?" she asked, while she waited alone in the library. "Please, open your eyes."

Emma held him upright, but she wasn't strong enough to lift him, and he hadn't regained consciousness. "Stay with me," she urged. "You're going to be well again, I promise."

But his skin was so very pale and cool, his breathing shallow. She clung to him, dimly aware of her own tears. *Don't leave me,* she prayed silently.

Somehow, this man had become the center of her life. His impulsive moments, his willingness to seize every chance for happiness, had filled their brief marriage with joy. No, she could never be the sort of countess his mother would expect. But it didn't matter anymore. All she wanted to be was his wife.

He can't die. I love him.

When the footmen came at last to lift him, Cormac never regained consciousness once. And dread dug its claws into her, making her fear the worst. Her emotions were scattered apart, and she tried to follow the footmen back upstairs. But her own strength was faltering, and she was starting to grow dizzy. When she reached the stairs, she held on to the banister for a moment, struggling not to faint.

Josephine hurried down the stairs toward her. Emma lowered her head, doggedly trying to take each step. But then, her mother-in-law came to her side. "Do you need a servant to carry you?"

Emma shook her head. She took one step, then another.

"What happened to him?" Josephine asked. "My daughter said something about a book?"

"I think the diary poisoned all of them," Emma said. "Your husband, then Finn, and now Cormac. It must have been something in the paint on the cover. We covered it with a handkerchief, in case we need to know what was in it—but we need to be rid of it."

"Dear God," the dowager said dully. "They read that book all the time. There was a bookbinder who tried to fix the binding, years ago, but it didn't work. The original paint was always coming off, so I paid him to add that green cloth binding." Her voice grew tremulous. "He was so proud of a new method he was developing. I watched him add a special powder to brighten the green paint." She let out a slight moan. "It—it's my fault that they died. And I accused my own sister when she did nothing wrong."

"I think Nuala will forgive you if you apologize," Emma said. "Right now, if you can. She may know a way to help Cormac before the physician arrives."

"I will," the dowager agreed.

The stairs seemed to spin, and Emma paused to try and catch her balance. "It's beginning to make sense now. He didn't have the diary on our journey here or in the cottage. I think that's why he got better."

"But we need to know for certain," Josephine said.

"I agree. We should have someone test the paint," Emma suggested. "And the physician should treat him for poison. I hope now he will never get sick again."

She continued up the stairs with Josephine at her side. The dowager remained at her side and said softly, "You really do care about my son, don't you?"

"I love him," Emma admitted. "And I never cared about whether he had a title or any wealth. Even if he had nothing but the shirt on his back, it would be enough for me."

Josephine rested her hand on Emma's back, guiding her upstairs. "I wasn't fair to you or kind when you arrived at Dunmeath. I am sorry for it."

"You were only trying to protect him," Emma said. She was grateful for the apology, for it meant they might truly begin to have a friendship between them.

"Does he know you're blind?" Josephine asked softly.

Emma froze at the words, startled that the woman had guessed. It must have been avoiding reading Josephine's list that had finally given her away. "I'm not fully blind," she said slowly. "But yes, he knows. And he's never made me feel less of a person because of it. He's good to me."

"He has a big heart, does Cormac," she said. "As do you, I suspect."

To Emma's surprise, when they reached the top of the stairs, the dowager reached out and embraced her. The familiar scent of verbena enveloped her, but it gave her such a sense of hope that she hugged the woman back.

"I'll help you," Josephine promised.

The physician was already returning, and he hurried up the stairs past them. Emma walked with the dowager into Cormac's bedchamber, but after she told the physician what she suspected, all she could do was sit and pray.

Chapter Thirteen

"**D**RINK," A WOMAN'S voice bade him.

Cormac felt as if his insides were raw, and the warm tea was soothing. It tasted odd, but the honey made it go down easier.

When he opened his eyes, he saw Nuala on one side of him, Emma on the other. His mother stood on the far side of the room, her hands clenched together.

"Cormac," Emma murmured, taking his hand. In her eyes, he saw hope, and he tried to squeeze her hand.

"What happened?" One moment, he had been searching his grandfather's diary for names, anything to discover a connection—and the next, he'd awakened here. He vaguely recalled being forced to drink something and the horrible nausea and sickness he'd suffered.

"You were being poisoned," Emma said. "By the diary." She went on to explain their theory about the book. He remembered how, years ago, the diary had been given to a German bookbinder who had offered to repair it for his father, the earl. Apparently, the bookbinder had covered the leather in cloth that had been soaked in green paint—paint that was brightened by a powder.

"Every time you read the book, you were touching poison," Emma said. "Your mother and sisters weren't affected by it because they never read it. And I touched it by accident that day."

Her revelation made sense, though he'd never expected such a thing. But he'd read the book frequently in London, for it had brought back good memories of his father, grandfather, and brother. Thinking back, it did seem that the moments he'd been sick had followed the times when he'd spent an hour reading.

"The physician treated you for poisoning, and Nuala made some tea to ease your pain. I believe that you're going to be well now." Emma's eyes brightened, and he felt the same sense of hope.

"Where is the book now?"

"We got rid of it," Josephine answered. She came to his side, and he saw the tears flowing down her face. "I only wish I'd thrown it out years ago."

"I'll miss the stories," he admitted.

"The stories are here." She touched his heart, then his head. "You can write them down again for your children."

At that, he glanced at Emma, whose cheeks were flushed, but she said nothing.

"Will you give me a moment alone with my wife?" he asked them. Nuala and Josephine nodded, and after they'd gone, he sat up and drew Emma into an embrace.

"I hope you're right about the book," he said.

"I am." She cupped his face between her palms and said, "I believe it, and I know you're going to live." Emma hesitated a moment, as if gathering courage. "I broke one of our rules."

"And what rule was that, *a stór?*"

"I'm in love with you," she answered. "I couldn't stop myself. From the moment you taught me to dance, to the moments we shared in that cottage . . ." Her words broke off. "And when I saw you lying in the office unconscious with that book, it felt as if someone had ripped my heart from my chest. I don't ever want to feel that way again."

Her words filled up his own heart, but he clasped her hands in his. "My heart is and always will be yours, Emma. I love you, too."

She leaned in to kiss him, and the touch of her lips was its own healing balm. He held her in his arms, so thankful that they would now have the gift of time together.

"I think we should be married again," Cormac suggested. "Here, in Ireland, with the family. And if you wish it, we could travel to London afterward to visit your family."

At first, she seemed nervous at the thought of another wedding, but she nodded. "If you'd like."

"My mother and sisters were not pleased that we didn't have a proper celebration." He drew his hands down to her waist. "And we could have another wedding night, if you're wanting to."

A shy smile spread over her face. "What about another honeymoon?"

"Aye. I think it could be arranged." He stole another kiss. "But I'll tell you, *a stór,* as soon as I'm well enough to leave this bed, I'll be bringing you back into it."

"I look forward to it," she whispered with a smile.

Summer

A DROPLET OF ink spilled on the paper, and Cormac paused to stare at it. He'd nearly finished writing the story about the time he and Finn as boys had spent the night outside during Samhain—both of them eager and terrified to see ghosts.

He'd begun writing a new diary—this one in a leatherbound book. He'd recorded the stories he could remember from his grandfather and father in the old book. And now, he was writing the stories about his brother Finn.

The sound of an infant crying broke through his reverie, and he glanced up to see Emma carrying their son. The shoulder of her gown was damp from the baby spitting up, and she offered a weak smile.

"You're still working on the new diary." She drew closer to him, patting the baby's back.

"Aye, *a stór*." He rose from the desk and grimaced when he saw three full cups of tea in various places around the library that he'd forgotten to drink. "One day, I want our Liam to know their stories." Although it had bothered him to lose the diary, he'd done what he could to preserve the memories.

"Come here, lad." He reached out to take the baby from her, and his son squirmed in his arms, fussing until Cormac started to bounce him.

"Hawkins told me that Lucy has invited us to London this summer," Emma said. "Her letter came this morning. I thought we could bring Nora with us if we go. She could attend a few balls or supper parties, even if she hasn't made her debut."

"I don't know if Nora will be wanting an English husband." His sister had strong ideas about what she didn't want in a man and wasn't afraid to voice them aloud.

"Possibly not, but it would be good for her to see London. And my father has been wanting to meet Liam."

The baby started to settle down, and Cormac swayed, holding their son in his arms. "And what of your stepmother?" he asked.

"I am . . . trying to forgive Lucy," Emma said quietly. "She intended to save my father, and she hosted the auction out of desperation."

He shifted Liam's position and saw that the baby's eyes had closed. "I cannot say that I'm disappointed in the outcome of that auction." With his free hand, he lifted her wrist to his mouth. "My beautiful, wonderful wife. I will ever be grateful that you agreed to marry me."

As they walked out of the library together, Emma teased, "So, I suppose you would bid on me again?"

"I would pay every last penny I own," he answered. "But some things are beyond price." He rested his hand upon their son's head in silent thanksgiving.

With a smile, she answered, "So, they are."

Author's Note

During the early 19th century, a new pigment was developed for books called "emerald green" that was, quite literally, poisonous. Also known as Paris green, Vienna green, and Schweinfurt green, the color was produced by combining copper acetate with arsenic trioxide, which resulted in copper acetoarsenite. According to *National Geographic*, the toxic pigment was commercially developed in 1814 by the Wilhelm Dye and White Lead Company in Schweinfurt, Germany. These toxic books were bound in cloth, and the paint was laced with arsenic. Many of these older books are still in existence, and the Poison Book Project was launched to locate and catalogue these "noxious volumes."

I took a bit of literary license with the time frame and the symptoms of arsenic poisoning. Although clothbound books came a little later, it's still possible that a German merchant could have been experimenting with the green color a few years earlier than 1814. Since Cormac was reading the book without gloves, the paint would have touched his hands and he could also have inhaled particles into his lungs. But thankfully, his exposure was not daily, and this would explain why he would get well for a time, only to become sick again after handling the book.

Even so, if you find yourself in an antique bookstore and discover a vivid green book, don't touch it without gloves!

Did you miss the first two books in the School for Spinsters series? Enjoy *A Match Made in London*, about Violet Edwards and Lord Scarsdale, or *Match Me, I'm Falling*, about Lady Ashleigh and Cameron MacNeill, wherever e-books are sold. If you would like to receive an email whenever Michelle Willingham releases a new book, visit her website at www.michellewillingham. com/contact to sign up for her newsletter.

About the Author

Michelle Willingham has published nearly fifty romance novels, novellas, and short stories. Currently, she lives in Virginia with her children and is working on more historical romance books in a variety of settings such as: Regency England, Victorian England, Viking-era Ireland, medieval Scotland, and medieval Ireland. When she's not writing, Michelle enjoys baking cookies, playing the piano, and chasing after her cats. Visit her website at: www.michellewillingham.com.

Milton Keynes UK
Ingram Content Group UK Ltd.
UKHW020700180823
427095UK00014B/445